S0-CEX-521

All-Night Pharmacy

ALSO BY RUTH MADIEVSKY

Emergency Brake

All-Night Pharmacy

• *a novel* •

Ruth Madievsky

Catapult
New York

This is a work of fiction. All of the characters, organizations, and events portrayed in this novel are either products of the author's imagination or are used fictitiously.

ISBN: 978-1-64622-150-9

Library of Congress Control Number: 2022951936

Jacket design by Gregg Kulick
Jacket photograph © Cat Thomson / Millennium Images, UK
Book design by tracy danes

Catapult
New York, NY
books.catapult.co

Printed in the United States of America

10 9 8 7 6 5 4 3 2 1

For Adam, my love,
and for my family

С вами хорошо, а без вас ещё лучше.
With you it's good, but without you it's even better.

—Russian proverb

1.

Spending time with my sister, Debbie, was like buying acid off a guy you met on the bus. You never knew if it would end with you, euphoric, tanning topless on a fishing boat headed for Ensenada, or coming to in a gas station bathroom, the insides of your eyes feeling as though they'd been scraped out with spoons. Often, it was both.

The first time Debbie took me to Salvation, she dressed me in a highlighter-pink bandage dress with cutouts up the sides. She wouldn't let me wear a bra.

"Nipple outline is part of the look," she insisted.

We were at her apartment, a dingy West Hollywood complex with permanent pigeon-shit stains on its maroon awnings. She lived there with her on-again-off-again "musician" boyfriend, Dominic, who was really just an addict with a guitar. He wrote songs with names like "Heroin Heroine" and "Salty Surprise." If he'd ever made money off his music, it left his hand before it reached his wallet.

I watched Debbie do my makeup in her filmy bathroom mirror. She held a smoky eye palette in her palm like a clamshell, lips parted as she painted my face. Debbie had big blue eyes and a pout that made men do stupid things. People said we looked alike, but no one ever mistook one of us for the other. Debbie wore her body like she owned it; for me, it was the other way around. She was only five foot two, but that made her more powerful; you could fall asleep spooning her and wake up with a screwdriver pressed to your throat. She was so alive it was scary. I could hear her heart beating from another room. Sometimes, she bruised herself sleeping—her blood was that close to the surface.

She powdered the corners of my eyes, and I could count every flag of dead skin on her lips. Her breath smelled of barbecue chips. She'd sucked the blackheads from her nose with a pore strip earlier, but she intentionally left a cluster above her right nostril.

"Making one imperfection visible makes another invisible," she explained.

So this was why she'd half-heartedly tweezed my eyebrows: to distract from the way my ears poked out of my hair, how my bottom lip was thicker than my top. I craned my neck to watch myself transform in the mirror.

"Stop moving," Debbie said, forcing my head back. "Keep your eyes on me."

She didn't want me to learn how to do my own makeup. It would upset our dynamic of her as artist and me as canvas.

I was eighteen and had just graduated high school. My plan was to do two years at Valley College and transfer to UCLA. I couldn't decide whether to study English or biology, so I was considering registering for classes in both. Debbie had planned the night out as a graduation present. "Drinks are on me," she said that afternoon, which meant she'd had a good shift at the strip club. I occasionally kept her company in the dressing room as an excuse to get out of the apartment

I shared with our mother. And, okay, maybe I got something out of the dressing room too. With so many tits, tattoos, and sequins flying against a fluorescent sky, it was easy to miss that the teen girl doing her homework hadn't flipped a page in the last hour. I watched the women as casually as I could, pretending I was checking out their outfits and not them. Occasionally, one of them held my gaze. I imagined following her out of the club, wrapping myself around her in the back seat of her car. Kissing her neck as she lifted my shirt, demanding to see me now that I'd seen her.

"Holy shit," Debbie said. "My best work yet." She stepped aside so I could see myself in the mirror.

My eyelids were a gradient from silver to galaxy black. The wings of my eyeliner sharp as needles. Lips the color of honey and more symmetrical than I'd ever felt.

"Do you like it?" she said. The uncapped lipstick in her hand was called Toxic.

I looked icy and confident. Unfocusing my eyes, I pretended I was looking at some other girl entirely. "It's perfect," I said.

●

Salvation was in a rapidly gentrifying part of East Hollywood, on the same block as a hipster coffee shop, karate studio, taqueria, and weed dispensary. The bar was nondescript from the outside, announcing itself with a flickering lime-green neon sign. There was no line. The bouncer asked for our IDs, and I slipped him my fake. He barely glanced at it before stamping my hand with a crucifix. I felt a surge of protest, a desire to declare I was Jewish, but the only Hebrew I knew was the wine prayer our father used to recite ironically. My discomfort at being inked with Christian insignia was half-hearted and came from the part of me that wanted to be rewarded for acting correctly. Being a person didn't come naturally to me the way it seemed to for others. People who were sure of themselves awed me. I studied them and tried to mimic their ease. Sometimes I got away with it, but never with Debbie. She saw through me down to my bones.

Inside was equally underwhelming. Red pleather booths, glossy pub tables, string lights, a dozen stools lining the bar counter, a jukebox. Salvation used to be a Christian bookstore by the same name. Aside from decorative signs like CHRISTIAN LIVING and USED BIBLES and the bookshelves displaying various liquor bottles behind the bar, it looked like any other dive.

The people were another story. Many looked like they'd wandered in after giving up on the lines for the gastropub across the street. A smaller contingent had the air of longtime regulars trying to ignore the bougie new clientele. I followed Debbie to the bar, where we claimed the only open stools. To our right, a woman was leafing through an enormous album of sepia-toned photos, a plastic pharmacy bag in her lap. To our left, two men were playing a card game where every card was the five of clubs.

"What's the deal with this place?" I asked.

Debbie ordered two Moscow mules before I could look at a menu. "You'll see."

We spent the night chatting up strangers and people Debbie knew from previous nights out. There was Grant, who'd moved to Los Angeles from Idaho to become an actor and had so far only booked a community theatre production of *Starlight Express* and gay-for-pay porn. There was Ashleigh, an energy healer who'd been wearing a jade egg in her pussy for two years to convert her traumas into sexual energy. And there was Karina, who gave us mystery pills as my graduation present. I'd tried a few things with Debbie before, but I'd known what they were ahead of time—weed, coke, acid, Molly, benzos, some opiates. This pill was round with the number 30 imprinted on it, a moody brown that reminded me of Venice Beach at dusk.

"So nice of you," I said with a plastered-on smile. "But I'm good."

"Really?" Debbie said. "Come on, live a little. We're celebrating."

Her eyes were bleary, and she kept licking her lips. She must have taken something before we went out.

"I'm not in the mood," I said.

She rolled her eyes at Karina, who was pretending not to listen. "I get it. College Girl is too refined to slum it with us." Debbie was waving her hands and knocked over the house of cards the men next to us had started building. They glared at her, and she glared back, until one of them whimpered.

"I'm not going to let anything happen to you," Debbie said. "Don't you trust me?"

I said nothing.

"Do you want me to ID the pill for you? Kind of defeats the purpose, but if it would make you feel better . . ." She pulled out her phone.

"Lower your voice," I said.

Debbie's laugh was a manhole cover scraping across asphalt.

"What?" I said.

"Nothing."

"Just say it."

She gave me a sad little smile. "How did I end up with such a narc for a sister?"

Karina bristled at the word *narc*. The men collected their cards and moved to a distant table.

"I'm not a narc," I said.

The light caught Debbie's extra canine tooth. In another life, she might have been a hunting dog or a vampire. "Prove it."

We both knew as soon as the argument started that I'd end up taking the pill. I still felt obligated to push back, even if my resistance was purely symbolic.

Once I swallowed the pill, Debbie grew softer and said, "Molodets," *attagirl*, one of the few Russian words our grandmother taught us. "There's the sister I know and love." She kissed me on the forehead and ordered another round.

The rest of the night is patchy. I remember Ashleigh gifting me one of her jade eggs. A man with shoulder-length dark brown hair intercepting me on my way to try it out. He was leaning against the wall, nursing a beer, people-watching. "Is that what I think it is?" he said.

He stuck out his hand, and I gave him the egg. He raised it toward the light, rotating it like a jewel. "Interesting."

He placed it back in my palm, fingertips grazing my wrist. I felt my nipples harden.

"I had a pet snake when I was a kid," he said. "One

day, out of nowhere, it laid eggs. One was dark green. My mom freaked out and showed her psychic, who said it was an omen. She said I was destined to meet a woman with a matching egg."

"And then what?"

His eyes flit over my chest. "That's for us to decide." He smiled gravely, our fate already sealed.

We spent the rest of the night talking. His name was Ronaldo but he went by Ronnie, and he had one of those faces that alternated between seductive and wholesome. His eyes went wide and angelic when I spoke, then narrowed with an impish half smile. The cumulative effect made me hyperaware of the nakedness beneath my clothes. He worked at an electronics store, and his life's goal was to start a self-improvement video game company. "Like therapy, but fun," he explained. For hours, we traded stories. Our fucked-up mothers and absent fathers. Our most embarrassing high school memories. His ninety-year-old customer who couldn't figure out how to access the kink channel she'd paid for. The household objects we'd transform into if we got zapped with a mad scientist's ray. We counted to three and named what we thought the other would become. I said futon. He said knife block.

Back at Debbie's apartment, I recounted my conversation with Ronnie, or what I could remember of it.

"What the fuck is a self-improvement video game? Do you pretend to pick up trash on the freeway?" Debbie laughed. "He sounds like a virgin."

We were lying in her bed still wearing our makeup. Dominic was out. I'd forgotten how much Debbie distrusted earnestness, preferring the company of known liars over loyal friends. I regretted telling her about Ronnie. I turned off the light.

"Did I hurt your feelings?" she said. "Sorry. I just think you can do better."

"You don't know him." I turned to face the wall.

"Neither do you. He's just some dude. And I'm your sister."

"What does that mean?"

She said nothing. Her heart went quiet like a cold-blooded thing.

Eventually, I asked if she was asleep.

"I planned this whole night for us," she said. "And you ditched me."

"I was fifty feet away. You could have joined us."

"And talked about snake eggs for two hours? Hard pass. He obviously made that shit up to get in your pants."

"So what if he did?"

"Relationships built on a lie are doomed to fail."

"Did you read that in a magazine at our pediatrician's office?" I felt rotten as soon as I said it, but I didn't take it back.

She didn't say anything for a long time. Then she turned so we were butt to butt. "I'm just looking out for you."

I waited until her breathing got even before reaching between my breasts for the jade egg. It was warm. I could feel Ronnie's fingerprints radiating from its surface. Energy healing was bullshit, but I worked the egg inside me. I pretended it was Ronnie, and I gripped as hard as I could.

I was tired of being a knife block. I wanted to be a knife.

2.

I ran into Ronnie at Salvation the next weekend, and an hour later, we were at his place, fooling around beneath a ceiling covered in glow-in-the-dark stars. "Those were the previous tenant's," he said, burying his head between my legs. His air conditioner was busted. A floor fan rotated its head like an owl.

"You like that?" he whispered.

I wasn't sure how to answer, so I groaned and closed my eyes. I tried to ignore the whirr of the fan blades, the mint of Ronnie's shampoo, the sweat pooling where his hand gripped my thigh. I liked to zone out when men went down on me. If I couldn't see them at all, even better. I didn't want to be complicit in the faces they made when they performed cool-guy-loves-eating-puss.

Sex with Ronnie was fine, or what I considered fine back then. What he lacked in skill he tried to compensate for in curiosity and gusto. Mostly, I liked being around him.

When we went to Salvation together a couple of weeks later, we shared greasy Parmesan fries, grinning at each other like toddlers. Ronnie pointed a fry at the bar counter. "What do you think he does when he's not here?" he said.

It took a beat to figure out who he meant. I was groggy from the night before; Ronnie had woken me at three in the morning to try a sex position he'd dreamt about. One of his signature moves, I would come to learn. The fantasy involved two wine bottles and a watermelon. Was it good? Not particularly. But it made me laugh.

"The guy in the striped shirt?" I asked.

He had a thin brown mustache and an urgently-seeking-love look in his eyes. His backward baseball cap tried to convey a playfulness of spirit, but I could sense the anxiety leaking out of him like carbon monoxide. He was flirting with a woman whose defensive body language made it clear she wasn't interested.

"I'm getting sad Little League referee vibes," I said. "Lives with his grandmother. Spends so much time with children and the elderly that he's forgotten how to relate to people his age."

"Tragic," Ronnie said, draining his beer. "What about that guy?" He gestured to a stocky man with a cavernous face, drinking alone in a booth.

"Retired cop," I said.

Ronnie laughed. "Definitely has an ex-wife he's obsessed with. Drives past her house twice a week just to feel something."

"Thinks 9/11 was an inside job."

"Ate dog food on a dare and didn't think it was half bad."

"Jerks off to videos of birds hatching."

"Jesus," Ronnie said, laughing harder. "You sick little fuck. Where did I find you?" He wiped his eyes and got up to buy more drinks.

●

I'd never had a real boyfriend before. In middle and early high school, the thought of introducing someone to my family was nightmarish enough that I kept things casual. What would I say? This is my mom, no one knows what's wrong with her, get ready to duck when the glasses fly. This is my dad, no he's not stoned, he's just dead behind the eyes because he's lonely in his marriage and finds parenting thankless. This is my sister, she's my best and my worst friend; you should be at least a little afraid of her—I am.

A few weeks in, Ronnie and I were spending most days together. Every sloppy grope, every food truck carnitas split in the park, the taste of horchata on each other's tongues, his hand in my back pocket on the walk home, the discordant piano violence of his teenage neighbor, a sign that my real life was approaching. A couple months after we started dating, Ronnie, Debbie, and I were wasted at Salvation, and Debbie went around telling everyone we were getting married. She thought this was the funniest thing—people buying us drinks, sharing their drugs, filling a Dodgers cap with loose bills for our wedding fund. She didn't mind having Ronnie around when she had a use for him.

"This is fucked-up," I told her.

"Since when are you one to turn down free shit?" she said, pocketing half the money and most of the drugs. "No one's going to remember this tomorrow anyway."

But they did remember. Every time we went to Salvation, people asked about our wedding. If we'd picked a date, a dress, a venue, who was going to walk me down the aisle. I could have said anything—that the wedding was off, or we'd eloped, or we were waiting until I turned nineteen. I couldn't do it. We'd taken their gifts and well wishes, and I had this sick feeling that I was in their debt. I wasn't sure I believed in karma, but the word *betrayal* kept popping into my head when I was trying to fall asleep or come.

"Are we horrible people?" I asked Ronnie. We were in bed, passing a joint back and forth.

"That was all Debbie," he said. "What were we supposed to do?"

"We could have said it was a joke. We shouldn't have let them give us stuff."

Ronnie shrugged. "It made them happy. Everyone likes to feel generous."

I couldn't let it go. The more I imagined getting married, the less unreasonable it seemed. I liked the idea of having someone to come home to—someone who would listen to me bitch about my family, and bring me tea when I was sick, and let me put my head in their lap when we watched television. Who was sweet and funny and had a rent-controlled apartment. Someone to step between me and Debbie. Someone who would understand me and make me feel known. Who wouldn't weaponize that knowledge against me. I wasn't sure Ronnie was all these people. I wasn't ready to get married, but I thought holding a gun to our relationship's head might expedite knowing if it was meant to last.

"We should move in together," I told him one night.

He didn't respond right away, so I tossed an empty beer can at his head.

"Fuck yes," he said, rubbing his temple. "Come here." He held out his arms.

I let him envelop me like a weighted blanket.

"This is going to be so great," he said, kissing my cheek. His breath smelled like buttered toast.

I envied his confidence, the golden retriever way he pawed through life. I couldn't imagine what it was like to believe in greeting card platitudes like *Things have a way of working out.* To think a pop psychology book or a video game could teach you how to live with yourself. It made him dear to me, but it also made me lonely.

Debbie thought moving in with Ronnie was stupid. I'd made the mistake of being honest with her about the sex, and ever since, she'd been hounding me to break up with him.

"Rushing into shit isn't going to make him sling better dick," she said. "If anything, he'll stop trying as hard once he's locked you down. A month in, he'll be going down on you in a Contreras Family Reunion 2009 T-shirt."

The two of us were eating popcorn chicken on Ronnie's couch. He'd bought dinner for me and him, but then Debbie had shown up and announced she was starving, so he'd left to buy more.

"It's so obvious that you're jealous," I said. "It's sad, really."

"You're deflecting," she said, trailing a greasy finger against the faux leather couch. It looked like a snail had begun crossing the couch arm before being snatched by an airborne beast.

"I'm not deflecting. I just don't remember asking for

your advice." I swiped at the oil streak with a napkin, making it worse.

She rolled her eyes. "Well, there's a place for you on my couch when things get ugly."

"Why are you so sure it's going to get ugly? This is what people do. They move in together, they get married, they rescue a poodle mix with an anxiety disorder. I didn't give you this much shit when you moved in with Dominic."

Debbie looked like I'd emptied my soda over her head. "That's not the same thing."

"You're in a relationship, aren't you?"

"I can't tell if you're being cruel or if you're just dumb." She picked at a patch of dead skin on her arm.

We both knew she had nowhere else to go, that living with Dominic was more a necessity than a choice.

"Okay, little sister," she sighed. "Move in with the first fuck who thinks you're special. Congrats on figuring it all out." She ate the last piece of chicken and began rifling through our pantry, breaking into a box of Pop-Tarts.

Debbie was always questioning my every move. I tried not to show it, but I wondered if she was right. I wasn't *not* rushing to commit to a guy I barely knew. I didn't have a plan for how to keep my mother from unraveling when I moved out. Buying school supplies was as far as I'd gotten in registering for classes. Navigating Valley College's financial aid portal, selecting classes that would set me on a path to becoming whoever I was going to be—all of it gave me palpitations. I knew these weren't the decisions of a well-adjusted person, but I was afraid that examining them further would collapse the popsicle-stick scaffolding holding up my entire life.

I didn't want to be like Debbie. I didn't want to rely on precarious jobs—or on men—to stay afloat. I wanted to live for more than fleeting hits of chaos. Ronnie was kind, stable, self-assured. He never wondered if he was unfit for society. I once caught him smiling at a fire hydrant as if its existence foretold mankind's ultimate triumph over adversity. I thought I could learn to be like him through osmosis.

◐

We celebrated moving in together at Salvation with Debbie and my high school friend Kim. I wore a floor-length lace sundress Debbie had shoplifted from a discount department store. Her way of making amends, I guess. My grandmother called, but I let it go to voicemail. My family didn't know about Ronnie. The less they knew about my life, the better. We spent the night doing shots, dancing to corny music from the jukebox, and lying to each other.

"This one time," Debbie said, giggling, "my sister fucked a gas station attendant, and he had to steal the boner pills from behind the counter to get it up."

The truth was that he worked at a car dealership and sold sex vitamins on the internet as a side hustle. He had no problem getting it up. He was in Debbie's high school class—she'd introduced us. But I didn't contradict her, even when Kim yelled, "Sad!" and Ronnie looked at me funny. The truth had no place at Salvation. Here, stories were everything. You'd meet computer programmers pretending to be social workers for the homeless, and skater kids claiming to be radiologists. Every person here was a liar and a cheat. They were lonely and sensed there was something incurably wrong with them. They were here because they didn't want to know what it was.

Kim spent half the night flirting with a guy who claimed to be an art buyer for a museum I knew had closed years ago. He kept touching her face and making nonsensical comments about where he'd shelve her portrait—between Jackson Pollock and Jeff Koons—and I wanted to say something to Kim, but I didn't. Who was I to stop her from blowing some loser, if that's how she wanted to spend her night.

Around one, Debbie followed some guy into the bathroom and came out with enough K to make me relive my childhood as a video game. There we were, walking home from elementary school after our mother forgot to pick us up again. The blinds dismembering sunlight onto the handyman's bedroom carpet. The strip club's signature smell of burgers and musky perfume. Fighting with Debbie over the television remote while our rabbit, Muffin, shook in my lap. Our mother slamming the medicine cabinet door, mirror shattering. Debbie and I rushing to clean the shards before she got to them. Our father sneaking out at midnight wearing the next morning's work clothes. Debbie teaching me to ride a bike. Debbie kissing my skinned elbow, telling me not to cry. Her friend Harriet punching me when I tried to call an ambulance the first time Debbie overdosed, my stomach bruising the color of grape Kool-Aid.

At some point, Ronnie asked where Kim was, and panic

pierced me like an ice pick, but I couldn't exit the game. I kept trying to push the *back* button, but the controls were jammed. Later, she'll tell me the last thing she remembers is getting in the fake art buyer's pickup. That she woke up the next afternoon under a tarp in his truck bed, her dress on backward, face stinging from sunburn. There was a searing pause during which I was too ashamed to ask what she thought happened, and she didn't tell me. She stopped returning my calls, or I stopped returning hers, or maybe there weren't any calls in the first place.

When I think about that night, I remember the champagne-bubbles feeling in my stomach and Ronnie and me dancing to the *Grease* soundtrack. Debbie slurring to Ronnie that if he ever hurt me, she'd juice his dick like a carrot. Ronnie laughing and kissing her on the head. People buying us drinks all night. Kim holding the train of my dress while I peed. The fake art buyer's voice a brick cracking in half. Smashing the *back* button, then all the buttons at once, over and over, but there was no way out.

3.

I told my mother I'd been awarded a merit scholarship that came with free room and board. That living on campus was mandatory, so I needed to move out. She had no idea Ronnie existed, that we were moving in together, that I hadn't registered for a single class. But she didn't doubt I'd earned a scholarship, which was affirming and soul-crushing. The only thing worse than concealing how adrift I was: when people I loved believed the lie.

I convinced my mother's insurance company to pay for a home health aide to come by twice a week. She would organize my mother's medications into pillboxes, make sure she took them, keep her company for a couple of hours. My mother's response was "Absolutely fucking not," but after a week alone with her thoughts, she acquiesced. For all her paranoia, she still had something of the socialite in her and did not like solitude.

Her aide, Janice, was a Black woman around her age. I supervised her first few visits. Janice was what my grandmother would call a yachna. She lavished my mother with ridiculous stories—she claimed her sister had been Basquiat's muse, her mother had invented the Bundt cake and been screwed out of the patent, and she herself had been a health aide to a dying conservative politician who admitted on his deathbed that he secretly voted blue. My mother was riveted. She told Janice stories I'd never heard, like the time a geriatric fortune-teller approached her in a park because of her "commanding aura."

Janice burst out laughing. "I try to avoid that woo-woo stuff, but now you've got me invested."

The vein in my neck throbbed as I watched them hit it off. It was bleak to see Janice accept my mother as she was, because she was being paid to. At least I was leaving her in capable hands.

"She'll be fine," Ronnie said the night I moved in, kissing my neck.

We were hanging my clothes in his closet. There weren't enough hangers, so I had to hang my dresses with his shirts, my tops with his pants. I wanted to go out and buy more, but Ronnie said he liked it this way, our clothes hugging even without us animating them.

"Try and relax," he said, pulling down the straps of my top. He kissed up my right arm and down my left. "I can literally feel the knots in your back."

"I'm fine," I said.

He kneaded between my shoulder blades with his fingers and then his elbow. "I wish you didn't feel so guilty for moving in with me. You deserve to have a life of your own. I'm sure your mom wants that for you."

His elbow felt like a blunt dagger. I leaned into the hurt.

Ronnie had never met my mother. He didn't know about her psychiatric history, that her moods were the weather of my life. She suffered terrible migraines and couldn't be dragged out of bed. Or she was up for days, making fifty PB&J sandwiches we'd spend the next two weeks eating, and monitoring the news for signs danger was imminent. These could be anything from newly approved medications for diseases she'd never heard of, to protests of any scale, to what companies were rising in the stock market.

She had a kaleidoscope of diagnoses no two psychiatrists could agree upon. The mix "possibly included" major depression with psychosis, schizoaffective disorder, delusional disorder, borderline personality disorder, and others I'd forgotten. When I was a kid, she kept the blinds drawn, making our apartment feel separate from the outside world, our own strange planet where only the people inside could be trusted. The allure of a private world hits different when you're six, doing a puzzle with your mother inside a pillow fort where "they" can't see you, than when you're twelve, lying to your friends that your mother has a rare immunocompromising condition that prohibits having people over. I maintained the lie with such conviction I sometimes forgot it wasn't true. Confessing to my friends that my mother was profoundly mentally ill, that I counted her pills and sometimes crushed them into her food as though my parent was a horse that needed to be tranquilized, was out of the question. I understood, in theory, that intimacy was built upon mutual vulnerability. My friends knew I was hiding something, and this knowing cemented us as "school friends" whose bonds rarely extended beyond the final bell.

Here was an opportunity to come clean to Ronnie. To be clear-eyed in our love. He wouldn't dump me for having a sick mom. Unless?

I decided to tell him another night. Or, fuck it, not to tell him at all. A woman is entitled to her secrets. Keeping things from him was arguably a feminist act. Why risk provoking a less generous version of him, when I could have this version, who teared up watching trivia shows where contestants lost all their money when they guessed wrong. His favorite show was a British cooking competition, where all the winners got at the end of each season was a cake stand and pride. I wanted to be more like Ronnie, whose brain dispensed serotonin like Halloween candy. Our life together was no different than the spreadsheets he filled out at work. Ronnie + me – my mother + health aide = happiness.

4.

I'd lived in Los Angeles my entire life, sharing a room with Debbie until our mother kicked her out when she was eighteen. I was sixteen. According to our father, our mother had always been paranoid. She didn't like entering stores with surveillance cameras, made our father taste the food first at new restaurants, and hid money inside a ceramic pot beneath a fake cactus. But she was beautiful and charming, a magnetic storyteller you could listen to for hours. The kind of woman always encircled by a crowd at parties. She'd introduced several friends to their future spouses. She was famous for her karaoke rendition of "I Will Survive," which could make a grizzled biker weep. It was after she had Debbie that her quirks became pronounced, and after she had me that she alienated her few remaining friends.

"She's always been a drama queen," my grandmother told me after an incident on my tenth birthday. It was my mother's idea to go bowling as a family, even insisting I invite a few friends. "I wouldn't do that if I were you," Debbie warned. But I couldn't help myself. My mother was in one of her lucid periods, and the three of us had spent the previous night bingeing on chips and ice cream in her bed, gossiping about who at school was kissing whom, which teachers drove fancy cars, which of my mother's friends had cheated on their partners. It felt like some maternal instinct to make my birthday special had overpowered her sickness. It was hard not to blame myself when, an hour in, she became convinced there were microneedles extracting our DNA inside the holes of our bowling balls. She tried to save my friend Marta by tearing the ball from her hand and ended up ripping off part of Marta's nail. Marta began howling, and Dena, the other friend I'd brought, threw up at the sight of her bloody finger.

"Pizdets," my grandmother cursed. She reached into my father's jacket pocket—while he was still wearing it—and withdrew a mini bottle of vodka none of us had known was there. She emptied it over Marta's wound. "Hush now, be a big girl," she said over Marta's shrieks. "I know it hurts, but it doesn't hurt as bad as when my great-uncle lost three fingers building railroads in the camps."

My father made Debbie and me spend the night at our grandmother's. It was a one-bedroom apartment with the thermostat set to eighty degrees to "prevent pneumonia and infertility."

"Maybe I shouldn't have encouraged her with all those family stories," my grandmother mused as the three of us sweat in her double bed beneath terry-cloth blankets and her airless Soviet duvet. "But she needed to know her history! How was I supposed to know she'd think everyone was KGB? Vey iz mir, she wasn't even born yet. If I can sleep at night, so can she." She began snoring moments after this declaration.

My grandmother was a hard woman who'd immigrated

from Saint Petersburg in her twenties with her mother; her father had been murdered a decade earlier as an enemy of the state for teaching Torah in their basement. "Or so we assume," she always added. She was at school when it happened, and her mother was at work. The family never actually received confirmation that he was dead. It was a neighbor who claimed to have seen the KGB break in, ransack the apartment, and drag my great-grandfather away. "For all we know, he might have been the one who informed on my father," my grandmother said, spitting with a loud *ptoo.* "I was twelve and studying to be a pianist. The KGB tore the keys off my piano, looking for money and jewels that weren't there." I felt a little sick when she described the piano's dismemberment. Soon after, she and her mother were evicted and reassigned to a two-bedroom communal apartment with three other families. They couldn't afford a new piano. Decades earlier, her great-uncles, great-aunts, and cousins perished in Nazi camps. Other relatives had fled and gone into hiding, and only some made it out. My grandmother retold these stories obsessively. And my mother, who was alive for none of this, trotted them out like prophecies to anyone who'd listen.

My grandmother saw her daughter's disability as a betrayal. If my grandmother could live with this history and function in society, why couldn't her spoiled American daughter do the same? What did she have to complain about? What about her life was so hard?

It was only when things got out of hand—when my mother broke into the apartment across the street to prove the neighbors were recording her in the shower and selling the videos, or when she swallowed three AAA batteries because she'd read on some message board that they'd scramble the signals of tracking devices—that she got medical attention. I secretly relished my mother's brief inpatient stints. I felt Debbie and I were partly to blame for participating in her delusions, because it was more tolerable to play along than to examine the ways we'd become our guardian's guardian. Not having to witness her instability made it easier to pretend it didn't exist and wasn't possibly coming for me too.

Her insurance preferred to subsidize occasional hospitalizations and a litany of generic psych drugs than commit to a more expensive solution like specialized therapy or a treatment program. When she actually took them, the drugs made her nauseous, gave her dry mouth and a hand tremor, "made everything flat." Her depressive periods were almost as bad as her manic ones. Each time, it felt like an ancient curse taking effect, my mother's life force draining her charisma down to that of a felled tree. Debbie and I muscled through her depressions, her manias, chasing the elusive stretches of lucidity we thought represented who our mother really was.

As I got older and realized she would never get better, I hardened myself against her. We all did. Our father left after she cheated on him during a psych hold when I was fifteen. Debbie and I mutely listened on the line as the night nurse who caught them informed our father.

"And you were—let me guess—on break while my wife was being penetrated by a stranger?" he asked. His voice hitched and became icy. A beer can hissed open and then another.

Meanwhile, he'd been having affairs for years. He was so half-hearted about hiding the evidence—leaving motel receipts in jacket pockets, taking "work" calls at all hours of the night—that it was all the more tragic that our mother had no idea. For someone with intense persecutory delusions, she was remarkably unsuspicious of the three of us. I suppose he felt entitled to do whatever he wanted as compensation for taking care of her all those years. But she had no right to screw around. It didn't matter that her doctor said impulsive sexual behavior was a manifestation of her illness. My father couldn't handle the shame of being betrayed by her, of his crazy wife not thinking *he* was enough.

He left a few weeks after she returned from the hospital. He wasn't much of a presence when we lived together, and once he was gone, the fact of him barely registered. He checked in with Debbie and me occasionally, and then less frequently, until we barely spoke at all. We lost touch like high school classmates who realized they had nothing left in common after graduation. I have no doubt he believed he was doing right by us by sending checks for Hanukkah and our birthdays. That he was "respecting our boundaries" by waiting for us to contact him. One of his core beliefs was that a person couldn't be held responsible for what they don't know. So he chose not to know us. Perhaps if I'd tearily confided how abandoned I felt, that I was constantly assessing myself for signs I too was going crazy, that I wasn't suicidal per se but felt only the dimmest zest for life, he would have intervened. But I didn't tell him any of that, and he didn't ask.

"Fuck that guy," Debbie declared a year after he left. She

stopped talking to him entirely, making me the family liaison. And then our mother discovered that Debbie was stripping and kicked her out. She'd overheard Debbie making fun of some customer who "looked like he did butt stuff with the family dog" to her friend Harriet on the phone. It was kind of shocking—we'd assumed our parents already knew, that Debbie stripping was this unspoken topic no one wanted to broach. I called our father, begged him to do something. He said we needed to "let things cool down." I heard a woman laughing in the background and understood why he didn't offer for Debbie to stay with him.

"You're not going to help at all?" I demanded.

A dog barked and he shushed it softly. "Your sister's an adult. She needs to take responsibility for herself." I heard the smile in his voice, the dog's pant.

Debbie threw some clothes and makeup in a suitcase. A man I didn't recognize pulled up in a dirty car. His hairline was receding, and behind his sunglasses was either a port-wine stain birthmark or a poorly concealed black eye. The wheel of her suitcase got caught in a sidewalk crack, and I dug my nails into my thigh watching her yank it out. She banged on the trunk until he popped it from inside the car. He didn't help with her bags. She got in and kissed him on the mouth, and then he sped off, leaving tire tracks. When they were gone, I touched the marks. I put my hand to my lips.

Our mother ended up allowing Debbie to move back if she quit the club, but Debbie wouldn't take her calls. She cut off contact with both our parents. She bounced around for a few months, couch surfing with friends and staying with men she had brief, volatile flings with that ended with her being left behind in a McDonald's parking lot and, at least once, being pressured into sex with their roommates.

Then, she met Dominic, who lived alone in a studio apartment. Years earlier, a B-list celebrity hit him while driving drunk, and she'd paid him not to go to the cops. The accident messed up his back, and his doctor prescribed Vicodin for the pain. He built up tolerance and began needing higher doses, his pills running out in ten days instead of thirty. Then, it was heroin, which was cheaper than opiates and didn't require making eye contact with a tight-lipped pharmacist who disappeared for twenty minutes to "see if we have any in back," which meant she was looking him up in California's controlled substance prescription database and snitching to his doctor.

Dominic wasn't a bad guy. He was generous and a surprisingly good cook. He was mostly harmless, other than the part where living with him meant constantly being around pills or heroin. Debbie wasn't some virgin from a Renaissance painting when she met him, but I doubt she'd ever tried heroin. She preferred pills to needles but would do what had to be done. I couldn't tell if Debbie even liked Dominic romantically. Their relationship seemed so transactional: he had an apartment, she was willing to workshop his bad acoustic guitar songs, they both liked to get high and didn't mind sharing what they scored. When I told her this, she laughed in my face.

"All relationships are transactional," she said. "Grow up."

5.

By late September, our sunburns faded, and days were becoming interchangeable. Ronnie would drive to the electronics store where he kept track of inventory and leave me behind to "research what classes to sign up for." He hadn't gone to college, and I'd convinced him it was normal to devote ungodly amounts of time to "doing my due diligence." Really, I was spending most days watching *SpongeBob SquarePants*, reading novels about unlikable women behaving badly, and masturbating into a vegetative state. Every time I thought about college, this drained-pool feeling went through me, starting in my stomach, and radiating out to my lungs and brain. I couldn't reconcile the me that might perform mass spectrometry in chem lab with the me that had a drug-resistant UTI from skinny-dipping in the LA River on Debbie's dare. Ronnie didn't like how much time I was spending with Debbie, who scared the hell out of him.

"She doesn't understand boundaries," he said. "She treats you like a toy."

"Don't you think that's kind of reductive?" I said, lobbing therapy-speak back at him.

We were yet again eating microwave quesadillas on the

couch. He didn't own a nonstick pan, and I didn't have it in me to spend ten minutes scraping off melted cheese in the sink. It's not that I thought our life together would be glamorous, but I wasn't prepared for how much living with someone entailed having fraught conversations while picking each other's eyelashes out of shitty food.

"I don't think it is," he said. "She's not a stable person. Half the time you're with her, you come home in a horrible mood. Maybe you'd be happier if you took some space."

How could I explain that whether I had fun—whether Debbie was a good sister or a bad one—was beside the point? I didn't like who I was when I was with her, but I didn't like myself any other time either.

"Took some space as in stopped talking to her? I know the nuances of sisterhood might be lost on you, but I can't just cut Debbie out of my life."

"I didn't mean you should become estranged."

He pronounced *estranged* like a mom with a Chardonnay problem and a house overloaded with As-Seen-on-TV crap. "You shouldn't let her have this much power over you." A rope of oily cheese hung down his chin.

"Enough, okay?" I said, moving my plate to the floor. "I'm figuring it out."

"Are you?"

He said this so gently, I pinched the meat of my thigh to keep from crying out. Sometimes I wanted Ronnie to lay hands on me, to block Debbie's number in my phone and only allow me to see her with him present. To control my finances and choose my classes and watch me do my homework.

"It's a little late to register for classes this term, but I've got a few months to figure my shit out for the next one," I said. "I won't have as much time to spend with Debbie once I'm in school."

"You know you don't have to go to college, right? You could get a job."

"You don't think I can pull it off?"

"Baby, that's not what I mean at all." He swiped at his cheesy chin and placed a greasy hand over mine. "I just want you to be happy. Books make you happy. What if you got a job at a bookstore or a library?"

"I don't know."

I didn't want to give him the satisfaction of knowing me better than I knew myself. But, also, I did want him to know me better than I knew myself, so that he could explain me back to me. I thought back to our first conversation, to what household items we'd become if zapped with a mad scientist's ray. If there was a knife waiting to burst out of me, maybe Ronnie could get it out.

◖◗

I tried to do things the right way. I took a job as a page at the Valley College library. This felt like a step toward enrolling as a student, a chance to spend time on campus before committing. I watched students sit in the same spot for hours, eyes sutured to their textbooks. I resented their focus, the effortless way they parked their asses in broken swivel chairs until they'd learned their money's worth. Ronnie would pick me up after work, and we would go to a drive-through for dinner or nuke something in the microwave (we'd moved on from quesadillas to hot dogs). We watched *Jeopardy!* or *Match Game* and shared a joint. Game shows were the entirety of our shared taste. I preferred dark comedies and erotic thrillers, anything with acidic people on the verge.

Some nights, Ronnie gave me driving lessons in the parking lot of the mall. I liked when he adjusted my hands on the steering wheel and reminded me to check my mirrors. "Careful, you'll schvark it," he'd admonish when I zoomed over a speed bump; in whatever language he thought he was speaking, to "schvark" was to scrape the underside of the car. There was something hot about him deploying a Yiddish-sounding word. I was most attracted to him when he was telling me what to do.

He tried to bring that same energy to bed, but he was too tender with me. I pulled his hair, bit his neck, demanded he tell me I was nothing. He looked adoringly in my eyes and came immediately. I pretended I'd also come, as a courtesy.

"Love you," he said, kissing my cheek, my neck, my shoulder.

By the time I remembered to say "Love you too," he was asleep.

I got myself off staring at the plastic stars on our ceiling. *What are you doing what are you doing what are you doing* rang through me like a fire alarm. I tried to quiet Debbie's voice telling me that moving in with Ronnie was stupid, that she had eggs in her fridge that would outlast us. He snored next to me, his body heat and sex smell making me want to shed my entire skin. Even consecutive orgasms couldn't empty me out anymore. I gave up trying to sleep. I put on clean underwear and went to Salvation.

It was almost one when I got there, my favorite time to be at the bar. People were rolling in from parties all over the city, showing off bloody new tattoos of cobras and generic female names. A mother and daughter were celebrating a joint birthday. The jukebox blasted nostalgic nineties music. Eight or so people huddled around a large table in back, laughing and hooting and throwing back drinks. Debbie was one of them. She took a shot and massaged a bruise on her neck. It could have been a hickey, but its garish color and resemblance to fingertips made my stomach twist. I had the urge to fireman's-carry her out of the bar.

"Hey!" Debbie shouted when she spotted me. "Come join us!"

It wasn't too late to turn back. To give her a quick hug and pretend I was heading home. It's not like she would have tied me to a chair. As I made my way over, my body felt like a shopping cart with locked wheels that I was forcing across a parking lot. She put an arm around me and squeezed me into the circle.

"Perfect timing," she said. "Justin's about to go."

They were playing the Wealthy Patron, a game where someone comes up with a weird, shitty thing a wealthy patron could pay to watch you do, and everyone else names their price. It was rumored to have been invented by the owner of the Christian bookstore that preceded Salvation.

Supposedly, the owner's wife walked in on him playing with his mistress, lost her shit, and cited the game in their divorce proceedings. Soon after, the bookstore was sold.

"Here," Debbie said, shoving two vodka shots in my hands. "Get on my level."

A skeletal hipster in wire-frame glasses tapped his fingers against the table, scanning the faces of everyone in the group. It was his turn.

"Cheers," Debbie said, taking the first shot with me.

"Okay," the hipster said, chewing his lip. "I've got one. How much would the wealthy patron have to pay to watch a stranger plug one of your nostrils and jizz in the other?"

Everyone groaned. "Yuck," said the woman next to me. Her hair was blue and closely shaved. She smiled when she caught me looking. I took a second shot. Debbie handed me another. The group went silent as we considered our answers. Debbie nudged me. I took a third shot.

"Ready?" the hipster asked. "One, two, three . . ."

We shouted our answers at the same time, so no one could pivot after hearing someone else's. I said four hundred dollars. Debbie said two hundred. Blue Hair said thirty. The loudest answer came from a man in a pale green T-shirt covered in bleach stains, who'd shouted two thousand dollars.

"Yeah right, Franklin," Debbie said. "We both know you'd do it for the lowest milligram of Percocet."

Everyone cracked up, Franklin included. "Debbie, I love you, but you're such a cunt," he said.

I'd seen Franklin around. He sold pills at Salvation, immediately blowing most of the money on drinks to hide the evidence. He had oily brown hair and looked a little like Ronnie if you lightened his skin and cranked his degeneracy up ninety percent. It disturbed me that I found this man, who was clearly headed toward either prison or an overdose, attractive.

We played the Wealthy Patron late into the night, laughing, drinking, toeing the edge of some abyss. There was something wholesome about the game. Most people couldn't handle such masochistic introspection, and our mutual craving for it bound us together.

"Tonight, I have many sisters," I remember saying, my arms around Debbie and the woman with blue hair. My memory short-circuits after that, minus a few flashes: the woman typing her number into my phone, Franklin doing a body shot off the notch in my neck, Debbie crushing two pills on a handheld mirror, a sharp pain in my leg.

I woke up the next day to my phone ringing.

"You okay?" Ronnie asked. "Did I wake you?"

It was noon. He was on his lunch break.

"I'm fine," I said. "Just sleepy."

I'd made it home at least. I shifted in bed and yelped when the covers rubbed against my left leg. There was a two-inch gash on my thigh. Someone—me? Debbie? Franklin?—had staunched the bleeding with a pantyliner and a hair tie.

"What is it?" Ronnie said.

"Muscle cramp," I said, breathing through my mouth.

I had unread text messages from Debbie, Dominic, and "sandra blu hairr." I opened Sandra's first. It was a nude, taken in Salvation's bathroom. The flash caught her sapphire nipple ring, which glowed like an all-seeing eye. With a jolt, I realized she was responding to a nude I'd sent her first.

"Did you go out with your sister last night?" Ronnie asked.

I didn't respond. I'd sent Sandra a full-body shot of me flat on my back in Ronnie's bed. In our bed. It wasn't even sexy—I looked like a cadaver in an anatomy lab. Eyes filmy, no makeup, hair inexplicably wet.

"Do I want to know?" Ronnie said.

"I couldn't sleep," I told him.

I opened Debbie's text, sent at three in the morning: *where are you?*

I opened Dominic's text. He'd sent a lone question mark, in response to the same nude I'd sent Sandra. I dry-heaved and dropped the phone.

Ronnie called out from the floor.

I didn't remember taking the photo or what had possessed me to send it to Dominic. I'd met slices of bread I was more attracted to. There was no way I'd been trying to fuck him. I'd sent the photo to hurt Debbie.

"What?" I said.

Ronnie sighed. "You sound so tired, baby. Maybe you should—"

"My mom's calling. I'll see you at home." I hung up and silenced my phone's ringer.

I could see Ronnie knitting his eyebrows, brainstorming a novel way to get through to me. How could I explain this thing between Debbie and me when I didn't fully understand it myself? My whole life, I'd had this compulsion to watch over her. My presence didn't stop her from doing what she wanted, but I felt the need to play witness. It was spiritual, how she magnetized me. How, where she went, dynamite followed. Being Debbie's sister was obliterating. It was also the closest thing to knowing who I was.

6.

Working at a community college library wasn't the cozy, literary fantasy I'd concocted in my mind. It was freezing, and the coffee machine was broken with no indication of ever being repaired. It was impossible to read during my shifts—there was always some beady-eyed grandma who needed help finding a whodunit, or a sweaty student waiting on me to fix the copy machine. Even if I'd had time to read, the library purchased only single copies of the dark, woman-authored novels I was interested in, and I'd been strictly instructed to save the fast-movers for library patrons. Reshelving books with crusted food between the pages, I wished I was home with Ronnie. But when I watched TV with Ronnie on our ratty couch, I wished I was at Salvation. It was only when I followed Debbie down a rabbit hole that ended in scar tissue and the deforestation of my remaining dopamine that my want quieted.

At the start of spring semester, leaves the color of pantyhose coated the ground. I'd intended to enroll as a student that term, but I'd watched the deadline come and go. Instead, I was promoted to library assistant. The pay was barely more than what I earned as a page and didn't make up for the extra duties like answering phones and computing fines. It wasn't hard, but settling into the work expended all the energy I'd allocated toward personal growth. Debbie's voice echoed in my head, asking the question beneath all her questions: *Who do you think you are?* I didn't have an answer.

In mid-February, I quit my job and blew my last couple of paychecks on a knife. It had a three-inch blade and a teal fish-scale pattern around the hilt. It reminded me of mermaids and gutted sea life, and there was something sexual about handling it that made me avoid the pawn shop owner's gaze. The guy who'd owned the knife had gotten throat cancer and pawned it to pay for chemo. He pawned his watch too, and a bronze statue of a woman fingering herself on the moon. It covered only his first month of treatment. The pawn shop owner didn't know if he was still alive. I paid for the knife, and, as he was ringing me up, told him to throw in the statue. I displayed it in my corner of the bedroom, using a folding chair as a pedestal.

"Hot," Ronnie said when he got home. "She kind of looks like you."

That's not why I bought it, I wanted to say, but then he'd ask why I bought it, so I said nothing.

Why did I buy it? It had to do with her expression, shameless and confrontational. I wanted to wear my agency that nakedly. I slept better than I had in weeks, knowing she was watching over me. And when the clawing emptiness kept me up and I snuck out in the night, she kept

Ronnie company. I still think about the statue, about the role it played in summoning everything that followed. It's hard to know which was the bigger catalyst. The more obvious answer is the knife.

7.

On my nineteenth birthday that February, Debbie and I went to a new bar in Hollywood named after a tool. Screwdriver or Wrench or something. The bartenders wore hard hats and there were nails and drill bits embedded in the walls. It was Debbie's idea.

"It looks like shrapnel," I said. "Like the bar was bombed and the owners decided it'd be too expensive to repair, better to just build a theme around it."

Debbie groaned. "Why is everything war to you?"

The bar smelled like Eurotrash cologne and neck sweat. It seemed as though everyone there was either a middle-aged man looking to ruin his life or a high school cafeteria lady with green streaks in her hair. Ronnie and I were fighting. I had asked for a new vibrator for my birthday, and he got mopey about it. He made me watch an eighteen-minute video about the effects of toxic family relationships on libido. I felt I had to prove I was still attracted to him, so I straddled his lap and pushed my underwear to the side, but I couldn't get wet, and it hurt even with his spit, and my grimacing made him go soft. I tried to give him a handjob, but he recoiled from my touch. I uninvited him from my birthday party, and he called me a child, and I called him a pedophile. I sobbed on the bus to Debbie's, and no one paid me any mind. Twelve other souls gliding alongside me in the dark, pretending I was an empty seat.

"Seriously, when are you leaving him?" Debbie said, two drinks in.

"Why would I leave Ronnie?"

"Because you don't love him. Because you're nineteen and shouldn't be glued to some dude. Because he's low-key a basic bitch and can't get you off."

"That's not true."

I was ready to deny everything: the fight with Ronnie, feeling invisible on the bus, and especially our sisterhood, which increasingly felt like Russian roulette.

"Which part?" she said.

"You need to be nicer to Ronnie. He's not going anywhere."

"Oh, yeah?" She stirred the ice in her cocktail with a finger, the rough-cut crystal of her ring scratching the glass.

"We might get married. We might have babies someday."

Debbie laughed.

"What?"

"Nothing." She bit the inside of her cheek.

"Ugh, just say it."

"I don't want to hurt your feelings."

I glared at her.

"You've never talked about having kids before." She shrugged. "I didn't think you were the mothering type."

Before I could answer, a man in a denim shirt bumped into me. "Shit," he said, dropping to his knees. He crawled under my chair, using his phone's flashlight to scan the floor. He cupped a white pill. We watched him make his way to a corner booth, where a man in a leather jacket waited with nail clippers. He split the pill in his palm. The men grinned at each other. Each took half.

"Aww," Debbie said, placing her hand over mine. It felt cold and bony, like touching a reptile. "It's like us."

She didn't blink for a long time. Her eyes were so glassy I could see my future in them.

"I think I'm ready to head out," I said.

"Already? I haven't given you your gift." She handed me a velvet pouch. Inside, a magenta Swiss Army knife that looked like the sort of thing you'd give a Girl Scout. "It's got nail clippers and everything. More practical than the one you're carrying, no?"

I hadn't told her about my knife. I hadn't told anyone. She must have followed me to the pawn shop or snooped in my bag when I was in the bathroom. Debbie was like that. She'd dig a lipstick out of my bag, apply it, then slip it into her purse right in front of me.

"Little sister, why do you have some old guy's knife?" she asked.

"For protection."

"Protection from what?"

I didn't know how to explain it. It—the feeling—was like eating chicken and realizing halfway through it was raw. I felt that way all the time.

I mumbled, "Don't worry about it," and buried my face in the drinks menu.

"You're ridiculous. This shit is why no one knows what to do with you."

A group of men turned to look at me. The one with a neck tattoo of Jesus said, “I’ve got a few ideas.” His buddies high-fived him.

Debbie smiled at them. “Prove it.”

•

An hour later, we pulled into the emergency room parking lot. There were six of us crammed in the sedan—Neck Tattoo was driving, Debbie was up front barking directions, and I was in back, wiping up the blood running down my legs with cocktail napkins.

We pulled up to the curb, and Debbie helped me out of the car. “How are you?” she asked.

“Fine,” I said, doubled over. My body felt like a period cramp plugged into an electric socket. “The bleeding stopped. We don’t need to go in.”

She poked the bloody spot in my lap and rubbed her fingers together. “Oh, sure. That looks normal.”

An SUV pulled over next to us. A woman got out, hyperventilating and clutching her stomach. The driver said something indistinguishable and drove off. He flew over a speed bump, schvarking the back of his car against the parking lot concrete. The sound made me tearful.

“We’ve got it from here,” I told the men from the bar. “Thanks for the ride.”

Relief smoothed out their faces. This was a story for them to tell on some gross couch, cracking a sixth beer, everyone drunk or high or heading in that direction, *this one time, some bar slut bled all over me in the bathroom, and I had to drive her and her crazy sister to the ER.*

"I can stay if you want," Neck Tattoo said, forcing a smile. "For like, support."

Forced intimacy made me light-headed. He looked grateful when I said no.

They sped off as though pursued at gunpoint. I wished Debbie hadn't told them, back at the bar, that I gave the second-best blowjobs in Los Angeles. That I hadn't insisted on proving her wrong—that I was number one—as if this was a long-held conviction. I'd never cheated on Ronnie before and was shocked at how little it took. It wasn't even because we'd fought. It was Debbie who'd pressured me into it, who'd been in the mood to watch something explode. I hated myself for taking the bait. I hated Ronnie for not coming out with us and preventing my betrayal. I hated everyone in the waiting room who was here for normal reasons. Most of all, I hated Debbie, for showing me yet again who we were.

◐

The triage nurse didn't think I needed immediate attention. She gave me Tylenol and suggested we "get cozy," directing us to the waiting room. We'd been waiting an hour when Debbie started getting jittery. She kept gawking at the people passing by in scrubs and white coats and sinking in her chair when they looked back.

"Motherfucker," she said under her breath.

"You okay?" I asked.

She ignored me.

I took her hand, but she flinched away.

"This is bullshit." She was shaking her head and speaking too loudly for an emergency room at three in the morning. Her pupils were pinpricks. "I can't take this anymore," she whisper-shouted.

"Can't take what, waiting?"

She groaned. She'd been chewing gum earlier, but she seemed to have swallowed it. "White coats, man. The fucking white coats."

"You're okay. They're not hurting anyone."

"I've gotta get out of here," she said, picking at a scab on her knee. It began to ooze.

"Calm down." I put my arm around her. "Everything's fine."

"No." She shrugged me off. "I have to go."

"It's my birthday," I whispered. I looked around to see if anyone heard. I don't know what I expected—a nurse to pop out with a cake, while the randos in the waiting room serenaded me?

Debbie made for the exit.

"Is this about Dominic?" I said. "I didn't mean to send that picture. Don't go. Please."

She peered over her shoulder a couple of times to see if she was being followed, looking everywhere but at me.

Then she was gone. I sank back in my chair, shaking. She'd forgotten her purse. I slung its long chain across my body. Now people were staring at me to see if I was about to make a shitty night even shittier. This was classic Debbie: following her high wherever it took her, dooming everyone else to soak in her mess. She used to come home blitzed from the strip club, pick a pointless fight with our father about feminism or our mother's illness, storm out of the house raving that no one loved her, and leave me behind as collateral. When I was sixteen, she "accidentally" abandoned me at a party in the Arts District. I accepted a ride home from a guy who kept insisting we go to his converted loft instead. I lied about being on my period. He said he "didn't mind a little finger paint."

Hours passed before they called my name. I left behind a bloody splotch on the seat. Wiping it with my dress only made it streakier. "Don't worry about it," a nurse said, taking my elbow. After that, I was dealt with quickly. Someone stuck a lubey wand inside me and said I was having a miscarriage. The ultrasound looked like black-and-white footage of a tiny hamster lying supine in its wheel. Why hadn't anyone warned me it would look like that?

I hadn't known I was pregnant and was relieved that, soon, I wouldn't be. Someone asked if I wanted a D&C, pills to shed what was left, or to wait for it to pass naturally. "We can't do the D&C here since it's not an emergency, but you can do it at your gynecologist's office," she said. What gynecologist? "Naturally," I mumbled. I was given another Tylenol and a thick pad and told to come back if I started fevering.

Someone patted my hand and gave me a pamphlet called "Self-Care After Miscarriage." It was just black-and-white text. No reassuring clip art of pastel hearts, teddy bears, or flower wreaths. My anger hardened around Debbie and Ronnie, fusing them to me like extra limbs. A sharp pang of want went through me, but want for what? Ronnie would have burst into tears if he were here. Debbie was too high to comfort me, even if she'd stayed. I wanted a specific version of her, the one who would make fun of the other people in the waiting room to make me laugh. The one who kissed my skinned knee after I fell off my bike. I'd believed that some sisterly intuition would activate when I truly needed her. How mortifying to be proven wrong.

The morning buses were running by the time I left. I avoided the driver's eyes and claimed a row for myself. There were three other people on the bus, women in housekeeping uniforms. One was nodding off, eyes snapping open each time her head slid down the window glass. Another had her hair in a tight bun and was playing sudoku. The third was sitting too far back for me to see what she was doing. When she caught me looking, she smiled. It made me feel ashamed for where I'd been and where I was going.

I dug inside Debbie's purse. Two lipsticks, both mine. Crumpled one- and five-dollar bills. A silver rabbit figurine with black crystal eyes, definitely stolen. It was covered in scratch marks. I untwisted its tail and poured its contents into my hand. There were nine pills—five Oxys, three Ativans, and a blue one I didn't recognize. The bus lurched, and I clutched them in my fist. I dry-swallowed an Ativan and an Oxy and took my lipsticks back. I left the Swiss Army knife behind on my seat.

8.

Debbie called the next morning as if nothing had gone down between us. She asked how I was feeling, and it was so breezy, you'd think I twisted my ankle rollerblading at the beach. I told her about the miscarriage. She was quiet a few beats. Then, "Do you promise?"

"Excuse me?" I said.

"You're not just saying that to guilt me?"

I waited for her to ask if I was in pain. If I'd known I was pregnant. If I was sad I wasn't anymore.

"Hello? You there?" she asked.

"I'm here."

"Well, how do you feel now?"

"Shitty. Everything hurts."

"Sorry. I guess you have an excuse to keep Ronnie off you for a while."

She kept talking at me, something about it all being for the best, about fighting with Dominic and did I want to go out tonight. Also, she needed her purse, I better not have left her purse at the ER. I hung up. I felt my pulse in my temples, my stomach. I took an Oxy and got back in bed beneath a heated blanket.

When she knocked on my door that night, I didn't

answer. I watched her through the peephole. She wore a black sequined minidress and hoop earrings, hair tied back in a high ponytail, lips glossed with the rose-gold shade she wore when she was on the hunt.

When I didn't answer the door, she called my cell. When I ignored her calls, she banged louder.

"I know you're in there," she said. "Let me in."

Ronnie was asleep on the couch with one hand in his pants and the other in a bag of Doritos. He groaned as the bangs grew louder.

"Will you get that?" he said, turning away from the door, chips spilling onto the carpet.

"No."

He sighed and rubbed his eyes, coating his brows in orange powder. "What's going on?"

When I didn't answer, he turned to face me. "Jesus," he said, sitting up. "Why do you have a knife?"

"Talk quieter," I said. "I don't want her to hear you." I pointed my knife at him, watched the overhead light dance up and down its spine.

Outside, Debbie was yelling, "Is this because I didn't stay with you last night? Let me in so we can talk like adults."

Ronnie looked from the door to my face to my knife like a cartoon character, mouth half open. I used to love that about him, how goofy he was.

"Where did you get that?" he said, backing away. "You're just trying to scare her, right?"

"Don't let her in here."

"I won't. I won't! Stop waving that thing at me."

He paced the living room in rubber flip-flops, side-stepping all our crap. His shoes were everywhere, their corn chip stench woven into the carpet. Junk mail, receipts, and college financial aid pamphlets were stacked on the coffee table and kitchen counter, were spewing out from under the couch. The hamper by the TV was so full it had fallen over. Ronnie's undershirts had yellow pit stains that reminded me of smeared insects.

"What happened last night?" he said.

He stepped over the piles of dirty clothes, his big toe hooking a lacy blue thong. He bent down and laid it, refolded, at the top of the pile. He did it so tenderly. You'd never know it was dirty, four-year-old underwear. The sweetness of that gesture, how casual it was, made me tear up. Ronnie was a good person. I couldn't decide if I wanted to embrace him, or kick him out of the apartment at knifepoint, or which of us deserved better than the other.

Debbie screamed, "If you're not going to let me in, at least give me my fucking purse!"

A short pause, her ragged breathing.

"Fine! Keep it. But don't expect me to treat you ever again. Fucking baby. Go pass a blood lemon!" She kicked the door so hard a flurry fell from the popcorn ceiling.

I waited for the sound of her padding toward the elevator, and then, for the elevator's ding.

"A blood what?" Ronnie said. "Is she high?"

"Probably."

When Debbie had an abortion her sophomore year of high school, she was warned that she may pass lemon-size blood clots. I'd gone with her to Planned Parenthood. I didn't abandon her in the waiting room. I stayed the whole time, studying for an exam on *Hamlet* while someone's infant pet my leg like a dog. I let her have window seat on the bus ride home. Our pediatrician had given Debbie some extra money on top of what she needed for the abortion, and we bought two popsicles each from an ice cream truck a few blocks from home. Debbie was ravenous. I let her finish mine. I got a C on the test, my worst ever grade in English. I'd been secretly hoping to qualify for Honors English the following year. But after the exam, my grade wasn't high enough, and my teacher "had concerns about my commitment." I told no one. It was less embarrassing to pretend I didn't care than to out myself as a failure.

I didn't tell Ronnie about the miscarriage, afraid it would bind me more tightly to him. He wanted kids someday, had even told me some names he liked: Rex, Scarlet, or "something to honor your Jewish heritage." The thought of being responsible for a child, when I could barely control where my own feet led me, was horrifying. Maybe Debbie was right—maybe I wasn't the mothering type. Maybe that was why I miscarried.

After the elevator dinged, I locked myself in the bathroom with her purse. I took another Ativan, another Oxy, and whatever the blue pill was. I shivered as they hit the back of my throat. Something stabbed my uterus with a trident. My fetus's ghost? I cried and told Ronnie that Debbie was a bear trap, that I'd been willingly chewing off my own leg.

"It's not your fault," he said. "Toxic people hijack intimacy into violence. Don't let her gaslight you."

It made me laugh, how ill-suited I was for someone like him, who quoted therapy memes he saw on Instagram, who loved me despite having little reason to. I held it against him. If I was what he loved, then there was something broken in him too.

He wasn't wrong about intimacy and violence going hand in hand. But sometimes it's better when these things aren't named. When I left the bathroom, Ronnie put his arms around me. I cried into his shoulder, still gripping the knife.

"I wish I could carry some of this pain for you," he said, kissing my head.

We sat together on the floor, Ronnie rubbing my back, me mimicking the motion against his leg with the blunt side of the knife. The overhead light illuminated the hilt, fish scales glinting like crashing waves. He told me if I wanted, I could cut him a little. He took off his sweatpants and offered his thigh. The blade was so sharp, it barely grazed him. I traced a spiral, and the blood surfaced delicately, like fresh buds emerging from the ground. When I looked up, he was watching me. He didn't yank at my shirt or try anything. He just sat there, running his hands up and down my back, whispering, "I'm sorry," whispering my name.

9.

I ran through Debbie's pills quickly and bought more from Franklin at Salvation. I needed a break from feeling so much all the time. Without my library job to keep me busy, and with Debbie and me not speaking, I spent days hitting *replay* in my head. Ronnie would leave for work, and I'd inch from our bed to the couch and back to bed, thinking about what happened with Kim and the fake art buyer, how Ronnie had no idea I'd miscarried his baby, all the times I should have stood up to Debbie and hadn't. The strip club dressing room. The time Debbie and I saw my father out and about with one of his secret girlfriends.

It was summer, I was twelve, Debbie fourteen, and we'd just shoplifted drugstore lipstick. My lips were Electric Cantaloupe, hers Blue Velvet. My jaw ached from smiling. There was nothing better than when Debbie and I played for the same team. We were taking the long way home, walking past banks and pet food stores and white-washed Mexican and Chinese restaurants with racist, pun-based names that would open and close in the span of a year.

"Let's cut across the park," Debbie said, linking arms.

That's when we saw our father and this red-haired woman picnicking on the grass, laughing, double-scoop ice cream cones in their hands. The happy-go-lucky look on his face was so foreign, as if the woman had slotted it in the way I used to with my Mr. Potato Head toy. This was a man who roamed our house like he'd just woken from a twenty-year coma. Debbie and I turned in the other direction and were silent the rest of the walk home.

We'd both known—but had never spoken of—our father's affairs. When his phone voice passed through our papyrus-thin walls at night, Debbie made a show of opening our bedroom door just to slam it. When he took us grocery shopping and bought almond granola, which none of us liked, Debbie and I exchanged looks. He shelved it with our cereals, but a couple of days later, the box was gone. For weeks, I caught Debbie eyeing the space where it had been. I was dying to know what she knew of his affair and how she felt about it. But I was afraid that speaking openly of our family dysfunction would make it permanent, and so I never asked. I sympathized so much with my mother then, who was right to be suspicious of what happened outside our home, and wrong to put her faith in family.

Replaying this memory, I kept wondering whether I was the same. I felt chemically bonded to Debbie, regardless of how much chaos she brought to my life. If genetics didn't usher in incurable mental illness, being Debbie's sister would. Chewing on these thoughts too long ended with me gasping for air, wondering if I was dying.

When the world's seams came apart, when I toed the edge of a me-shaped hole, I took the tail off the rabbit. I couldn't unscrew it fast enough. I left new scratches on the surface, knocked out its dark crystal eye. The Ativans were dainty white disks with a score down the middle for splitting. I took them whole. Sometimes I dissolved them under my tongue or snorted them, but that felt too close to the behavior of an addict. I needed them, but I didn't like knowing I needed them. It helped to take them preemptively, before the needle-pierce of dread.

The Oxys were a warm bath. They came in beautiful tropical colors—marigold, seafoam green, ripe peach—and turned my brain into cotton candy. Boundaries blurred, time stretched like taffy. My breathing slowed, and sometimes I couldn't tell if I was asleep or awake. I felt less like a hunted animal. Objects around me—our dirty laundry, the kitchen scissors, Debbie's purse—were no longer malevolent containers. I could stare at them all I wanted without feeling doomed. When I saw things on TV that reminded me of the pills—white plates, party balloons, a blue eye—I felt protected. I understood why people wore evil eyes and rosaries and red string bracelets. The pills didn't cure me of the drained-pool feeling. But they pumped a little helium into everything.

I told Ronnie my fatigue and occasional loopiness stemmed from depression and anxiety. When he was home, I took the pills in the bathroom. But a month after my miscarriage, I fell asleep clutching the rabbit and woke to its contents splayed on the comforter between us. Ronnie was pinching an Ativan between his fingers and pill ID'ing it on his phone.

"Hey, it's okay," he said when I started to cry. "Whatever's going on, we'll figure it out."

"I don't know what's wrong with me," I said. "I'm scared all the time."

He pulled me into a hug. "How long have you been taking these?" he asked into my hair.

"Once a week maybe, when I've really needed them," I lied.

I could feel his suspicion in the way his breathing hitched.

"They're Debbie's leftovers," I said. "This is the last of them."

"Fucking Debbie," Ronnie said, shaking his head. "I'm glad you're staying away from her. I'll take care of you."

He gave me vitamin D capsules and a book called *Codependent No More.*

I started going to Salvation while Ronnie was at work. I bought more Oxy and Ativan from Franklin and told people I got fired from the library. It didn't feel like a lie. People started buying me drinks again. The stakes got higher when we played the Wealthy Patron, now that I had no income and needed to lower my rates. Sometimes, a finance or real estate bro would overhear us playing and yell, "Sold!" when I lowballed. Sometimes, I let them do stupid things to me. One had me yell degrading garbage at him while he jerked off for forty dollars. Another paid me seventy to swap underwear. He tucked mine in his wallet, but I had to wear his green boxers decorated with Christmas wreaths under my dress. Laughing with people who meant nothing and everything to me, humiliating ourselves under the guise of self-knowledge—this was the most I could imagine for myself.

Weeks passed with no contact from Debbie. I began to worry. It was April, and we hadn't spoken in two months. I considered going to her apartment, but I was afraid of what I'd find. In my twilight sleep, I saw her dead on the bathroom floor, flies buzzing in and out of her mouth.

I decided to call her. It went to voicemail. I tried Dominic next.

Debbie was okay, he told me. She was in rehab.

10.

The following week, someone called from a rehab clinic to say Debbie was leaving early. She'd claimed I was coming to get her. It was as though she'd known I'd called Dominic looking for her, and she'd been waiting this whole time for me to crack. When he first told me she was in rehab, I wondered if she was getting clean because of me. If, after another cycle of self-degradation, she realized how badly she'd betrayed me and decided to get help. That theory lasted less than the time it took to swallow my morning pills. Maybe she'd gotten busted and chose rehab on some public defender's advice. I wondered what it meant, legally, if she was ducking out early. Then the pills kicked in, softening the edges of everything like an oil painting, and I found I didn't care.

I debated standing her up, letting her rot in the waiting room for hours, the way I had the night of my miscarriage. How long before she gave up and walked to the bus? I wanted her to be the deserted one for once.

I agonized all afternoon over whether to pick her up. Ronnie was against it. He said nothing had changed between Debbie and me, that I had no reason to believe she was any different.

"Don't you think going to rehab signals a kind of

change?" I asked. "Maybe she's done some work on herself. Don't you think I should find out?"

"She's leaving early!" He shook his head and poured more milk in his "late-afternoon cereal." His Froot Loops dyed it a sickly green. "And she's the reason you're hooked on pills."

"What?"

Ronnie sighed. "Don't lie to me. I know you're still using."

"Rarely," I mumbled.

"Stop it," he said, nearly yelling. "Stop lying to me."

"For someone obsessed with mental health, you're awfully judgmental."

"I'm trying to help you. You're obviously going through something, and I don't think sketchy pills are the best solution."

"Oh, you don't think? Okay, I'll just keep taking your vitamins. I'll be fixed in no time."

He groaned and massaged his head. "Give me a minute to think. I'll come up with something."

"Is it a video game?"

Ronnie's eyes got big. "Don't be like that. I'm on your side."

"Because you love me, or because you want me to stop spending money on drugs?"

"You're not the only one this affects." His eyes watered. He bit his lip in a hopeless attempt to look tough. "I feel like I'm in love with a coma patient."

"Excuse me?"

"Don't pretend you don't know what I'm talking about. Those pills turn you into a zombie."

"They do not." I fixed my posture like I was back in middle school, my grandmother tying a broom to my back.

"They do! Having sex with you is like fucking a corpse. You just lie there with your dead eyes all tiny and unfocused. It's creepy. You make me feel like a pervert."

"Maybe you are a pervert." I took a steadying breath, willed my pupils to widen. "Maybe fucking you makes me feel dead."

"What?" He held his spoon suspended in midair, the colorful faces of the Froot Loops looking on with their mouths agape.

"Maybe dissociating is the only way I can stomach it anymore. Have you considered that?"

"You don't mean it." Again with the baby seal eyes. It was exhausting being around someone who was always acting as if you'd knocked him to the ground.

"You're right." Was I yelling? "It's not a new thing. It's the only way I could stomach it ever."

He stood so fast his stool tipped over. Any theatrics he hoped to achieve were undercut by the soft sound of our carpet absorbing the stool's fall. He stormed into the bedroom and slammed the door. I hadn't thought for a second that he'd hurt me. I almost wanted him to. It would be a relief for hands to close around my throat. It would be an excuse to fight back.

I wiped my eyes and left the apartment. I considered borrowing Ronnie's car, but I was afraid he might do something crazy like report it as stolen. Admittedly, that wasn't his style. He was good to me, though I wasn't giving him much reason to stay that way. I left his keys on the hook and boarded the bus red-faced and panting. As we pulled away from the stop, I took another pill.

The whole way there, I considered what to say to Debbie. What I wanted from our sisterhood. The months apart hadn't delivered clarity. I hadn't enrolled in school, or gotten sober, or worked on my relationship with Ronnie. Had Debbie been giving me space, or was she angry with me? Who had ditched whom? Worst of all, I missed her. Teachers used to write in my progress reports that they were *concerned about Debbie's influence.* That's what I wanted: for Debbie to keep her influence to herself. How could I know what kind of person I wanted to be when she was always forcing me to see myself on her terms?

"Back the fuck off," I mumbled.

An elderly woman in the row ahead turned around. Whatever she saw in my face made her move five rows up.

When I got to rehab, Debbie was waiting for me to sign her out. She'd gained a little weight, and her hair was greasy, and she didn't have any makeup on. She wore jeans, one of Dominic's checkered shirts, and a sagging purple backpack. It was unsettling how little she looked like my sister. She could have been anyone.

On the bus, she wouldn't explain her early departure. "It doesn't matter," she kept saying, which made me certain she'd gotten kicked out.

"What did you do?" I asked.

"Nothing," she said. "It just wasn't for me."

"Did you hook up with someone who worked there? Did they catch you using?"

"What? Are you serious?" She flinched as if I'd grabbed her by the hair.

"So, you decided sobriety's not for you?" I burrowed my finger into a hole in my seat, tearing the cheerful rainbow fabric.

"It's none of your business," she snapped. "You haven't spoken to me in months, and now you want to know my life?" She faced the window. "I can't believe you think I fucked someone on staff. Who am I, Mom?"

I sighed. "I don't know, Debbie."

She shook her head but didn't say anything more. She didn't ask how I was doing, and I didn't tell her. If she noticed any change in me—my slower response time, how I kept checking to make sure I hadn't lost my bag—she didn't show it. When she pulled the stop request cord at Hollywood Boulevard, I followed her off the bus. It wasn't the stop for her place or mine. We walked in silence, passing weed dispensaries, Thai restaurants, cheesy souvenir shops where, if your name was "American enough," you could find a keychain with it printed on a Walk of Fame star. I thought she was heading toward a liquor store with a bright yellow marquee, but she ducked into the laundromat next door.

Inside, it was packed and chilly, the air conditioner on full blast. Children chased each other around metal benches while their mothers scratched off lotto cards with quarters. Old men read the newspaper. A tight-faced woman yelled something about bean dip into her phone. Two dour teenagers scrolled Snapchat and shared a bag of Flamin' Hot

Cheetos. Debbie unzipped her backpack and started loading one of the washers.

"You want to wait here for two hours until your laundry's done?" I said. "What's wrong with the laundry in your building? Do you not live there anymore? Are you still with Dominic?"

She didn't answer. She was scoping out the people around us.

A girl about our age loaded a dryer with beautiful lingerie. She had bleached-blond hair with black roots and the kind of lips white girls from our school paid hundreds of dollars to emulate. She wore a denim jumpsuit and gigantic gold earrings with BITCH dangling inside the hoop. A rainbow assortment of bras, underwear, and negligees flew into her dryer. One cream-colored garment had a rust stain in the crotch. It made me feel tender toward her, like we shared a secret.

"Wait here," Debbie said. She did a lap around the laundromat. When she reached the entrance, she left.

I didn't have it in me to follow her. I was drained from arguing with Ronnie and wanted one drama-free day with my sister. I couldn't remember the last time we'd had that. Debbie liked to say, "If you're not asking yourself, *Am I about to ruin my life?* at least once a day, you're not living a life at all."

The girl with the lingerie applied holographic lip gloss and checked her Instagram notifications. Only nine new likes. She scrolled through a library of selfies; a couple were nudes. I watched her obscure her nipples and vagina with flower and unicorn emoji. After a while, she left the laundromat too.

Debbie returned wearing a droopy smile. She'd obviously taken something.

"Where did you go?" I said.

She waved me off. "How long ago did that girl with the underwear leave?"

"I don't know, ten minutes?"

Debbie scanned the room. Then she reached inside the girl's dryer, withdrew a fistful of lingerie, and stuck it down her jeans. Her oversized shirt concealed any lumps. The whole thing took twenty seconds. No one but me saw.

"Your turn," she said.

"No way. She's going to notice if half her stuff goes missing."

Debbie rolled her eyes. "Please, did you see how much crap she shoved in there? She's not going to notice a couple missing thongs."

"I don't want to."

Debbie's washer finished its cycle. She sighed and began transferring her clothes to a dryer. "It's good to see you, little sister." She took a seat next to me on the bench. "Even if you're still a narc."

"I'm not a narc," I mumbled.

"Whatever you say." Debbie lit a cigarette and started pacing the laundromat, blowing extravagant puffs of smoke.

The owner, a middle-aged Russian woman who'd been chatting with the lotto ticket mothers, said, "Ey, what are you doing? You can't smoke here." Her hair reminded me of the angry swirls our mother scribbled across the mirror when her meds ran out.

"Sorry," Debbie said. "I didn't see a *No Smoking* sign."

"Please," the owner said, pointing to the door.

Debbie took one last drag and killed the cigarette on her arm.

The owner gasped. "Are you crazy?"

Debbie smiled and stuck the butt in her pocket. People stared. One of the mothers summoned her children. The owner seemed to be deciding whether to kick Debbie out. She shook her head and muttered something in Russian. While this was happening, I eased open the dryer and stuffed a handful of lingerie down my pants.

•

Back on the bus, Debbie was bragging about being molested by our pediatrician.

"I've heard this so many times, I feel like I'm the one he molested," I said.

"I wasn't molested. I was sixteen."

We'd had this argument before. Debbie refused the role of victim, and I refused to recognize their gross friends-with-benefits arrangement as consensual.

"Every psychologist on the planet would agree that what happened to you was fucked-up," I said.

"What's fucked-up is how much you worship authority. You can't stand when people with power don't behave the way you want them to."

"You're right," I said, throwing my hands in the air. "It's

so weird of me to not want my doctor to fuck my underage sister."

"Don't be such a prude. I pursued him. Would you care this much if I hadn't gotten pregnant?"

"Of course," I said, though there was something extra violating about him rooting in her body. Picturing his self-satisfied expression when he handed Debbie the money for her abortion was revolting. The smugness of parting easily with hundreds of dollars, of reassuring himself he was a decent man in a pickle, one he'd be out of soon enough.

"It's not like he felt me up during my physical. He came to the club not knowing I worked there. He barely knew who I was—I'd seen him, what, a few times before that? He was hot, so I went for it. I made the first move."

"Debbie, come on. He knew you were sixteen. If he cared about you, he would have done something."

"Done what? Reported me to some agency? Turned me into a sex trafficking victim? Gotten me expelled from school and sent to juvie? You're right, that would have made my life so much better."

Across from us, a young woman with an Afro put noise-canceling headphones on.

"He was basically extorting you. He knew you didn't want it getting out that you were underage and using a fake ID. He had power over you."

"No, I had power over him. I could have gotten his medical license revoked. I could have gotten him thrown in prison. I still can."

Neither of us spoke after that. We both knew if she came forward, it would be her word against his.

"You act like he's this terrible monster," Debbie said eventually. "But I wanted to be with him, and he always treated me nicely. What happened to you was way worse."

Out the window, a little terrier licked pink ice cream off the sidewalk. Her owner yanked the leash, and she looked up with a blend of puzzlement and devotion. It made me nauseous. I closed my eyes.

"What?" Debbie said. "You disagree?"

"I didn't get pregnant. He didn't penetrate me."

She scrunched her nose. "I hate that word." Then, more gently, "You act like you're over it, but it's okay if you're not. You were so young. Is that why you get so upset about me and Dr. Matthews? Is it triggering?"

"The fact that you still call him Dr. Matthews should tell you something."

My insides felt like loose teeth. Everything was rattling, trying to scratch its way out. I wondered what Ronnie was up to. Why, all my life, I'd felt like a dead animal with its skin still on. Both Debbie and I had been assaulted, by different men, before we were out of school. Debbie with the pediatrician when she was sixteen. Me with the handyman when I was nine.

The handyman worked in the building where my childhood best friend, Nina, lived. He had a kind smile and was an excellent listener. He gave me an unfamiliar brand of attention, the kind I'd seen in movies about teenage cheerleaders and red-lipped women. One afternoon, he invited us over for lemonade. He said he had a gift for us and pulled a Victoria's Secret bag out from under his bed. Nina and I cat-walked across his bedroom in frilled baby dolls. Then we all got under the covers. It was kind of like playing Doctor. I liked being looked at. I liked being touched. He made me feel important. I was there because I wanted to be. This happened a handful of times.

When I told Debbie a few months in, I was bragging.

"That's disgusting," she said. "Never do that again."

I didn't understand, and she wouldn't explain. The next day, she cornered Nina in the bathroom and told her to stay the fuck away from me. Then she punched her in the mouth.

Nina's tooth punctured her lip, which looked like a bloody steak for a week. Debbie got suspended, and Nina's parents forbade us from hanging out. When she passed me in the halls or washed her hands next to me in the bathroom, she pretended not to see me. I hated Debbie for taking away my best friend and an adult who made me feel special, for leaving me with no one. I kept thinking about her saying, "That's disgusting." I was disgusting, I was sure she meant. She was the only person I'd told.

It was only in high school, emboldened by weed, that I let the internet tell me that children can't consent. That there is a word, *grooming*, for what the handyman did.

Debbie refused to see any parallels between the handyman and the pediatrician. But what hurt me most was that we both thought we'd wanted it, whatever *it* was. We both thought what happened was fine, but it wasn't fine, and only the other immediately recognized that. We never seemed to understand each other, or ourselves, at the same time. One sister's clarity was the other's delusion. That was the tragedy of our sisterhood. As soon as we came close to a mutual understanding, one of us changed, or both.

"Do you have my rabbit?" Debbie asked.

I pulled the figurine from my bag and unscrewed its tail. I took two pills and offered it to her. She shook out a handful and took three, all different colors.

"Keep it," she said, placing the rabbit in my palm. She curled my hand into a fist.

◐

Hours later, we were at a house party by USC. We dropped acid with a mustachioed frat boy who looked like an eighties porn star and ditched him when he started pawing at our shirts. He called us teases, and we laughed at his stupid porn-stache and ironic Hawaiian shirt his mom probably bought at Saks Fifth Avenue. We stumbled into a bedroom and flung open all the drawers. Debbie found a handle of vodka and we took pulls from it on one of the twin beds. The sheets were rough and smelled like weed and sunscreen.

"Who does that creep think he is?" Debbie said, passing me the bottle. "Like I'd ever let him near my little sister."

Eardrum-annihilating trap music pulsed through the walls. A cobalt betta fish circled its bowl like a patrolling cop.

"Sister sister sister sister sister," I mumbled, the words leaving my mouth as purple vapor. They encircled me like a protection spell.

◐

I must have passed out. Someone must have carried me out of the house. I came to alone in the back seat of a car.

My head throbbed and I could barely turn my neck. The emerald negligee Debbie pressured me into stealing was draped over my clothes. I stuck my hand down my jeans, fishing for the rest of the lingerie, finding only the period-stained cream panties. I tore off the negligee, threw it and the panties to the floor. I felt inside my underwear, crying out in relief that nothing hurt, that I was dry.

Receipts and empty water bottles carpeted the floor. I heard a whoop and saw Debbie out the window with two men I didn't recognize. They were standing at a cliff's edge. We were parked on an overlook off Mulholland Drive. A sign read NO PARKING AFTER 9 P.M.

"Take that, motherfuckers!" Debbie screamed, pitching something small and dark into the canyon. I listened for the sound of it landing, but there was none.

Debbie was having the time of her life, while I was passed out in a stranger's dirty car. While I wondered if I'd been violated and reassured myself the answer was probably no. I was afraid of what would happen when I got out of the car. *Something terrible*, the canyon whispered. I wanted to carve myself out of the night as if from a sheet of construction paper. Some animal inside me whimpered, and then drew its teeth. I dug through my cross-body purse, relieved I still had my knife. I stumbled out of the car.

One of the men had his arm around Debbie's waist, resting on a sliver of bare skin.

"Your turn," she told me, holding out her hand.

They were tossing batteries enveloped in gum wrappers into the canyon, hoping to blow something up.

"Where we come from," the man touching her explained, "it's a virtue to rid yourself of anything that doesn't serve you."

He was tall with spiky black hair and gray eyes. The other man was shorter and had the wiry blond beard of millennial folk musicians. The men claimed to be disgraced Icelandic princes. I was pretty sure Iceland wasn't a monarchy, and I thought I recognized the shorter one as a substitute teacher from our middle school. I couldn't remember if I'd tried this particular Oxy-Ativan-vodka-acid cocktail before. The folds of my brain had been set aflame and sprayed down with a firehose. My body was a lumbering animal I wanted to shrug off. Or remove forcibly, if it came to that. And it did feel that it may come to that.

The canyon extended its arms. My heart knocked the back of my throat, telling me the night wouldn't end until someone went over the edge.

"Is she okay?" the tall prince said.

"Don't worry about her," Debbie said. "She's just being dramatic."

They were laughing at me.

"She's freaking out," the short prince said.

"Yeah, she does that," Debbie said. "Take it easy. Everything's fine."

Beneath us, the city splayed open like a surgical patient. The red glow of its open arteries an ultimatum. The canyon demanded a sacrifice. It was me, or Debbie, or the princes.

"Whoa," said the short prince when he saw my knife.

"What are you doing?" said the tall prince.

"Fuck you," I said, willing my eyes to focus on Debbie's face, which forecasted no fear, only amusement.

"Okay, little sister." She looked at the princes and the three of them giggled. "Maybe we should find you a ride home."

I pointed the knife at her. Her eyes considered the blade. I could see them reflected there, glowing blue and otherworldly. We'd awakened the knife's spirit. There was no turning back now.

"Oh, please," Debbie said. "Give it a rest."

"You give it a rest," I yelled.

Debbie flinched, my voice more threatening than the knife.

"For once in your life, you give it a fucking rest," I repeated, breathing hard. "You have no idea what it's like being your sister. I've never had a day of rest in my life. Chasing after you like a dog. Leaving pieces of myself behind. And every time, you act as if that's how it's supposed to be. You lead, I follow, no questions asked. It's not fucking working for me."

"Okay, you've made your point," she said, twirling a strand of hair. "Can we talk about this later?"

"Shut up," I said. "This is what I'm talking about. You don't take me seriously. I'm not a real person to you. When have you ever been there for me? You abandoned me in the emergency room when I was bleeding out, and then you disappeared for months." My words came out funny, as if I had paper towels in my mouth. "I thought it would be different this time. I thought rehab meant something."

She went from looking amused to looking hurt. *Not hurt*

enough, the knife whispered. I shouted louder. I don't know how long it lasted. My entire body was a mouth, my knife a tongue prodding the space between us. Then, abruptly, I was done. My armpits clammy and cold against the wind. The sweat reminded me of Ronnie's dirty laundry scattered across our apartment, and I was crying now, the princes looking at each other like, *We sacrificed the throne for this?*

Then, Debbie was saying something, the wrong thing, and I was laughing in a voice that sounded like it came from elsewhere, from the hellmouth of the canyon itself, and I was thinking about what the prince had said, that *it's a virtue to rid yourself of anything that doesn't serve you*, and I was lunging at Debbie with my knife. She was slapping my arms away, and the men were laughing and cursing, and I sunk the blade into something supple. The slapping stopped.

Wind rushed through the low grass. My knife stuck out of Debbie's upper arm at a ninety-degree angle. *Right triangle*, I thought. We stared at it in silence, as though paying our respects to a historic monument.

And then one of the princes said, "Shit, shit, fuck, shit."

Debbie eased the knife out at the same angle it had gone in and handed it back to me. I wiped the blood off with the hem of my shirt and returned the knife to my purse. We watched the sleeve of her tan denim jacket turn the color of raspberry jam.

We looked at each other.

11.

The princes dropped us off at the emergency room and screeched away the moment we left the car. In the ER, they dressed Debbie's wound and gave her morphine and antibiotics. They asked questions, and I left to buy coffee so I wouldn't have to hear. She was wheeled upstairs to a shared room with an old lady who looked like a baby chick with its fluff torn out. Someone gave me a bottle of Pedialyte. I slept in a stained armchair in the corner, waking each time one of them moaned in their sleep. Around four, I took another Ativan, and that knocked me out until morning.

When I awoke at nine, Debbie was gone. Her breakfast tray untouched. I ate her lukewarm oatmeal and drank her orange juice. Her elderly roommate was gone too, maybe in surgery or the morgue. I could have stopped by the nurses' station, asked if Debbie had bolted or been transferred to another unit. I could have called her or gone by her apartment. Instead, I pocketed her blueberry muffin and went home. What was there left to say? We'd dumped the body of our sisterhood in that canyon.

At home, Ronnie was playing video games in his underwear. He drove a convertible through a destroyed city, an animated slut with enormous breasts in the passenger seat cheering him on. I announced that I was leaving him, that I couldn't play house anymore. He crashed the car. The woman flew through the windshield. We fought, we cried, he told me I was the love of his life, I told him not to be ridiculous. He told me I'd never loved him, I told him I had, I really had, and we both knew I was lying. He started raving about Debbie, and I told him never to say that name in front of me. I rubbed his back through the crying spells. I made him chamomile tea and, at his request, reopened the spiral cut on his thigh with my knife. Neither of us acknowledged that the blade was crusted with someone else's blood.

The next morning, I asked if I could keep living with him until I could afford a place of my own. He agreed right away, sensing an opportunity to convince me to stay. That night, he threw out his stained undershirts and sorted our mail. He called his grandmother to transcribe a mole recipe, which he cooked while I took a forty-minute shower, most of it locked in a staring contest with the drain.

For weeks, every day looked like that. I forgot about finding a new place to live. I began doubling up on my pills, which made me prone to spontaneous naps and dizzy spells where everything fizzed like television static. I kept picturing my knife slipping from the shower caddy down the drain, accelerating through the pipes, and then shooting out of someone else's drain to stab a grocery clerk or a Holocaust survivor or my mother.

The pills made the visions worse, but the queasy doom that set in when I waited too long between doses—the shaking and the nausea and the suicidal smack of my heart against the walls of my chest—left me little choice. Ronnie stopped asking if I was okay after an incident involving spaghetti marinara and his favorite Lakers jersey. He treated me like something volatile, a dictator or a thawing lake. We slept butt to butt, not touching, and when his foot grazed mine in the night, he drew back as though electrocuted. He even dropped me off at Salvation some nights. Tragically, all this had the opposite effect he'd intended, cementing him more as abused assistant than lover.

I did call Debbie a month after the hospital. By then, her phone was disconnected. Dominic hadn't heard from her since before rehab and didn't expect to the way they'd left things. I let myself into their apartment one night when he was out. Debbie's stuff was untouched. The strip club said she hadn't shown up for work in months. When I called her friend Harriet, she said Debbie was probably wreaking havoc on some investment banker's marriage in the Florida Keys. They weren't speaking. I asked around Salvation, shoved her picture in people's faces. No one was concerned that one of their own was missing.

"Oh, her," some said. "Haven't seen her around in a while."

Others didn't remember her at all, asked if I was sure this was the right bar.

I searched her name online and found nothing. I called her rehab, some nearby strip clubs, the women's prison, a few homeless shelters. Debbie was nowhere. I stopped by my mother's on the off chance Debbie was there or she'd heard from her, but she was too consumed with determining if her neighbor had threaded cameras through the vents to engage. I called my grandmother and asked as casually as I could whether she'd talked to Debbie.

"Ha! I'll be lucky if she attends my funeral. That brat didn't even wish me a happy birthday."

Had I? I couldn't remember.

I even tried my father, but I got his voicemail. When he called back three days later, he wasn't concerned.

"Your sister is very dramatic. When people don't give her what she wants, she cuts them out of her life."

"You don't think it's weird no one has heard from her?"

A loud sigh. "With Debbie, I don't know what's weird and what isn't. She's probably doing this for attention."

"Maybe."

I waited for him to ask how I was doing otherwise. To invite me to lunch or introduce me to his latest girlfriend.

"Well, I should get going," he said. "Unless there's something else you need."

A blender whirred in the background, the wet clang of crushed ice.

"Enjoy your margarita," I said, and hung up.

I didn't call the police or report Debbie as missing. It wouldn't take much detective work to learn I'd been buying drugs and engaging in borderline sex work, and I was not about to risk hefty fines or jail time over Debbie's bullshit. My gut told me she hadn't been abducted, that wherever she'd gone, it was by choice. Vanishing without a trace was dramatic, but Debbie wasn't above anything.

"Do you think she might have . . ." Ronnie said. "You know."

"Debbie doesn't have it in her to commit suicide," I told him. "She's too self-absorbed."

"What does that have to do with it?"

"Can you talk quieter?" I'd mixed up my pills and hadn't slept in two days. "She's not introspective like that. To her, other people are always the problem. Besides, she needs an audience. If she'd killed herself, I'd know."

For all his unsolicited theories, Ronnie had been right about one thing: I was addicted to Debbie. That night on the overlook was more than a culmination of my rage—it was me carving a path toward recovery.

I took my pills, sunk into the sofa cushions, and decided to stop looking for Debbie. To give myself the gift of quitting her cold turkey. It was the first decision I'd made without her foot on my neck. *Going to the police is for narcs*, I imagined telling her. For once, I couldn't hear her retort back.

Something had been decided the last time we saw each other. We'd cut ourselves open and bared our meat. Debbie didn't open wide enough, so I did the cutting for her. It was my turn to be the artist, hers to be the canvas. In a demented way, I'd honored her. You can't reach a mutual understanding without spilling blood. She taught me that.

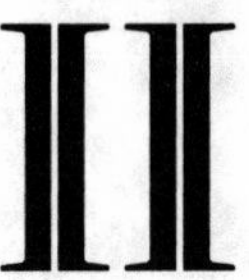

12.

Franklin was in his midthirties and had the soft, guilty eyes of someone who'd managed to puke his way out of a handful of overdoses when several of his friends hadn't. He was the only Salvation regular who didn't shrug me off when I'd gone around looking for Debbie. He offered to help me look, and then he offered me Oxy, no charge. Two months after Debbie disappeared, I moved in with him. He was "between places" and was renting a room at the Stardust Motel. We had two twin beds that we pushed together, a window facing a concrete courtyard where guests went to smoke or cry, and a small shower where we fooled around. It was too hard in the bed with the halves moving apart. When I asked him to cover the drain with his foot so it couldn't make eye contact with me, he acted like this was a reasonable request. "Anything for you, m'lady," he said, kissing down my chest.

It was June, and the air was thick with night-blooming jasmine. A couple of times a week, we popped into Salvation to drink rum and cokes in our bathing suits. Then we took Franklin's van to Venice Beach. He'd sold most of the seat belts, and the radio was stuck on a channel that played sad Spanish folk songs. I called Franklin mi cabrón. I didn't know what it meant, but it sounded like *my cat* or *my heart.*

At the beach, we drank whiskey from a thermos, and I wrote messages on Franklin's back with a shell. I looked for homeless people along the boardwalk. "Want to make fifty bucks?" I asked.

Franklin was buddies with a pain management doctor named Jeff. He'd been married to Jeff's sister, before she cheeked eight fentanyl lollipops and walked off the Vincent Thomas Bridge. Some bond had formed between Franklin and Jeff after that.

"The only way to really see a person is to lose everything you have in common" was how Franklin put it.

"But then you have the losing in common," I said.

"Right." He gave me a sage smile.

They had an arrangement where Franklin brought in the homeless folks we met on the beach, and Jeff wrote them prescriptions for opiates, benzos, and stimulants. Franklin then drove them to pharmacies all over the city to fill the meds. Each homeless person got fifty bucks and a sandwich. The pills went for ten, twenty, thirty dollars each. Every day, I waited for us to get busted. For some CVS pharmacist to catch on, cops swarming our van while I waited in the parking lot, singing corridos. Franklin and Jeff split the cash two ways, and Franklin gave me half his share. Jeff never wrote scripts for fentanyl.

•

One night, a guy brought a goat to Salvation. One of the regulars bought the goat a beer and tipped the bottle into its mouth, everyone laughing when it burped. I couldn't remember the last time I'd been so happy. I hugged the goat around the neck, whispered how much I loved it in its floppy ear. It was trying to tell me something. I was going to be okay. I was exactly where I needed to be. With Debbie gone, my real life could begin. Then, the goat started making this sound like a penny in a blender, and the bartender said it had to go. Franklin tried to buy me the goat, but he only had twelve dollars. His owner said I could come by to see the goat sometime, but he didn't give me an address and I forgot to ask. The goat's name was Sherman.

•

Franklin never told me he loved me. I told him once, but I don't think I meant it. He made me come four times in the shower and we were lying naked and wet in bed. A jacaranda bloom had latched in his hair—I dissolved the purple bell on my tongue. The pills peaked, and I felt that we had just been born together. I squeezed his hand, and he squeezed mine back. Blood shuttled between our hearts as if we were one body. *I'm exactly where I need to be*, I thought again.

"You know why I started selling at Salvation?" he asked.

It was a supermoon. Light poured through the flimsy blinds like milk.

"Why?" I asked, though I knew the answer.

"'Cause those sad motherfuckers can't afford more than a couple pills a night, and they always take 'em right away. Nothing to trace, nothing to repossess. The owner's brother being some bigwig for the po-po doesn't hurt either."

"Brilliant," I said, as though I didn't personally know

several others who'd sold at Salvation for the same reason. I willed him to stop talking.

"We could do this a long time."

I said nothing. I imagined dipping a giant chocolate chip cookie into the puddle of light on the floor.

"I'm serious," he said. "A few more years, and we can get our own place."

"You don't think we'll get caught?"

"Never. Shit's airtight."

I stared at him, wondering what kind of person he would become in prison. He'd probably piss someone off and get shanked early in his sentence. Or he'd run drugs for a sleazy guard. Maybe he'd get into gardening and Catholicism. It was impossible to know a person.

"You know what they'd do to a pretty girl like you in prison?" he said.

I spat my gum and stuck it between the blinds. "Show me."

•

A week later, a pharmacist made a fuss over a thirty-day supply of Vicodin, and the homeless man we paid to pick up the prescription bolted. He didn't get caught, and we paid him extra for his trouble. But calls were placed to Jeff's office, a complaint filed with the Department of Justice. Jeff denied knowing anything about the Vicodin and submitted a police report claiming his prescription pads had been stolen. He called off the scheme, saying we needed to lay low. Franklin, having lost his main source of income, bribed a

Walgreens pharmacy clerk into pulling six bottles of narcotics off the shelf.

If he'd run his plan by me, I would have talked him out of it. I would have warned him that clerks aren't the ones who fill prescriptions, that you have to account for the pharmacy's mandated pill counts, the triplicate sheets that were sent to the DEA. All the things I'd learned from spending time with Debbie and Dominic.

"I heard the police kicked down his door when he was on the toilet," someone at Salvation said.

"I heard they didn't have sufficient evidence for a drug charge, but they got him for staging car wrecks."

"I heard he skipped town and is hiding out with his half sister in New Mexico."

"New Mexico? I heard Nevada. Benny swears he saw him panhandling on the Strip."

"He's definitely in prison. My uncle at Twin Towers said there's a new guy who got busted for robbing a pharmacy."

You could ask five people at Salvation the same question and get five different, equally confident answers. It was my favorite thing about us. Our loyalty was to story, not reality.

"Well, which is it?" they asked me.

I shrugged. How should I know? I cleared out of our motel room as soon as I heard what he'd done. I couldn't stand by anyone who was that stupid. Say what you will about Debbie, but she was strategic. Destructive, selfish: yes. But she was no fool.

13.

Jeff owned a few units in an apartment complex in West Hollywood, and he gave me a break on rent after our scheme fell apart. I think he believed I was terribly heartbroken over Franklin's arrest. Maybe I reminded him of his dead sister, and he wanted to help me the way he'd never gotten to help her. I leaned into victimhood, crying about my financial precarity. He gave me a thousand bucks and a steep discount on a five-hundred-square-foot studio with big windows facing a palm-tree-lined street. I felt a little guilty for playing him. Then I remembered what Ronnie said after Debbie lied about us getting engaged, and we accepted all those gifts: "Everyone likes to feel generous." I split a pill with my knife and toasted to Ronnie's unexpected wisdom.

Without a job or direct access to pills, I had to ration my remaining supply. The situation was dire. My tolerance had gone up the last few months, and I needed higher doses of Oxy and Ativan to reach the same lightness as before. Rationing was unsustainable, withdrawal a guarantee. On top of that, the hospital kept sending outrageous bills for my miscarriage. After I ignored the first few, they became threatening. At Salvation, the Wealthy Patron led to increasingly disgusting offers for depreciating prices, and I found myself considering them. I needed a job.

I couldn't stomach going back to the library or asking Ronnie if his electronics store was hiring. He checked in sometimes, but mostly I screened his calls. When Jeff told me about a nearby hospital that was always short-staffed, I applied to be an emergency room secretary. It sounded easy enough—answering phones, scheduling follow-up appointments, updating medical records, coordinating transfers from the ER to other floors. *Ability to provide family-centered care and tend to the needs of patients and their families is a must*, the posting said. Why not get paid for what I'd been doing my entire life?

I took just enough Ativan before the interview to take the edge off, to come across as charming and capable. My interviewer was a middle-aged woman with close-cropped fake blond hair and bags under her eyes the size of marshmallows. She looked like the default administrator character in a sitcom. Her name was Ellen. She checked her phone every few minutes, and I appreciated the open acknowledgment that I barely mattered.

"What about this position appeals to you?" Ellen asked.

I spoke about my passion for administrative work and my desire to help people through their worst moments.

"I'm a people person," I heard myself saying. "I'm great in a crisis."

Ellen took notes on a legal pad I was sure she'd chosen to look serious. "How do you handle conflict?"

I thought of when my mother believed her pills were

mind-control devices, and how I crushed them into her pudding. I thought of the last voicemail my father left me, asking me to call him when I had a moment. It was three months ago, and I had yet to call back. I thought about refusing to let Debbie into my apartment the day after my miscarriage. I thought about stabbing her. I told Ellen about corralling difficult library patrons and caring for my "chronically ill" mother.

"Is there anything else I should know about you?"

"I have a strong work ethic and am deeply committed to personal growth. I see this position as a critical stepping-stone in my path toward higher education and lifelong learning. I've always dreamed of becoming a primary care physician. Firsthand experience in an emergency room, helping our community's most vulnerable, would be an invaluable learning opportunity."

It sounded like the kind of aspirational shit someone sipping coffee from a mug that said *CELEBRATE* in curly gold font wanted to hear. Ellen smiled at me. I knew I had the job. She warned me that the last secretary quit because she couldn't handle how depressing it all was, how everything was literally an emergency. "That doesn't bother me," I assured her. And it didn't. She offered me the job the following day.

I taped a plastic bag of Jeff's pee to my stomach to pass the drug test. The testing center woman took one look at my white skin and business-casual cardigan and decided she didn't need to wait outside the curtain while I peed. "Just don't flush when you're done," she said. *Joke's on you*, I thought, pouring Jeff's pee into the cup, not bothering to draw the curtain all the way. I emptied the rest of the piss in the toilet and took the Oxy I'd hidden in my bra right there in the bathroom.

The first few days were orientation. I sat in a chilly conference room with forty others, straining to focus on the slideshows about HIPAA, workplace harassment, the twenty-four-hour pharmacy, the hospital's health insurance plans. Each visit with a mental health professional was ten dollars out of pocket, and generic medications were highly subsidized. I sat up straighter, skin tingling. I knew then what I would do. I'd make an appointment with the first available psychiatrist and get them to prescribe me Ativan for my anxiety. Then I'd tell them about my chronic back pain from a "gymnastics injury" and see if they'd order me Oxy too. It felt good to show myself tenderness. With a steady supply of pills, I could do it more often.

A sweaty man in a collared shirt to my right said, "Sounds pretty good, eh?" He had kind eyes and looked like a father, the type who picked up pizza for his family on his way home and wiped the grease from his daughter's mouth and drank a beer on the couch, just one, after the kids went to sleep. I flashed him an innocent smile and said, "I think I'm going to like it here." I couldn't picture his wife on the couch with him. I saw a burn mark instead of a face.

14.

I spent two weeks shadowing the outgoing emergency room secretary, Tam, as she went through the motions of her day. Tam was a young Vietnamese woman with pointy, acrylic nails decorated with geometric shapes. The dagger-like wings of her eyeliner were more immaculate than anything Debbie could pull off, and she exuded the bored competence of a teenage babysitter.

"Here's how you dial another unit in the hospital," she said the first day, clacking her nails against the phone. She eyed my unpainted, bitten-down nails and frowned. "You should take notes. When I'm out of here in two weeks, you're on your own." She handed me a pen and two sheets of scratch paper with someone's bloodwork results on the back. Several values were printed in red, flanked by the word *HIGH*.

"What happened to this guy?" I asked.

"Huh?" Tam looked at the paper. "It's anyone's guess." She opened a drawer beneath our desk full of uncapped pens and takeout menus. "You can leave your notes here when you go home. Don't take anything with patient identifiers with you. The hospital just settled a multi-million-dollar lawsuit after someone left a bunch of chart notes in an Uber." She rolled her eyes and pulled out a menu. "This Armenian place is good."

An elderly man approached our desk, clutching his chest. Tam ran me through the motions of asking what brought him to the ER, filling out the appropriate forms, telling him to please take a seat and that someone would be with him shortly. We did the same for a nursing student with a needlestick injury, a limping woman who cussed us out for taking too long, a construction worker who'd fucked up his hand. We answered calls from patients' families and said things like, "I'm sorry, I don't have any updates at the moment." When the same person called more than twice in an hour, Tam screened their calls.

"Don't let patients bully you," she advised. And, "Befriend the nurses. Otherwise, they won't share their snacks."

I didn't get the sense that she was leaving because the job was too depressing, as Ellen had said. When I asked her on our last day together, Tam said Ellen was thinking of a volunteer. "Gloria's Chinese and a foot taller than me."

"Ugh," I said.

"Well, that explains why my goodbye present was a subscription to a meditation app," Tam said, deadpan. "I'm leaving to do an MBA."

I waited for her to tell me what she wanted to do with her degree, before realizing I'd only asked the question in my head. The moment had passed. Tam was now texting in several group chats. One was in Vietnamese, and its most recent entry was a photo of a miniature poodle eating a blueberry.

"Aw, is that your dog?" I asked.

"My brother's," she said.

"Are you guys close?"

She shrugged. "Sort of. We talk most days."

Sort of? I'd thought of closeness as a binary, like being pregnant: you either were or you weren't. She returned to texting, shifting her posture so I could no longer see her screen.

We ordered from the Armenian place for lunch, and I began to panic at the thought of handling the desk alone come Monday.

"You've got this," Tam said, dipping a kebab in garlic sauce. "Just don't look up any celebrities; the compliance people track that shit. One time, I accidentally opened Robert Pattinson's chart instead of Robert Patterson or whoever, and I got a call two minutes later, demanding I explain myself."

"So the hospital keeps pretty close tabs on everyone?" I asked.

"Nah. Just don't do anything that'll end in a lawsuit or a TMZ article, and you're fine."

I was too anxious to finish my food and dissolved an Ativan under my tongue in the bathroom. Next to my foot, a miniature gin bottle nestled against a mound of toilet paper like a washed-up message in a bottle. It was empty. I wrote, *I was here and so were you*, on a shred of toilet paper, but it kept tearing, and instead of slipping it in the bottle I flushed it down the drain.

•

After work, I stopped by my mother's to give her my leftovers from lunch.

"It's me," I said, unlocking the door. "I brought food."

"I'm in bed," she called.

She was in pajamas, a cool washcloth on her head.

"You okay?" I whispered.

"Migraine," she said.

"Sorry. Did you take your medicine?"

"Janice gave it to me earlier."

I checked her pillbox and saw that today's pills were gone.

"How's my working girl?" my mother said, patting the bed.

I crawled in next to her. "Fine. I'm on my own starting Monday."

"Wait, did you—?"

"I showered after work," I lied.

"Good. Hospitals are cesspools. You're sure you weren't followed?"

"I'm sure. We're safe."

I tucked my arm behind her neck. She leaned into me. She smelled like warm vanilla, and her earring tickled my cheek. The gold hoops had belonged to her great-grandmother. I used to think she never took them off to honor her, but now I suspected it was a way of ensuring she had her most valuable possessions accessible in case she needed to flee the country. She wore a necklace with a small diamond bauble that my father had given her on their first anniversary for the same reason.

"You like the job so far?" she asked.

"It's fine. The pay is shit, but it's a little more than I was making at the library."

"Don't let them work you too hard. School comes first."

"Agreed." I rested my head against her shoulder. "So, listen. I know you and Debbie don't really talk, but I wanted to tell you she's living abroad now." This was the lie I'd manufactured now that Debbie had been gone five months.

"She's what?" The washcloth slipped into her lap.

"She's doing the Peace Corps. Or something like that. We got into a dumb fight, so I don't have all the details. She doesn't have cell service or internet most of the time."

"The Peace Corps," my mother snorted. "You actually believe that?"

"What do you mean?"

"Does your sister seem like the kind of person who'd join the Peace Corps? Sounds like she told you some bullshit story to get you off her back."

"I . . . guess that's possible."

"Classic Debbie," my mother sighed. "She probably ran off with some guy. Or maybe she and Harriet are up to something. I never liked that girl."

"Maybe." I was surprised by how well she was taking this.

"Well, she knows how to take care of herself," my mother said. "I don't have the energy to keep up with her antics. I'm sure she'll turn up when she needs something." She readjusted her eye mask and snuggled into my shoulder.

"You're probably right."

"Thank you for telling me." She kissed my cheek. "Does your dad know?"

"He knows Debbie and I aren't talking."

She smiled. "I bet he offered to drop everything and help, right?"

"Oh yeah, you know it. Dad the relationship expert."

We laughed, and then she clutched her head, and I went to get her a fresh washcloth.

"Don't tell Grandma you and Debbie are fighting," my mother said. "Tell her what you told me—that she's in the Peace Corps and can't be reached. The less she knows, the better."

Our most beloved delusion: that lying to each other was a kind of love. The rules of my family weren't so different from the rules of Salvation, where I could watch a soccer mom pretend she was drinking gin and not mouthwash while I pretended to take pills recreationally and not as life support. The difference was mutually assured destruction feels a lot better among relative strangers than family. Speaking our fears aloud wouldn't save us. The last time I'd done it, Debbie ended up with a hole in her arm, and I ended up without a sister.

15.

My first week covering the waiting room alone, I talked on the phone with the family of a guy who'd been clipped in a drive-by shooting. I babysat the husband of a woman who'd overdosed on Tylenol, and I reassured him that, yes, we carried the antidote. I discharged people and made follow-up appointments. I transferred a woman to the ICU with a catheter up her urethra and a tube down her throat. Or, as I thought of it, "spit-roasting." Debbie would have cackled. She was the only person who wouldn't judge me for thinking something like that.

I wasn't allowed to look up patients once they transferred, so I never got closure on what happened to them. I worked from seven until three thirty with an unpaid thirty-minute lunch. When it was busy, the day passed in a flash. When it was slow, I found myself jonesing for a car accident or a listeria outbreak, anything to drown out the rattling in my skull. I timed my pills so I was just lucid enough to do my job, and doubled up thirty minutes before the end of my shift. On the bus home, I closed my eyes and pretended I was floating in a lake.

I was quickly dispelled of the notion that I could leave work at work when a woman came through the emergency room complaining of Shoah grief. Her parents had each lost their entire families in the Holocaust. Siblings, parents, grandparents, aunts, uncles, cousins. They survived by hiding in the crawl space of a neighbor's boot factory.

"They never spoke of it, so I don't know if there were rats," she told me. "Probably there were—my parents avoided the subway for fear of them, and one time, my mother burst into tears when a trick-or-treater snuck up behind her dressed as the rat from *Ratatouille*."

There was no one else to triage, and I didn't know how to end the conversation. I kept my eyes on my computer, clicking random icons to look busy.

"They refused to wear boots," she continued. "Can you imagine? I grew up in Chicago, and they never wore boots. When I tried to talk about what happened, they just stared like I was speaking a foreign language. And now they're gone. They wanted to take their experiences with them. They didn't understand how silence creates golems."

"Creates what?" I asked.

"Golems. Something inanimate that's brought to life. In Jewish folktales, they're made from clay or mud, but I don't think you need to see a golem to know it's there."

I coughed and shifted in my seat.

She continued, "Golems are alive, but incompletely—their souls are unstable. They can be a force of protection or great destruction."

She explained how the trauma of the Holocaust had been transmitted from her parents, how it lived in the spaces between her ribs and her untattooed arm and the part of her brain that should be making serotonin.

"You're Jewish, right?" she said.

I hesitated before nodding.

"You carry this grief too."

I didn't know what to say. I believed similar things had happened to my family in the same way I believed water was made of hydrogen and oxygen. That I accepted this did not mean I felt close to it or understood its relation to me.

"I was like you once," the woman said. "I went to work, I watched critically acclaimed television, I got drunk at parties, I put leave-in conditioner in my hair. Then, one day, it was too much. The mask slipped. I haven't been able to wear it since."

My left thigh sweat against my right, the sliver of dress wedged between them growing damp. I wanted to tell her I knew the membrane between mask and face was razor thin. There were many moments like this when Debbie was around. A night would go from a generic boozefest to a near-death experience. One moment we were dancing in a nightclub, and the next Debbie was walking the balcony railing in her stilettos, men with vape pens recording her on their phones, leopard-printed women screeching for her to come down, the ground beckoning thirty feet below. Or we were at her and Dominic's place, watching a stupid rom-com, and I don't know how that transitioned into Debbie tying a cell phone charger around her arm to enlarge her vein. Me begging her to go out looking for pills instead of shooting heroin, or to at least use something safer, a condom or the tights I was wearing, as a tourniquet.

If our great-grandfather hadn't been murdered, would

Debbie have climbed the railing? If our mother hadn't internalized these stories, would Debbie and I have finished the movie and gone to bed? If our mother wasn't unreachable. If our father loved us enough to stay. If the pediatrician hadn't. If the handyman hadn't. If our grandmother had been born here. If we had family money. If Debbie could afford her own apartment. If I hadn't moved in with Ronnie. If I hadn't abandoned Kim. If I hadn't taken Debbie's pills. If I hadn't stabbed her.

I didn't know how to tell the woman any of this. I said I hoped she felt better and that someone would be with her shortly. And then I slipped beneath my desk as though I'd dropped a pen, and I didn't get up until the Ativan dissolved beneath my tongue.

16.

The job was fine. I didn't love it, I didn't hate it. I witnessed recovery and death and, more often than you'd expect, something startlingly in between. It was beautiful, and it was devastating, and every day was different.

The worst part was the people in the waiting room who saw me as a hostess or a personal assistant. They bitched about the magazines, demanded I change the channel on the television, asked truly bizarre questions. Not just esoteric medical questions, though there were plenty of those—they wanted to know how bad it was that a certain organ had been perforated, how long it took to remove a gallbladder. I could always tell who was going to spend hours interrogating me. I clenched when the doors opened to an older man with an angry mustache or a white lady with a dresser-size leather purse.

But these aren't the questions I mean. There was often some weirdo who wanted me to get them coffee, or to pop over to the pharmacy for cough syrup. People asked for a menu, like we were in a goddamn Olive Garden. They asked, "Can I smoke in here?" and lit up before I answered. Then there were the ones who tried to know me. They set up shop at my desk, leaning their elbows on the lip of the counter, drumming their fingers on the fake wood paneling. How did I end up here, they wanted to know. Did I have another job on the side? Had I gone to college? Did I have a boyfriend? Did I hope to become a nurse? They wanted to feel superior to someone. I told them my sister was dead and that I'd had a promising career as a sculptor until the rheumatoid arthritis got me. I said my father was sick, that I had to pawn his knives to pay for chemo. I was willing to be an object of pity if it helped someone get through their day. It was an act of charity, my way of making people feel less alone.

Management liked me because I gave them no reason to think about me at all. I showed up on time, and there was always ink in the printer, and when my coworkers needed someone to vent to, I wore a concerned look and said, "That's ridiculous," in all the right places. That was all anyone wanted in a coworker, in an inferior: someone to wipe their ass and pretend their stories were interesting. I had no intention of attending the happy hours and holiday parties, and it was the doctors who said, "We missed you last night!" while wearing loafers that cost more than my rent. I didn't have it in me to make strained small talk about the latest musical to hit the Pantages Theatre, LA traffic, the economy.

Debbie once boycotted Salvation for a few weeks because she was sick of "drunk dipshits explaining the economy to me." We tried other places—a rowdy club decorated with Soviet propaganda, an Irish pub that reeked of sausage. We walked into upscale bars and left in the same breath. We didn't want to drink anywhere near a crystal chandelier. We couldn't afford the drinks in places like that and only sometimes had the energy to convince some talent agent to treat us, and then hightail it before he dragged us back to his Malibu bungalow. There was a glamour to those aborted evenings. Debbie doing my makeup, lending me a push-up bra and five-inch heels. Strutting into some bar or club in a sixty-dollar outfit like it was worth a thousand, making eyes at whoever looked the most tragic or wore the most expensive-looking watch. When we were on, we were on. It didn't always end terribly. Some nights, we bought bacon-wrapped hot dogs from street vendors. One time, Debbie wouldn't take back the tassel earrings she'd lent me, slurring, "You deserve nice things!"

Another night, Debbie told people Ronnie had amnesia and didn't recognize his own wife. We got blitzed on free drinks, and I made out with a cute girl on the dance floor while Ronnie was in the bathroom. Her hair was so soft it kept slipping from my fingers. She smelled like a spicy flower and touched me the way you would something vulnerable, an unframed painting, a paper crane. I began plotting ways to take her home. I hadn't told Ronnie about my attraction to women, assuming it would come up organically in a situation like this.

"Don't worry about him," Debbie said. "You deserve this. I'll tell him she's into both of you."

At the end of the night, the woman offered me and Ronnie a ride home. She pulled up to our place, and I invited her inside for another drink. Ronnie giggled like a loon and said, "Unless you're a sleepy girl!" I wanted to pummel him with my heel. She laughed and kissed us both on the cheek. And then she clicked the *unlock* button and wished us a good night. I was too drunk to stay mad at Ronnie, to feel much of anything at all. Even the sex that night was decent. We were half asleep, and something about that took the pressure off. We pawed at each other with sloppy abandon. "You really wanted to hook up with her, didn't you?" he giggled, which made me giggle. We fell asleep holding hands. I was so hopeful that weightless feeling would last. That the highs of my relationships with Ronnie and Debbie could negate, or at least justify, the lows.

The sweetness of that memory caught me off guard. I wasn't ready to reminisce about Debbie, to contemplate whether I missed her, whether I'd made a terrible mistake. I ate my nails to keep from hyperventilating. *I'm exactly where I need to be*, I told myself, shaking as I unscrewed the rabbit's tail. From that day forward, I tried not to think of Debbie, not to closely examine my life at all. When I slipped, pills were my dimmer switch.

•

My health insurance kicked in on my first day of work. A month into the job, I told the first in-network psychiatrist I could get an appointment with—a white woman in her forties with sensible gold jewelry and coffee table books about trauma—all about my anxiety. Forty minutes later, I had scripts for Ativan and an antidepressant I had no intention of taking after she warned it could cause sexual dysfunction. It took so little to earn her trust.

The only wrinkle was that she couldn't prescribe Oxy. She referred me to a pain management doctor whose next opening wasn't for weeks. I had to keep re-upping from an Uzbek guy I met through Franklin who sold his grandparents' extra pain pills. He made Medicare fraud look like a tender tribute to the people who raised him, honoring them through the provision of nice shit: a glass coffee table, a flat-screen TV, a Pomeranian named Biscuit.

The pain management doctor was a short man with tortoiseshell glasses. He asked thoughtful questions without any detectable suspicion and showed genuine empathy for my alleged chronic pain. I thought I had him. But he insisted we start with physical therapy and crap like lidocaine patches and nerve blocks before he would feel comfortable prescribing opioids. There went my shot at immediate-release oxycodone, let alone the long-acting OxyContin I was used to. Maybe I could have gotten it out of him after "trying and failing" his cadre of non-opioid options, but it wasn't worth the effort.

Soon after, the best part of my job revealed itself like a speakeasy beneath a mediocre bar. I had a sinus infection, probably from snorting something I shouldn't have. One of the medical residents examined me and sent an antibiotic prescription to the hospital pharmacy. When the pharmacy tech handed me my prescription, something metaphysical passed between us. There's a Russian expression I learned months later—"narik narika vidyet bez fanarika"—a junkie can spot another junkie without a flashlight. The Russian version of "game recognizes game." She saw my ID badge and asked if I was new. I said yes. "I'm Shirin. We should grab lunch sometime," she said. "I'll tell you all the hot goss."

The following week, we split a Southwest salad and a

frankly offensive excuse for a burrito, even by hospital cafeteria standards. Shirin was petite and had a soft voice that reminded me of wool sweaters, but there was something cutthroat about her energy. Her eyes had no empathy behind them. But then she pulled foil-wrapped baklava from her bag for us to share, and I second-guessed my assessment.

"My mother-in-law made these," she said. "She likes to warn me that her son doesn't like fatties and then bring over a mountain of dessert." Shirin was so slight that if her diamond studs were any bigger, she'd tip over.

We bonded over our immigrant baggage—she was Persian, and I exaggerated how recently my family came over from Russia.

"I bet your parents drop by your place unannounced all the time, right?" Shirin said. "And if you ask them to give you a heads-up first, they act like you literally shot them."

"Always," I lied. "There are no boundaries in my family."

"Boundaries?" Shirin laughed. "I don't know her."

"Does your family unload the most depressing stories on you? Like, you'll be having lunch for your grandma's birthday, and suddenly you're transported to 1930s famine-stricken Ukraine, where fat kids are being chased through the streets by desperate men with forks?"

"Literally every day," she said. She was cutting her burrito into bite-size pieces with the exactitude of a surgeon. "But they also lie constantly to 'protect us.' One day, Great-Grandpa dies a war hero, and the next he dies of a stroke."

I doubted my grandmother had lied about her father being murdered, but I hadn't considered the everyday stuff. Who knew if her mother actually had fourteen abortions, if her grandmother spent two years in a psych ward after a traumatic stillbirth, if my family evacuated their prewar apartment the literal day before the Jews who stayed behind were rounded up.

"And they wonder why we're so fucked-up," Shirin continued. "They think if we do all this American dream crap like get married and buy a condo in Encino, we can sleep without Ambien and fuck without wine. Like we can shoo away all that trauma with an Hermès scarf."

She was currently wearing a red Hermès scarf. When she caught me looking, she laughed. "I mean, you can't blame a bitch for trying."

Another time, Shirin told me she had a software engineer husband who bored her, and that she'd recently embarked on a side hustle reselling designer clothing that had "fallen off a truck." Her cousin dropped off a suitcase every few weeks, and she hooked her friends and family up with the goods. Two-thousand-dollar dresses went for three hundred; leather jackets with the tags on for eighty.

"At this point, I'm just waiting until I have enough money to leave," she told me. Her crimson lip gloss left a bloody smear on her straw. "My husband's not abusive or anything. I'm just sick of doing the same goddamn thing every day. I'm twenty-nine, and I feel like I'm going to spend the next sixty years of my life washing this man's socks until one of us dies."

"I know what you mean," I said, thinking of Ronnie as I offered her the rest of my fries.

"It's going to take years, man." She stuffed three fries in her mouth. "Pharmacy tech pay and a thousand bucks after my cousin's cut isn't enough to live how I want to live, you know? This hospital's so fucking stingy. I've been doing the pharmacy's waste disposal for a year and get paid fifty cents an hour more than my coworker who spends half her shift reading porny werewolf novels on her phone."

"I get it. I really do."

And when the idea came to me, I swear the cafeteria fluorescents flickered like cartoon lightbulbs above my head.

◐

Few people know that medications are still effective decades past their expiration dates. One study found that twelve out of fourteen drugs tested were at least 90 percent active twenty-eight to forty years after they'd "expired." Still, pharmacies must dispose of all medications at the time of their manufacturer-determined expiration dates. This was Shirin's job. Expired noncontrolled substances like blood pressure and diabetes pills went in one bin. Controlled substances like opiates, benzos, and sleeping pills went in another. Those with the highest abuse potential—like OxyContin, fentanyl, and Adderall—also had to be inventoried through a manual count and comparison to the previous tally. If the counts didn't match when Shirin's manager documented them in the white binder she kept in her office, she would need to report this to the California Board of Pharmacy and the DEA. So long as everything added up, inventory was reconciled.

No one, however, was digging through trash cans to count how many expired pills were actually destroyed. So when I asked Shirin to pocket some for me, it wasn't so different from reselling clothes that "fell off a truck." She took what she could from a supply that had already been reconciled. I kept what I wanted and sold the rest at Salvation to mostly the same people who used to buy from Franklin. I gave Shirin a third of the profit. I also let her borrow my apartment to cheat on her husband. Though I could never guarantee what pills she would swipe, it was enough to cover my bar tabs and my own supply. A perfect arrangement. Debbie would have been proud.

17.

New Year's came and went with all the fanfare of a menstrual cycle. I worked the holiday for the overtime pay, tending to those who'd drank too much or not enough. The next few weeks were rainy, the sky the washed-out gray of old sweatshirts. It seemed to foretell a year devoid of luster and miracles.

I came to Salvation one night partly to sell, partly because I was lonely. It was the nine-month anniversary of Debbie's disappearance, and a year since my miscarriage. I tried to drown thoughts of her in cheap cocktails, but I kept flashing back to my knife sticking out of her arm. Blood seeping through her sleeve. The blankness on her face when she looked up at me, the O of her mouth.

As though he'd read my mind, the bartender refilled my drink and asked, "What's your sister up to these days?"

"No idea," I said, trying to keep my voice casual. "I haven't seen her in almost a year."

"Whoa. You used to come here with her all the time. You get in a fight or something?"

I gulped my cocktail, which tasted like sad watermelon. "She kind of just disappeared one day."

"For real?"

I nodded.

"That's crazy."

"Is it though? You know how Debbie is." I couldn't muster up an eye roll. The righteousness I'd felt when I decided to stop looking for her was fading. It had stemmed from my conviction that Debbie would grow bored of whatever scheme she'd fallen into, whatever guy she'd holed up with. I hadn't prepared for the possibility that nine months later she would still be gone.

"I don't know, man," the bartender said, cocking his head. "I hope she's okay."

I tried to focus on the task at hand, finding someone to sell to. That's when I noticed three men shooting tequila at the other end of the bar. I could tell at least one would end up in my emergency room before the month was up. Debbie and I had always been perceptive like that. We could tell by looking into a man's eyes if he loved his mother. If he'd thought about killing himself, if he'd ever tried and how. The pills reminded me of our gift and told me to take it seriously. With Debbie gone, it was my intuition that got the last word.

"I'm going to give you the number of the guy I used to find my birth mother," the bartender said. "You know, if you ever want to look for Debbie."

I handed him my phone. Whatever would make him drop the subject faster. When he finished, I beelined for the men at the other end of the bar and took a seat next to the one wearing a duct-taped bomber jacket. The other two—I could see now they were twins—gave me a once-over. One had a fat lip; the other, a bloody fist. Both had bitten their nails down to the meat. They looked vaguely familiar.

"Hey," the one with the bloody fist said. "You work at that hospital. We were there a few days ago. We, uh, had an accident."

His brother smiled, revealing a wet gap where his front teeth should have been.

They had a couple of years left together, tops. One of them would be too drunk to call 911 when the other puked blood outside the bus depot. Or the other would go into cocaine-induced cardiac arrest, and his brother would forget the steps of CPR. I couldn't sell to them now that they knew where I worked. I was about to make an excuse to leave when I realized the other reason I thought I recognized them. They had the same chin cleft and dirty blond hair as the man my mother had a fling with at the psych ward. He came around a couple of times, but their affair fizzled out quickly. I suspect he was into her for the pills. She didn't have anything particularly exciting—it was mostly antipsychotics, antidepressants, and seizure medications some psychiatrist hoped would "organize her thoughts." But below the sink was an expired bottle with ten chalky Percocets left over from a failed migraine treatment, and I found it empty one night after he left. He never returned. But these men were a decade younger and significantly sleazier than the man I remembered.

I felt woozy, untethered. Everything in the bar was obscuring its intentions. I was confident that these men switched places on women they were sleeping with, taking turns and comparing. If not with my mother, with someone else.

"I'm going home," I said.

"See you soon," the twin with the black eye winked.

Back at my apartment, I cracked open a window and listened for the screeches of neighborhood crows. They were quiet that night, and I felt terribly abandoned. I examined the private investigator's name and number and hovered over his contact. I unscrewed my rabbit and took a few pills before getting into bed and pulling my knees to my chest. "Mother yourself," I commanded, which only brought me closer to tears. Upstairs, someone turned on their shower. I felt the vibration of my drain stretching to the size of a manhole. Debbie clawing her way out, coming for me. I grabbed my phone and searched *how to cure addiction to another person*. It drew up 437,000,000 results.

Codependence, manipulation, and constant tumult are an addictive relationship's bread and butter, one website claimed. *The person you think you love does not exist, may never have existed. You are obsessed with a projection that will never love you back*. My hands shook as I article-hopped. *You must quit your addiction cold turkey*, the invisible experts warned. *Cut off all contact so you can heal.* I began to cry, overwhelmed at the confirmation I'd done the right thing by ditching Debbie. *Confide in a friend when you need support. Do not let cravings for your loved one threaten your progress.* "I won't," I said to no one.

18.

A week later, I was trying to read a novel without my co-workers noticing, when a blond woman with green eyes approached the reception desk.

"There you are," she said.

She took my hand in both of hers. The book slid off my lap to the floor. She looked around Debbie's age and smelled like sugared lemons. Her thin, silvery voice reminded me of a barspoon with a twisted handle I'd coveted at a flea market.

"I'm here now," she said. "It's going to be okay."

For a moment, I sensed every hair on my body. Then the feeling passed, and it was just me and this beautiful stranger, holding hands while an old man eyed us and grumbled about waiting for two hours.

"Sorry, who are you?" I asked.

She smiled. "I'm Sasha. You don't know it yet, but we were destined to meet each other. I'm your amulet."

"My what?"

"Your amulet."

"And what is that exactly?"

Sasha laughed. "Think of it as being spiritually akin to a knife."

I pulled my hand from hers and scanned the room to see if anyone heard.

"It's okay," she said. "I'm here to help you."

"What are you talking about?"

"You've walked off a map the universe intends to keep you on. I'm going to help you find your way back."

She wasn't dressed like the Scientologists who proselytized in ill-fitting, caterer-like uniforms. With her sparkly eyeshadow, low-cut mint sundress, and gold gladiator sandals, she didn't look religious or culty at all. I had the sense that my search for cures to Debbie-addiction had summoned her. *Take advice only from those who have your best interests at heart.* Despite being an atheist, I fell asleep praying I'd find someone like that.

"I know it sounds kooky," she said. "Give me a chance to explain."

"I've got two more hours in my shift," I said, surprising myself.

"I'll come back. We'll take a walk."

And then she was gone.

"Is that what I've gotta wear to get some medical attention?" the old man said. "Christ."

I jumped at the sound. "Someone will be with you soon."

My hands were shaking. I sat on them until it hurt.

◆

Sasha told me she was psychic as we circled Echo Park Lake.

"Not like palm-reader-at-a-fair psychic. I'm not going to

compliment your robust love line and tell you what a generous lover you are," she laughed.

Couples floated by us in swan boats. Ducks navigated between clusters of lily pads, nipping at bread crumbs.

"Psychic how, then?" I asked.

"I know your past lives and future incarnations. I know the faces of people who have treated you like a by-the-hour motel room. I know when you'll attempt sobriety and when you'll relapse."

If someone at Salvation had said this to me, I would have laughed them out of the bar. People at Salvation *did* talk this way, but from Sasha, it didn't feel like an act. I sat down on the grass. She sat next to me and took my hand in hers again.

"I know this is a lot," she said. "We won't do anything you're not ready for."

"But what do we do, exactly? I probably can't afford whatever you have in mind."

She smiled and interlaced our fingers. A tiny crystal winked at me from her canine tooth. "Here's how it works: we hang out, and I tell you what you need to know. There's no charge. Think of me as a spiritually connected friend."

I stared at our clasped hands and tried not to sweat. A little girl rolled down a hill, squealing. "Wait for me!" her younger sister said, rolling after her. My chest was hammering, bathing me in warm blood, and I felt I was having what I could only describe as a "good heart attack." If Debbie were here, she'd have ditched Sasha like a bag of oregano disguised as weed. "This crazy bitch is after money or drugs or a place to stay," she would have said. "Two months from now, she'll be running a dry shampoo pyramid scheme out of your apartment and claiming squatter's rights." It was classic Debbie to believe premonition existed only between the two of us.

Sasha squeezed my hand. "It's weird, I know. In time, you'll learn to trust me."

The thing was, I trusted her already. I knew liars, and Sasha didn't strike me as one. I didn't care if Sasha was a "real" psychic, if real psychics even existed. I didn't care if Debbie, who had iconically poor judgment, approved. Mostly, I was excited Sasha wanted to be my friend.

•

A few days later, Sasha was waiting outside the hospital at the end of my shift. She wore another sundress, lilac this time, fringed along the bottom. Her winged eyeliner was silver, and she was holding a pink box.

"Want to take a walk?" she said. "I got us ice cream sandwiches."

We fell easily in step with each other, some current between us synchronizing our movements.

"Where to?" I asked.

"There's this neighborhood I love a few blocks from here. It's always exploding with bougainvillea. Not just the pink kind—sherbet orange and yellow too." She handed me a chocolate chip ice cream sandwich with a cookies and cream center—my favorite.

"So, you're into flowers?" I asked, taking a bite.

I could hear Debbie laughing at me: "Oh my god, are

you flirting? You sound like a seventy-year-old trying to connect with his granddaughter."

Sasha buried her face in a tulip the same shade as her lips. "The poet Marie Howe has this line about tulips, how their face and their sex is the same."

I'd never heard of Marie Howe; I almost exclusively read fiction, a fact that suddenly embarrassed me. "Wait till she finds out about flamingo lilies," I said. "I'm pretty sure this girl I went to high school with used one as a dildo."

"No," Sasha laughed and gripped my wrist. Her nails were round and painted emerald; they gleamed against her tan like jewels washed up on shore.

"It was a fake ceramic one, like from TJ Maxx. She kept it in a vase on her nightstand and got super weird if anyone tried to touch it."

"You've had some childhood," Sasha said. She licked mint chip off her upper lip.

"Yeah," I said. "Well. I guess you know all about it."

"Bits and pieces. I'm not omniscient." She took another bite and caught the cream dripping down her wrist with her tongue. "Usually, it's like remembering a dream. Cloudy, but if I concentrate, the more significant details emerge. Sometimes, it's a vague feeling about someone I see on the street. Other times, a dense narrative, as though I'm watching a documentary. But it's never the whole picture."

"Have you been psychic all your life?" A ridiculous question, but I was fascinated by her. She had this authentic verve that none of us at Salvation could pull off. No matter how coolly we sold the lie of ourselves, our need for others to believe it was the tell.

"No," she said. "Not my whole life." She worked the purple beads of her necklace with the hand that wasn't holding the ice cream sandwich.

"Oh, how old were you when—"

"This isn't something I talk about when I'm getting to know someone. It's very personal." She released the necklace, beads striking her collarbone.

"Sorry. Of course. That was stupid of me."

"It's okay. I'll tell you more another time." She smiled and tossed the ice cream box in a trash can. "When we know each other better."

We walked in comfortable silence, admiring the fauna. I stopped before a house with an impressive array of cacti guarding the front yard. There were prickly pears and golden cereuses and enormous saguaros. My father bought a book on California cacti when I was eleven, and I remembered being perplexed by the sight of it on our living room bookshelf. He'd never shown interest in cacti before. I flipped through the book under the covers at night, obscuring the names of the cacti to see if I could identify them by image alone. I thought, if this was his new hobby, maybe it was something we could share. I concocted this whole scheme where, after I became a cactus expert, I'd ask him to take a walk around the neighborhood with me. I'd casually identify the cacti around us, letting him know I was part of the club too.

A couple of weeks later, I returned home from school to find the book gone from our shelf. I turned the house upside down, even dug through the trash. That's where I found the plant nursery receipt for an *Echinocereus pectinatus rubispinus*, also known as a molted candlestick tree. It was a gorgeous cylindrical cactus with plum-colored spines that, when in bloom, sprouted magenta flowers with a lemon-yellow center. I'd never seen one in real life. I waited giddily for him to bring our new friend home.

He got home late, when I was already in bed with my teeth brushed. I greeted him in the living room, wanting to catch him bringing the cactus in. He was already on the couch, drinking a beer, watching a *Seinfeld* rerun. There was no cactus. *Maybe it's a surprise*, I thought. Weeks later, when the cactus and the book never materialized, I realized I'd been right. It had been a surprise—for someone else, probably some woman he was seeing.

"What are you thinking about?" Sasha asked.

We'd been hovering in front of the house for several minutes. "Sorry. Just some family bullshit."

She resumed walking and I kept apace. "Has anyone ever told you about your past lives?"

"No, but my sister, Debbie, used to say I must have been a police informant in a past life. But that's just her being an asshole."

Sasha laughed. "Boring. Your past lives are way more textured than that."

"Like what?" I balled the ice cream wrapper in my fist.

"Where to start," she said. "Okay, in one life, you cleaned rich people's houses in Germany. You amassed an impressive collection of discarded objects—paintings they'd grown tired of, tarnished jewelry you were able to restore. You saved your favorites and had a side hustle selling the rest. It was all well and good until one of the women you worked for suspected you were fucking her husband. Which you weren't, but she made working there hell for you. Immature shit like dumping food on the carpet and leaving shards of glass in places she knew you'd blindly stick your hand in to clean. You only left after the husband *did* try to fuck you. Which sucked, because the money was good, and they had this amazing cat named Sybil."

I had no idea what to say to that.

"You've retained your endurance from that life," Sasha continued. "You're capable of tolerating a lot. Frankly, more than you should."

"Wait, what year was this? And was it East Germany or West Germany?" I didn't exactly believe in past lives, but I couldn't not press her further. "Was I Jewish?"

She raised her palm. "This isn't a Q&A, love. Take a deep breath, and just listen."

She began to speak of another life where I died young from poorly sterilized surgical instruments. "That's why you self-harm with pills and sex instead of knives."

I wanted to ask if all my past lives ended tragically, if this life would be more of the same.

"There it is," she said, stopping me with a hand on my shoulder. We stood before a white Spanish-style house draped in highlighter-tone bougainvillea. Magenta, neon yellow, atomic tangerine. It was 80 percent bougainvillea and 20 percent house. "Isn't it beautiful?"

The coolness of her hand felt otherworldly on my shoulder.

"What were you saying about using pills and sex instead of knives?" I asked.

"Later," she said, squeezing my shoulder. "Let's just be here together."

I would soon come to learn this was classic Sasha. She revealed only as much as she wanted and rarely entertained follow-up questions. Her revelations were casual, atmospheric, and shockingly specific, leaving me with more questions than answers. Yet, walking with her among the flowers that day, I didn't mind. I had a friend. A bold, funny, mysterious friend who was as interested in me as I was in her. Friendship could be a slow burn. I didn't have to consume her like a drink at last call. I was too afraid to ask what the other ways I'd used my knife meant.

19.

A couple of weeks after we met, Sasha was keeping me company at work, reading a book in the waiting room, when an elderly woman checked herself in. She was drenched in sweat and spoke frantically at me in Russian. I couldn't understand a word she said. "No English," she insisted, before launching into another anguished plea. I called the translator line, but it kept ringing and ringing.

"Please," the woman said. "There's an elephant on my chest. I can barely breathe."

I asked a few questions and got her triaged. Only after she was wheeled into the emergency room did I realize we'd spoken entirely in Russian. I knew a handful of Russian words, yet entire sentences had tumbled out of me. At least, I thought they had. My jaw ached after, as though I'd borrowed an ancestor's tongue. *What the fuck*, I mouthed to Sasha. She smiled and shrugged.

After work, Sasha and I walked to see the bougainvillea again. She seemed frustrated and was more forthcoming than usual. She said something about the president of Moldova's powers being suspended over his refusal to appoint government-backed ministers.

"Doubt it'll make a difference. Dodon's a pro-Russian

hack. And a virulent homophobe, not that that makes him unique," she said. "Last year, when Moldova's LGBT march was shut down, Dodon said, 'I have never promised to be the president of the gays, they should have elected their own president.'"

"Gross," I said. My knowledge of Moldova began and ended with my grandmother telling me there'd been several pogroms there in the early twentieth century. That the police "watched Jewish babies get torn in half and did nothing."

Sasha was a Jewish refugee from Moldova and kept up with past and present politics. Which made sense and also didn't. It rubbed unpleasantly against my conviction that she did not have a birthday or an immigration status or an ancestral homeland in a strict geographic sense. This meant she also had a mother, and blood cells, and taxes. I liked imagining her as an independent contractor for the universe, filing a 1099 form addressed to the wind.

•

I timed my pills just before visiting Sasha's apartment for the first time. Mortifying, how lived-in it felt compared to mine. My apartment was a hodgepodge of Craigslist furniture, flea market tchotchkes with no unifying design scheme, and floral Soviet-style throw blankets my grandmother had given me that violently clashed with everything else. Sasha's apartment was so intentional. There were poetry zines, essay collections, and books with holographic covers and titles like *Queering Spirit Work* piled everywhere. Plants rested atop them like sunning cats—monsteras, fiddle-leaf figs, cacti ranging from a two-foot saguaro to a bunny ears cactus the size of my thumb. Bushy green-and-purple plants she called wandering Jews hung from the ceiling and snaked across surfaces. Her walls had been taken over by unsettling abstract paintings that looked the way a panic attack felt. She had an iguana named Apples. She owned more clothes and makeup than my sister. My stomach dropped when I spotted the clamshell eyeshadow palette Debbie used on me the first time we went to Salvation together.

A mirror with a squiggly pink frame leaned against the wall opposite Sasha's bed. The placement felt a little sexual, and she smirked when she caught me looking. She patted the space next to her on the bed. I sat, smiling at our reflections.

"So." She lit an amber candle perched on a mercury glass dish. "What do you want to know?"

I spat out a litany of questions. Was my sister alive? Would my mother ever get better? Was the handyman still in Los Angeles? Would I get sober, and would it last?

She wouldn't answer directly. "If only it were that easy, right?"

We spent hours talking about Debbie: our childhood dramas, my miscarriage, how her absence alternated between feeling like I'd excised a tumor and like I'd lost an essential organ. The lightness in my chest—the physical sensation of unburdening myself to Sasha—was not unlike the relief I felt with my pills.

Sasha opened up too. She told me her parents lived in Philadelphia and didn't believe in her power.

"They think psychics are hacks," she said. "That they're no better than the scammers they knew back in the Soviet Union who billed old people for polyclinic visits they'd never had."

"They think you're faking it?"

"I don't know what they think. They're so wrapped up in the narrative that they pulled themselves up by their bootstraps after immigrating here—my mom's a dental hygienist and my dad owns a pawn shop—that they can't imagine any other way of existing."

She fluffed her pillow and reached behind me to fluff mine. Her hand brushed the tender space between the tops of my shoulder blades, igniting every pore.

"They don't believe in psychics, yet they're so fucking superstitious," she said. "They yell at me if I leave my purse on the floor because it means we'll run out of money. They won't let me sit on cold surfaces like the sidewalk because they think it'll make me infertile."

"Oh my god, my grandma believes that one too. It must be a Soviet thing."

Sasha rolled her eyes. "Can't sit at the corner of a table or I won't get married for seven years. Had to wear a red string bracelet my whole childhood as protection against the evil eye. When my mom was afraid someone put the evil eye on me, she'd chase me around the apartment with a pair of used underwear, trying to rub it in my face to dispel the bad energy."

"She and my mom would get along."

"Aw, you think?" Sasha asked.

"I mean, to a point," I said, tracing the path her fingers had taken across my back. "She'd probably think your mom was a spy. She thinks everyone is a spy."

"I never believed in any of their superstitions," Sasha said. "But I played along to keep the peace. They weren't all bad. My dad used to hand me a quarter to flash at the full moon, to invite abundance into our home. When I put a shirt on inside-out, my parents said that meant I was going to be beaten, and they would pretend-hit me before anyone else could do it for real."

"That's sweet."

"But I played my cards wrong. If I'd been more openly skeptical of their superstitions, maybe I'd seem credible. Maybe they would think, *Well, shit, if our cynical, occult-allergic daughter says she has this power, we should believe her.* It's not like I get paid to do this." She tied her hair into a high ponytail, uncovering a tattoo behind her ear: a tree branch bearing sour cherries.

"What, uh, do you do for money?" I asked.

Sasha smiled. "You haven't figured it out?"

She clearly didn't work a nine-to-five if she kept showing up during my hospital shifts. Scanning her room didn't reveal any uniforms, test prep books, framed diplomas.

"I'll give you a clue: I work for myself."

"Something creative, right?"

She nodded.

"Involving . . . plants?"

She laughed. "Try again."

Her candles didn't look homemade, and I couldn't spot a sewing machine or any other tools. The mirrored sliding door of her closet was partly open. Inside, an easel leaned against a stack of shoeboxes. Above her headboard hung a painting of overlapping abstract splotches in pastel tones. It reminded me of naked cells under a microscope, cold words like *endoplasmic reticulum*. The figure was vaguely woman-shaped—I spotted what could be breasts and an ass—and it felt like what you'd get if you forced Matisse and my unmedicated mother to make a collaborative painting. There was something sinister about its peach, mint, and cloud-colored tones. It was like looking up the lyrics to a pop song and realizing it was about watching your parents murder each other.

"You're an artist," I said.

"A painter, mostly. I tried sculpture first, but my pieces always came out looking like sex toys from Mars. But enough about me. Are you hungry? I need a snack."

We migrated to her living room. She turned on a horrible Russian talk show where women bickered over sexual propriety. A nineteen-year-old girl with an eighty-four-year-old husband brought her mother on to spar about marriage and family honor. The audience yelled out questions about the couple's sex lives. The host was a middle-aged woman with hair dyed the color of menstrual blood, and she sided with the disgusted mother. There was a musical interlude by a Russian pop star whom, according to Sasha, everyone knew to be gay but pretended otherwise for political reasons. There was a pseudoscientific diet advice segment, peppered with bold and irrelevant claims like "Halloween is a celebration of evil." I found myself rooting for the couple, for the way their relationship was a fuck-you to acceptable sexuality, though I didn't believe they would make each other happy, and picturing this man two years from the grave atop his teenage bride made my throat close.

"Do you like this show?" I asked during a commercial break. A man with a handlebar mustache was holding several tiny pairs of pants. I couldn't tell if he was advertising weight loss pills, washing machines, or children's fashion.

"Absolutely not," she said. She dipped a chocolate wafer into her tea and took the whole thing in her mouth.

"It seems pretty fucked-up."

"Oh, it's the absolute worst." She dipped another wafer.

"Should we put something else on?"

Sasha laughed. "I don't watch for fun. It calibrates my attunement to human suffering."

"Oh."

She hadn't explained the ground rules of this amulet thing. I didn't want to piss her off with invasive questions, but I suspected she could see through my transparent attempts to play it cool.

"What else calibrates your attunement to human suffering?" I asked.

"So greedy," Sasha said, kissing my head. "That's enough answers for one day."

"Aren't you supposed to be advising me?" I teased. "All we've done is vent about our families, watch trash TV, and drink tea."

"Fine," she said. She closed her eyes and rubbed her temples. "Invest in a 401(k)," she said in a spooky voice. "Don't walk into oncoming traffic. Call your mother." She burst out laughing.

I rolled my eyes.

"I don't know you well enough yet," she said, handing me a wafer. "Tell me more about your thing with drains."

"It's not just drains," I began, wary of how unwell I sounded. "It's sewer gutters, the garbage disposal, the trash chute. After I . . . stabbed Debbie, I started having these creepy visions whenever I was alone around holes."

"What kind of visions?"

"My knife getting sucked down the drain and shooting out to stab someone. Or, lately, I keep seeing my ear cavity getting bigger. Swelling to the size of a marble, an egg, a grapefruit. And then—sorry, this is gross—this dark mass shaped like a dust bunny slips out. The drain swallows it whole."

"Interesting."

"Do you think it's a guilt thing? I stabbed my sister, so now I have a fraught relationship with holes?"

"Could be. Or maybe it represents a desire you're afraid to act on."

"What kind of desire?" I ate several wafers in quick succession.

"A fraught relationship with holes? Sounds very queer to me."

I picked the crumbs out of my lap and looked up to her scanning my face in a manner that was almost mathematical. "What do you suggest I do about it?" I said.

The talk show returned from commercial break. Instead of elaborating, Sasha turned up the volume.

20.

How did I go from having no close friends to spending several days a week with Sasha? She had all of Debbie's larger-than-life-ness, but without the dangerous edge or the bitter comedown. Her stories were more colorful than anything I'd heard at Salvation. I barely had the urge to go there anymore. When I did, I bolted as soon as I sold my pills and took the bus straight to Sasha's. I was using less. I still took Oxy and Ativan, but not so much to dull my sensitivity to the world as to avoid withdrawal. Sasha made me want to feel things, some things, again.

I avoided eye contact with her paintings, which made me anxious if I looked too long. One night, I fell asleep on her couch and awoke to her evaluating a piece still wet with paint. A cobalt shape that was both erotic and ruined. It reminded me of rough sex, birds of prey, drowning, bone marrow. The painting felt like a personal indictment. A road map to the ill-fated decisions Sasha was trying to save me from. I had the sense that if I fucked things up with her, I would become this doomed splotch.

"What do you think?" she asked.

"It's cool," I said.

She laughed at whatever she saw on my face.

"What?" I said.

"It freaks you out."

"Only a little. But don't listen to me. I don't know shit about art."

She made a *tsk* sound and dotted my cheek with blue paint. "You sound like my parents."

This was definitely not a good thing. "How so?"

"They know I support myself with my art but don't want the specifics. They feel similarly about my sexuality, by the way." She cleared her throat and dotted my other cheek. "They tell me they don't understand my art, and then a week later my mom calls to say their bathroom needs something bright, and can I send them a painting. Which, of course, I always do."

I pictured their house in Philadelphia, its leather couches and cabinets full of crystal glassware clashing spectacularly with Sasha's paintings.

"They never compliment my work. I don't even know if they've hung it up unless my dad texts a picture of my mom posing next to it, unsmiling."

"Sounds like they're proud of you."

Sasha shrugged. "I always tell them when I sell a piece, since child-pride is the life force powering every post-Soviet parent. They still try to convince me to go to dental school every other month. But as long as I don't expect them to support me, they're fine." She dotted my chin, the bridge of my nose, and above both eyebrows with her paintbrush. "And if they don't know about my lovers, they can pretend there aren't any."

I was a little jealous. I wanted parents who took offense

at my life choices. Criticism is still a cousin of attention. Beyond Debbie, the only person who spoke to me that way was my grandmother, but she unloaded so many depressing stories in the process that I left her company anemic and dead-eyed.

I wanted to know more about these lovers too.

"All of that's to say," Sasha continued, "you don't have to pretend to like something just because I made it."

"I do like it," I said. "It just hits too close to home in a weird way."

"So say that." Sasha took my chin in her hand. She traced my face with her finger, smearing me with paint. "I know you crave being told what to do. It kept you attached to your sister, and it's why you like being around me. Well, part of why you like being around me." She flashed her crystal tooth. "But you don't have to settle for being a person that things happen to. You have desires. Act on them."

"Is it free will if you're telling me to do it?"

Sasha laughed. "Bitch, does this look like an Intro to Philosophy seminar?"

Art supplies were strewn about her apartment. Underwear in highlighter tones hung from her drying rack. One of the thongs was crotchless. I wondered who she'd worn it for.

Her phone alarm went off, rain hitting wind chimes.

"Time to give Apples his medicine," she said.

Apples suffered from some kind of iguana anxiety disorder. He often looked like he wanted to fuck something and then to destroy it and be left alone forever. Our interactions had been brief and fraught. He whirled his head around when I pet him, watching me with slits for eyes. Every morning, Sasha fed him bread soaked in Lexapro.

"You have to drop the pill in the syringe and suck five milliliters of water inside," she explained. "It takes a couple minutes to dissolve. Then you expel it on a slice of brown bread, preferably from the Russian store. You can't let him see you do it, or he won't eat it. Here, hold this."

I gripped the syringe in my fist, thumb pressing lightly against the plunger.

She wrapped her hand around mine, my pulse throbbing into the soft skin of her wrist. The lavender of her detergent fused with the spiced amber of the perfume I'd begun wearing. "Ready?" Her thumb pushed into mine, depressing the plunger. A white slurry dripped onto the bread.

"Now fold the bread to spread the medicine."

I did as she said until the entire surface was damp.

She didn't withdraw her hand. There was an aura of complicity between us, and I grew slick with the force of it.

"Um. You can put it in his cage now," she said.

Neither of us moved. Apples turned to look at me and began to hiss.

Sasha pulled her hand from mine. "Who's mama's favorite asshole?" she cooed.

There was something human in the judgmental looks he gave me, in the restless way he paced his cage. He demanded attention but was deeply distrustful. When I tried to hold him later that day, he whipped me with his tail.

Nice try, dipshit, he was probably thinking.

He reminded me of Debbie.

In the bathroom, I saw that Sasha had painted my face in the shape of a heart.

•

Sasha rarely exhibited at galleries and didn't advertise. How buyers found her, and what they had in common, was mysterious to me. There was a bug-eyed white woman who'd left her husband to join an exercise cult, a Sikh man in his thirties pursuing a PhD in eco-poetics, a formerly homeless couple who'd won the lottery. I suspected people responded as much to Sasha as to her art. She was young, beautiful, a cipher. She invited them into her home and let them touch the paintings. Sasha was often braless in a flowy dress or crop top. Music played, candles burned, giving off traces of cassis or sandalwood. Once, I watched as two strangers became so undone looking at one of her pieces—a chain of wobbly pink circles—that she invited them to use her bedroom if they wanted to fuck, and they did.

When the eco-poetics PhD began eyeing the cobalt painting, Sasha told him it wasn't for sale.

"It belongs to her," she said, looking at me.

At her insistence, the painting went home with me. It lorded over my apartment, visible from every angle. There was no other art on the walls to dilute its dominance, and I found myself spending less time at home to avoid it. When I felt its curves scrutinizing me, reminding me of limbs whose bones had been replaced with olive oil, I took the bus to Salvation or to Sasha's. Yet I loved the painting just as much as I was repelled by it. It was the first thing Sasha had ever gifted me. When, a week later, my fire alarm went off in the middle of the night, her painting was the only possession I grabbed.

"Drunk idiots," my elderly Ukrainian neighbor with emphysema said, out in the hallway. "No fire."

"Thanks," I said.

He scrunched his face at the painting.

I turned before he could get a good look, pressing Sasha's gift to my chest.

"Can I ask you something?" I said one morning.

We were on Sasha's couch. I was reading the Marie Howe book with the tulips poem, while she read *The Lonely City* by Olivia Laing. It was the one-year anniversary of Debbie's disappearance.

"How old were you when you realized you were psychic? How did it come to you?"

She didn't look up from her book.

"Sasha?"

She was so quiet, I could hear Apples chewing from across the room.

"Sorry," I said. "Too personal. We don't have to talk about it."

She sighed. "I've never told anyone this before." She sat up and crossed her legs. "I was eight. It wasn't long after we immigrated. My mom walked in on me naked with a girl my age. We didn't know what we were doing, obviously. We were kids, and we were curious."

"Of course," I said. "What happened?"

"My mom completely freaked out. She sent my friend home, and then she screamed at me about what a terrible life I would have if I chose to be a lesbianka. How I would never get married or have kids to care for me in old age, how I'd always be lonely, all the shame I'd bring my family."

"That's fucked-up," I said, stroking her arm.

"I didn't even know lesbians existed. For weeks, I felt this horrible anxiety that I was doomed, that my life wasn't worth living. That I was a curse on my family, on the whole world."

I linked our elbows. She stiffened but didn't extricate herself.

"One night, not long after that, I woke up from a nightmare. It was raining, and the floorboards were creaking, and it sounded like they were talking to me."

"What were they saying?"

"It's you."

"What?"

"That's what it sounded like. *It's you it's you it's you it's you*. The next morning, I had this certainty I'd never felt before. That I was powerful. That I had purpose." Her arm in mine was stiff as a crowbar.

"And you think that's related to getting caught with your friend?"

I knew as soon as I said it that this was a miscalculation. That I came from mercurial people who punished me for trying to know them, and I was taking advantage of Sasha's candor, prioritizing what I wanted to know over what she wanted to tell me.

“Who knows if one catalyzed the other?” Sasha said sharply, loose waves half-mooning her face. “Can you pinpoint the exact moment you knew you were queer?”

I thought about a girl from my middle school swim team untwisting my bra straps in the locker room. My first sleepover, two girls giving me a makeover, their fingers all over my face.

“What matters,” Sasha said, “is I knew then that I belonged in the world.”

“You did nothing wrong.”

She wriggled out from my grasp and went back to reading her book.

21.

I hadn't seen my grandmother in months and was surprised when she invited my mother and me over to celebrate her birthday. She used to host birthday lunches every year, before my mother kicked Debbie out and the dynamics got too complicated. I called Sasha in a panic.

"What are you afraid of?" Sasha asked.

"That I won't be able to handle being around her and my mom at the same time."

"What else?" She was chewing something. A pita chip or a pretzel. The crunch and the wet sound of her licking crumbs out of her teeth lowered my blood pressure.

"I feel guilty that I don't make much effort to see her. She's not an easy person. The last time I saw her, she wanted me to dye her hair. They didn't have her shade at CVS, and I had to schlep to two other drugstores. Turns out, she called Valley College pretending to be me and learned I'd never registered for classes. The whole time I'm dyeing her hair, she's telling me how thankful she is her parents didn't live to see their great-granddaughter squander the opportunity to get a college education. How I'm wasting the gift they paid for with their lives. As if her father woke up one morning and thought, *Maybe I should get murdered by the state so that, sixty years from now, my great-grandchild will feel a moral obligation to get a bachelor's degree.*"

Sasha laughed. "I've heard this song before."

"I feel bad for her—her daughter lives on another planet, half her friends are dead, and she lives in a country that has no use for her—but that doesn't make it any easier to be around her. She's never asked what I want out of life."

"What's stopping you from telling her?"

"Not worth the drama." How could I articulate my desires to such a difficult person when I couldn't articulate them to myself?

When I arrived at her apartment, absolutely snowed on Ativan and Oxy, my grandmother greeted me with a *tsk* for not wearing a jacket. "It's like you *want* to get pneumonia," she said, draping a woven cardigan that had immigrated with her from Saint Petersburg over my shoulders.

"It's eighty-five degrees out," I said. "I literally got sunburned on the walk from the bus stop."

"My cousin Basya died of hypothermia in the summer," she said. "All the girls crying into her coffin were jealous of her tan."

My mother was already there, drinking sour cherry juice on the couch.

"Hi, Mom," I said, kissing her cheek.

"Hi, honey." She squeezed my shoulder. And then she got up to relock the door I'd already locked behind me. She stood watch at the peephole until it was time to eat.

The meal went as expected. My grandmother gloated about being on her feet all day to cook for us and shoved chicken soup, gefilte fish, and eggplant salad in our faces with no reprieve. Each time I protested, “That’s enough,” she dolloped another portion onto my plate, daring me with cataracted eyes to fight back. The chicken soup was good. The fish smelled fishy, but we forced it down. My mother was and wasn’t there, alternating between silence, small talk, and questions about thieving neighbors and why my grandmother hadn’t bought a water purifier for filtering out radioisotopes. My grandmother brushed off these obvious signs her daughter was unwell and pivoted to bullying me about not having married a doctor yet.

“You modern women have no sense of priorities,” she said. “You think you have all the time in the world. Even on Russian shows now, they’re all *career career career.* But they’re training to be dentists, lawyers. They’ll find husbands like that.” She snapped her fingers. “You work at a hospital, surrounded by single doctors! What are you waiting for? That perky tuchus isn’t going to last forever.”

Then she compared my ovaries to a box of dusty raisins and excused herself to abuse laxatives. While she was gone, my mother and I stared at each other as though we couldn’t decide which of the three of us was the circus animal.

When my grandmother returned, she asked about Debbie.

“She’s abroad on a service trip, remember?” my mother said. “The Peace Corps or something.”

“She could have called,” my grandmother said. “I haven’t heard from her in I don’t know how long.”

“They don’t have phones there,” my mother said.

“What kind of farkakte country doesn’t have phones?”

my grandmother said, frowning. “My neighbor Fanya just immigrated from a village with no name. She’d never seen a banana or a toilet in her life. But she knew how to use a phone. The Peace Corps.” My grandmother spat onto her greige carpet. “Why did my family give up everything to immigrate here if my granddaughter was just going to return to a hole worse than the one we left?”

No one had an answer for that. I downed the rest of my sour cherry juice, launching half of it down my trachea.

“When is she coming back?” my grandmother asked, beating my back until my coughs subsided.

“Who knows?” my mother said. She spread eggplant salad on seeded bread. “I think she likes it there.”

“What’s to like about communal apartments and buses so crowded your seat is inside someone’s armpit?” my grandmother asked, shaking her head. “It’s disrespectful. We went through hell before we came to this country. You princesses have no idea what it was like. My own father dragged out of the house and shot in the street like a dog. Before him, my mother’s first husband was killed in the war. She gave up her clothing atelier to go into hiding on a collective farm. She was one of the best seamstresses in Leningrad—she made pageant dresses for the Romanian queen, for god’s sake—and she ruined her hands digging for radishes.”

We all looked at the plate of radishes between us. My grandmother bit into one caustically. I couldn’t tell if her father being “shot in the street like a dog” was a detail she’d concealed from me, or if she was filling in the blanks of what she herself did not know.

“My mother’s first daughter contracted typhoid on the

farm," she went on. "She was three years old and died thousands of miles from home. My only sister, dead before I was born. She was so calm and thoughtful for her age. She loved being read to. My mother used to say she would have grown up to be a professor. You're named after her," she said to me, phrasing this last part as an accusation. "I grew up with no siblings and no father. You and your sister are so spoiled to have each other, and she abandons you to dig for radishes."

My stomach heaved. This whole time, I thought I'd quit Debbie. That I was in recovery. That every day, I made the conscious choice not to let her back into my life. Was I mistaken—was she the one who'd abandoned me?

There was nothing to say after that. A Russian New Year's concert from a decade earlier played in the background, the same closeted pop star I'd seen on Sasha's talk show serenading a cheering audience in a gold sequined tuxedo. My grandmother cranked up the volume.

As we were leaving, she gripped my shoulder and said, "You know, my only aunt died of unexplained kidney failure in her fifties, and her infertile husband took all the jewelry she'd been saving for me. At her memorial dinner, the waiters stole and resold half the food. My mother saw one of them in line to buy pantyhose a month later. She tapped his shoulder and said, 'Only God forgives.' He laughed in her face. A week later, he fell through a crack in a frozen lake."

"What happened to your uncle, the one who stole the jewelry?"

My grandmother scoffed. "He lived to be eighty-nine. My aunt is buried alone in the Jewish cemetery, but he gets to spend eternity with the mistress he dressed in her jewels." She took a swig of juice. "Jewish luck."

The takeaway of these stories seemed to be that our legacy was one of humiliation and suffering. Life treated those who came before me with relentless indignity, and I had a moral obligation to live better than them. Living better than them did not mean making my own choices. It meant honoring the choices my ancestors would have wanted for me.

I'd assumed this lunch would leave me clawing for my silver rabbit, but I was calm exiting my grandmother's building. The sky was the hopeful blue of toilet bowl cleaner, and I felt a shrugging indifference to the possibility that withdrawing from Debbie wasn't the grand gesture of agency I'd thought it was. A woman with matted hair was washing the building's driveway with an invisible mop. I offered her my grandmother's leftovers, and she disappeared with them around the corner.

"Hey, love," Sasha answered on the first ring.

I softened like butter. "What are you doing? Can you pick me up?"

While I waited for Sasha, the woman returned with a bird-of-paradise. "For you," she said, tucking the stalk into my tote. Its violet-and-orange head was still perched on my shoulder when Sasha pulled up.

"My favorite," Sasha said, hugging the flower to her chest. "How did you know?"

22.

Sasha never told me how long she'd be my amulet. I was afraid to ask, in case acknowledging what was building between us dispersed it like vapor. Her protection cast an aura that reminded me of waves lapping a pebbled shore. Drains began to behave as drains again. A squirrel approached me in the park and offered its acorn. Every electron in my apartment vibrated when Sasha was around. I felt hopeful, though I couldn't verbalize what exactly for.

I wasn't reaching for emergency doses of my meds and was even considering getting sober. But people at Salvation told stories of stopping cold turkey—how they relapsed once they realized that, if the endless vomiting and diarrhea didn't kill them, the suicidal thoughts would. I couldn't live like that, much less hold down my job. If I lost my job, my only income would be from selling pills, but if I wanted to stay sober, I'd have to stop selling entirely. Thinking through the mechanics of sobriety usually elicited so much anxiety I ended up taking more pills. It was easier not to think about it at all.

Sasha didn't drink or use drugs but she never demanded I abstain. One evening, emboldened by her retelling of a past life in which I lived in exile as a political dissident, inscribing my diaries into my dirt floor, I searched *how to get sober* online. I read about addiction specialists, Narcotics Anonymous, methadone and Suboxone. *You will need strong social support during this challenging time*, one website warned. *Seeing a therapist is highly recommended.* My psychiatrist refilled my Ativan every few months, but those visits lasted eight minutes, and I would sooner flee the city than admit I'd been grifting her. I logged onto my insurance company's website and searched for therapists who were accepting new patients. Most were women in their sixties with names like Rhonda, Barbara, Shirley. I emailed the ones whose photos didn't terrify me.

Pauline was several decades older than her photo. Her home office smelled like a drugstore candle, and her jewelry resembled something you'd get at Mardi Gras for showing your tits. She wore these purple and yellow beaded necklaces, one on top of the other, and the more personal her questions got, the more she tugged on them, so that by the time she got to "Have you had any thoughts of self-harm?" her fingers were covered in honeycomb-like indentations. Pauline's first order of business was insisting I take more walks. Something about endorphins and how they trick your brain into thinking you're on a morphine drip. She also referred me to an addiction specialist.

Dr. Ramos was tall and makeup-free. Pretty in the I-went-to-graduate-school way I realized I had hoped to be. Her nails were neon yellow, which suggested to me that she had friends. Gothic line drawings of misshaped faces wallpapered her office. Probably the work of her children, but I liked imagining that her creative outlet was crudely drawn pencil art.

"So," she said, scanning my chart. "I see you already have a prescription for Lexapro."

"I've never taken it," I said.

"Why not?"

"I was told it causes sexual dysfunction."

She tucked her hair behind her ears, revealing a cartilage piercing. "It can, but not for everyone. And it's manageable. It's not a reason to avoid SSRIs altogether."

"Speak for yourself, bitch," Debbie would have responded.

"So you've just been taking Ativan for your anxiety?" Dr. Ramos said.

I nodded. "The OxyContin helps slow my brain down too."

"Treating anxiety with Ativan and OxyContin is like yanking the emergency brake every time you want to slow down. You're going to ruin your car. Lexapro is your brake pedal. A more sustainable long-term solution."

Debbie would have joked that the doctor must own Lexapro stock. But she was the reason I was addicted to benzos and opiates in the first place.

"Are you willing to give Lexapro a shot?" Dr. Ramos asked. "It'll help us taper off the Ativan. After that, we can tackle the OxyContin."

"What are the other side effects?"

"Some people have a little stomach upset at first. Nausea,

diarrhea, some mild headaches. These tend to decrease over time."

"Okay."

She placed a bony hand on my shoulder. "I know it's scary. We'll start slow, and I'll check in with you regularly."

When I told Sasha about the appointment, she burst out laughing. "You and Apples *would* take the same antidepressant."

●

Dr. Ramos wasn't the squishy mommy figure I'd secretly hoped for, but she checked in each time we decreased my Ativan dose. A few weeks in, we scaled back too quickly, and my anxiety got so unbearable I called out of work. I felt like my organs were cannibalizing each other. "Go back to your higher dose from last week," she instructed. "We'll take it slower this time."

We went on like this for eight weeks before the Ativan was out of my system.

"This next part is kind of medieval," she warned. "I want to start you on Suboxone—it's a partial opioid agonist, meaning it binds your opioid receptors enough to feed that craving, but not so much that it gives you a high. You're going to have to stop taking your OxyContin—and any other opioids—and let yourself go into withdrawal. If you take your first dose of Suboxone too soon, the withdrawal is going to be very intense." She sent me home with a starter pack and an instruction sheet.

Medieval wasn't far off. I had to wait until I was nauseous, crampy, and couldn't stop shaking. I sat in my underwear on Sasha's floor, sweating against the rough gray fibers of her couch. She brought me Tylenol, nausea pills, glass after glass of ice water with lemon, half of which ended up on the floor.

It took forty-five minutes for the Suboxone to kick in, and by then, I felt like I was hanging by my hair from the ceiling.

"How did I get here?" I whined. "That's not a rhetorical question. I'm actually asking."

Sasha draped a cool washcloth around my neck and wrote down the time I took my first dose on the instruction sheet.

"How do you feel?" she asked an hour later.

"A little better. Still shitty." The cramps were receding, but I was fifty-fifty on whether I'd keep my breakfast down. The full-body chills had mostly localized to my left hand.

Sasha scanned the instructions. "Dissolve a second dose under your tongue."

"Then what?"

"We wait another two hours. If you feel okay, we're done for today. If not, you take another dose. You're doing great," she said over my groans. "I'm really proud of you."

I felt better an hour after the third dose. Sasha made me a bowl of couscous, and I fell asleep in her bed. We went on like this for three days, increasing the Suboxone dose based on my withdrawal symptoms. I called the addiction specialist's office every day, Sasha listening on speakerphone and taking notes. On day four, we settled on what Dr. Ramos called a "maintenance dose." I took the same dose every day and was supposed to call if my symptoms returned.

This was day seven. On the phone, I told her I felt mostly okay. She didn't know about my rabbit, the remaining pills I planned to sell at Salvation.

•

When Sasha was busy, and I was afraid to be in the same room as my rabbit, I took the bus to random stops. I liked walking around neighborhoods I didn't know. I tried to infer the kinds of danger people faced in different parts of the city by examining gas station over-the-counter medicine displays. I strolled through residential areas, wondering which were the types of places where people kept their blinds open, and when I found them, I wrote down what I saw. Sometimes I hitchhiked. Attempting sobriety, doing a good job at work, cooking vegetarian dishes like Greek orzo salad with Sasha—I could hear Debbie laughing at how boring I'd become. "What's next, the Peace Corps?" Hitchhiking gave me that hit of danger I craved. Most of my encounters were uneventful—older women who mistook me for a high-schooler whose parents had forgotten to pick her up, acne-pocked bankers who thought they had it in them to make a move but didn't. I kept my knife in my bag, its hilt crusted with Debbie's blood. It's not that I wanted to get hurt. I wanted to know that I could.

On my fifteenth day of sobriety, I spent the morning at an open-air market downtown, where vendors sold quinceañera dresses, knockoff purses, and caged rabbits stacked in a pyramid. The older rabbits had eye crust, long yellow nails, and fur that went gray like human hair. The baby bunnies enthusiastically nibbled browning lettuce in a way that made me think they'd accept anything you gave them. I wondered what would happen if I slipped one of my pills through the bars. A gift from one rabbit to another.

"Fifteen dollars," a woman who looked a hundred years old said to me. "Twenty-five for two."

I didn't know what formula a person would use to determine an animal's worth. I said no thanks and bought a bowl of Tajín-spiced mangos from a fruit vendor, and then I got a ride from his cousin to my mother's apartment. We listened to top 40s the whole way, shyly bopping our heads in lieu of making conversation. He dropped me off a couple of blocks from my mother's and said, "May God watch over you," before driving off.

My mother was watching a black-and-white film on the couch. Propaganda newspapers piled atop her coffee table. ILLEGALS NOW OUTNUMBER AMERICANS, read one headline. MOST PHONES ALREADY TAPPED, SAYS GOVERNMENT SOURCE, read another. In whatever Western she was watching, men chased each other on horseback. Shots were fired. Women in bonnets cried. I joined her on the couch, and we passed a bag of barbecue chips back and forth.

When the film ended, I asked if she wanted to watch *Nu, pogodi!*, a *Tom and Jerry*–esque Soviet cartoon she used to play for me and Debbie. It was one of the few bits of

Soviet media we could understand, as there was barely any dialogue.

She laughed. "God, we haven't watched that in years. Sure, pull it up."

I loaded a random episode on her laptop, and we scooted closer to each other. She draped a fuzzy blanket over my lap.

Each episode centered on chain-smoking Wolf's obsessive pursuit of Hare. This one took place at the beach, Wolf trying and failing to capture Hare using a trident, a speedboat, his bare hands. Each unsuccessful attempt sees Wolf harming only himself: falling from a tree onto a family of hedgehogs; nearly drowning when a bird sits atop his snorkel, cutting off his oxygen. I was struck by how homoerotic Wolf's obsession was, how unmistakably twinky Hare was rendered with his petite frame and green booty shorts. Observing this aloud would have made my mother laugh, but then I might have to explain why I knew so much about gay culture. She wasn't overtly homophobic, but I didn't want to test the limits of her tolerance by telling her about Sasha, the strip club dressing room, the time I nearly obliterated the family computer with lesbian porn.

"Have you been sleeping, honey?" my mother said. "You didn't have bags under your eyes like that a couple weeks ago."

I'd been having nightmares about Debbie conjuring pills from her mouth and making me eat them. I felt her planting thoughts in my brain, telling me to do things I didn't want to. Pauline frowned when I shared that.

"I'm not hearing voices," I told her earlier that week.

"You don't understand. This is exactly what Debbie would do to me if she were dead."

"You think your sister is haunting you?" Pauline asked.

"I don't know. My relationship with the occult is . . . complicated."

"Is this connected to that patient you told me about? Shoah grief?"

"I don't know. Her whole thing was that the past is the present, or something like that. Now that I'm off pills, I can't stop thinking about Debbie. My sobriety feels like this violent difference between us, like I've betrayed her. I don't know how much longer I can pretend it's no big deal that, a year and a half later, I have no idea where she is."

"Well," Pauline said, looking at the clock. "That's where we are. We'll continue next week."

Sometimes I stared at the private investigator's number in my phone until my chest filled with cement. I was terrified of knowing if Debbie was dead or alive. Of, once I knew, what would happen next.

●

"Are you really considering looking for your sister?"

We were at Sasha's place, making pizzas, while Apples glowered at us from the counter.

"I don't know," I said, slicing a mozzarella ball. "Doesn't feel like the best move, sobriety-wise. Even now, just talking about it, I've got that caved-in feeling in my stomach. If I was alone right now . . ."

Sasha didn't comment. She was scrubbing the grit from

a mushroom, humming Tegan and Sara's "Closer" under her breath.

"But I feel guilty," I said. "I keep replaying that statistic they always quote on TV—every day a person is missing decreases the likelihood they'll be found alive."

Sasha's back was to me. She put a clean mushroom in a bowl and reached for a dirty one.

"Then again, who knows if that statistic is real," I continued. "It's such a horny sentiment. Movies and TV trot it out whenever there's a missing white girl. If she's dead, the camera loves her brutalized body, naked, throw in some antlers or other culty shit. They love telling us exactly how she was violated."

"The desecration of her beauty and whiteness being the real tragedy," Sasha said.

"Right. And wouldn't there be a washout effect at some point? If Debbie survived the first year of her 'disappearance,' it's not inconceivable that she'd be alive today, right? Which would probably mean she wasn't taken, but that she'd left by choice. That's what I think happened—Debbie ran away, and it's not on me to bring her back. Does that make sense?"

"Does it make sense to you?"

"I can't tell if I believe it or if I'm making excuses for myself."

"Let's say you do look for her," Sasha said, slicing mushrooms. "Let's say that private investigator tracks her down. Then what?"

"I just want to know where she is. Maybe if I knew she was waitressing in Oakland or something, I could move on."

"Sure. But that's best-case scenario, right?"

"What do you mean?"

"Well. You said yourself there's a possibility she's not alive. Can you handle that?"

Her back was to me, so I couldn't read her expression.

"Are you trying to tell me something?"

"Stop reading into everything I say," she said. "I'm trying to help you figure out what you want."

"Sorry," I said.

Outside, a crash like a dumpster falling over. Someone screaming, "I'm a person! Fuck!" Sirens.

"I hope that wasn't an omen," I said.

She groaned. "Not everything is a sign." Then, more gently, "Sometimes I wonder if it's healthy how much meaning you see in things."

"I was joking."

"I mean in general. You're always waiting for the universe to hurt you or to love you. Usually in that order."

"That's how it was with my family," I said. "Reading the room was a survival skill."

"I know. But you're your own person now." She looked at me so tenderly then. It was unbearable.

I flung a bell pepper at her.

"Rude!" she said. "You're going to regret that when you see my pizza."

This whole time, she'd been blocking my view. She stepped aside, grinning. The dough was a perfect circle. The sauce and cheese arrayed so symmetrically it was almost religious. It was the most beautiful pizza I'd ever seen.

"Do you like it?" she asked.

She'd written my name in mushrooms.

23.

Working night shifts at the hospital was my therapist's suggestion. I couldn't "fall back into substance abuse" at Salvation if I was chaperoning emergency room patients and their entourage five nights a week. At least, that was the idea.

"How are you adjusting to the new schedule?" Pauline asked a few weeks in.

"It's fine," I shrugged. "Quiet until it's not. The overnight shifts draw a different crowd."

"Oh?"

"People who can't wait until morning to get checked out because they can't afford to miss work."

"Hmm." She twirled her necklaces.

"Plus drunk people, overdoses, car accidents."

"Is it difficult not to get emotionally invested?"

"It is and it isn't," I said. "They enter my day so dramatically, and then they're gone. I spend hours consumed by the lives of complete strangers, and sometimes I take the bus home wondering if they existed at all."

"That sounds disorienting."

I told her about how, before I met Sasha, there was a woman who'd shared my waiting room after her husband broke his legs stringing Christmas lights. We didn't talk much, but there was an energy between us. It was a little angry and a little sexual. She disappeared while I was on break, but one night at Salvation, I thought I saw her sipping a martini at the bar. I downed my drink and decided to talk to her. Halfway to the bar, I slipped on a lighter someone had accidentally, or intentionally, left on the ground. When I righted myself, she was gone.

"Have you been to Salvation since getting sober?" Pauline asked.

I shook my head.

"That's great." She smiled with her teeth. The glow of her gaze sizzled me like an ant beneath a magnifying glass. "Is something wrong?"

I told Pauline it was starting to hit me that Debbie might be dead. Before I got sober, Debbie alternated between dead and alive in my imagination, but I hadn't assigned an image to *dead*; the real-life implications of her not being alive didn't register.

"Her disappearance felt abstract," I said. "I thought, *Debbie might be dead*, the same way I thought, *I could get in a gruesome car accident today.* It was almost superstitious: by acknowledging the possibility, I was inoculating myself against it."

"But you don't normally drive, do you?"

"I hitchhike."

"Hmm. It's interesting that you use the example of a car accident. You mentioned seeing a lot of car accidents at work, and your patients are proof that they happen all the time."

"I'm not sure I get the connection."

"When you hitchhike and *don't* get into a car accident, does that feel like evidence that your sister is alive? Is hitchhiking another way of inoculating yourself against the possibility that something terrible has happened to her?"

"I don't think it's that deep."

"Maybe it isn't. You tell me." She tightened her necklace around her finger like a garrote.

◐

That night, I spent the first half of my shift babysitting the cousins of a woman who was getting her stomach pumped.

"Tricia never does this," one of them kept saying, while the others nodded alongside her, as though I had some say in how hard the doctors worked to revive her.

The one with penciled-on eyebrows was crying when she picked up her phone. It was her husband, telling her they were out of hot dogs and Bud Light and mayonnaise and could she pick some up on the way home.

"Tricia is *dying*," she whisper-shouted. "What is wrong with you?"

I took my break around one in the morning, the best time to roam the halls. Someone was always exalting their gods or condemning them, crying for their mother or becoming a mother, bargaining, whimpering, making noises I had never heard before and would never hear again. Every floor had its own smell. The NICU was fabric softener, the emergency room rubber and antiseptic. A night nurse told me smell could trigger psychosis, which was why the psych ward smelled like nothing. Its essence had been sucked out, leaving an absence that reminded me of watching an empty washing machine run.

Back at my desk, the cousins were gone, the only traces of them a pile of picked-over parenting magazines and their nightclub musk.

•

The next day was Thursday, my day off, and I took the bus to Salvation to sell the last of my pills. I wasn't lying to Pauline—I hadn't been in months, not since getting sober. I snagged my favorite spot: a booth facing the jukebox, where I could watch the faces of my people, my brothers and sisters, as they sang along with the songs that reminded them how it felt to be loved.

Only, something about Salvation was different. The vibe was off. Women dressed like wannabe influencers were taking selfies in front of the CHRISTIAN LIVING sign. One of them said, "They're giving out avocado fritters if you check in on Yelp." "Yaaaaas," the others replied.

In the next booth, two middle-aged white men were heckling a young Black woman.

"That's how the game works," one of them insisted. Aviator sunglasses dangled from the collar of his golf shirt.

"You said it was pretend," she said.

"All right, I see where this is going," the other man said. He had the whitest teeth I'd ever seen. "You want to change your answer."

"What I want is for you to leave me alone," she said.

"You better not be here when my sister comes back from the bathroom."

"Two hundred," Aviators said, grinning.

"Fuck you." She stood, yanking her purse over her shoulder.

"Two fifty," Teeth said.

"Are you playing the Wealthy Patron?" I interjected.

All three of them looked at me.

The woman groaned and said, "Oh good, another one."

"What's it to you?" Aviators demanded.

"You're playing it wrong," I said. "It's a game. Not a contract."

The woman rolled her eyes. "Here's an idea: Why don't the three of you play with each other?" She stuck her phone in the waistband of her leather leggings and pushed her way out of the booth.

"Fuck off," Aviators said, glaring at me. He downed what was left of the woman's drink.

The men stared me down as I walked toward the bar and took a seat next to a woman in an ugly Christmas sweater.

"Hey, Sharon," I said. "Been a while."

"Debbie," she said. "Thought you'd skipped town."

"I'm her sister. I used to hook you up, remember?"

"Hmm," she mumbled. "Yeah, that's right. Sure, I do."

"What's new?"

She could barely keep her eyes open. I thought we'd catch up, but she kept tilting in her chair and catching herself just before she fell. I looked around for anyone else I recognized, but there was no one. Several couples had laid claim to the pub tables. One pair, also in Christmas sweaters, was splitting a bottle of wine and doing a crossword. Another were on a first date. "I *love* cauliflower," the woman said. "Samesies," the man replied.

Then Sharon tipped over, her enormous purse plummeting with her. Out spilled loose bills, a half-empty bottle of mouthwash, breath mints, a rubber pig keychain with MAMA markered across it in child's handwriting.

"Oops," Sharon said from the floor.

I started to help her, but the woman sitting on her other side jumped in. "It's okay, I've got her," she said. She crouched to help her up. "You're okay. Take it easy."

"Christ," the bartender said, looking at Sharon. "Usually she holds it together until ten."

The woman pocketed the loose bills before returning everything else to Sharon's purse and placing it on the bar between us. When she caught me staring, she flashed a guilty smile. "My fee," she winked.

I didn't have it in me to fight a stranger over a few dollars. I gave the bartender a twenty to put toward Sharon's tab and went back to scanning the room for someone, anyone, familiar. Aviators and Teeth were gone. The woman they'd been harassing and her sister had returned to their booth and were taking pictures of each other. Then, by the jukebox, I spotted one of my regulars, a former insurance agent who'd been cut off by her doctor after her pain needs exceeded the CDC's maximum opiate dosing standards.

I rushed to her, realizing in that moment I didn't know her name.

"I'm so glad to see you," I said.

Her eyes were empty fishbowls.

I offered her all sixteen of my remaining pills, no charge.

She didn't seem to hear. She mumbled something about supplies for the rapture, and where will all the animals go.

"It'll be okay," I told her.

"You don't know that."

I thought about tucking the pills into her shaky fist or finding someone else to sell to. I ended up flushing them and calling a car.

I felt queasy and bereft. Maybe the Thursday crowd had always been like this; if I came back late on a Saturday, it might be just as I remembered. But as we rounded the corner of my street, I knew I wouldn't return. It's not that I'd bought into the fantasy that you could leave your race and class at the door, that at Salvation we were all equal in the eyes of an apathetic god. But I'd believed our shared degradation afforded us fellowship, if only conditionally. That what we did there—and what was done to us—didn't count. I understood then that a bunch of fuck-ups under one roof didn't constitute a family. That, at this moment, Debbie might be hog-tied in a ditch, grass overtaking her final resting place. I puked on a palm tree in front of my apartment, wishing I hadn't flushed the rest of my pills, grateful that I had.

24.

At work, I was forced to entertain Joel, a former copyeditor who'd picked at his skin so badly he developed a staph infection.

"Don't ever work for a music weekly," he advised. "Super toxic culture, no healthcare, and everyone thinks they're the next Phoebe Bridgers, when, at best, they're the next Patricia Hamburger."

"Who?" I said.

"Exactly."

He was so pleased I'd walked into his joke, I felt I'd done a public service.

"Anyway, I'm all about being my own boss now. I'm writing this screenplay about a food delivery gig worker who fights crime. It's about turning late-stage capitalism into a hero origin story."

"Cool," I said, flipping through a pile of papers meant for shredding to look busy.

"You want to see it? I could use some beta readers. When it's done, I mean. I'm in the pre-outline stage."

"I'm not much of a reader," I said.

He raised his eyebrows at the novel propped open on my lap.

"My girlfriend's," I said.

"Cool, cool." He picked at the weeping rash on his arm. "Right on. Love is love."

I nodded toward the seating area, and he left me alone the rest of the night.

Calling Sasha my girlfriend, even as a lie, turned my blood into seltzer.

Guess what I just did? I texted her.

Made someone's terrible night a little better? she replied instantly.

I told some guy you were my girlfriend to get him to leave me alone, I started to type. Then I deleted it.

Something like that, I texted her. *Gave some guy notes on a screenplay that will either never get made or will become a cult classic, until he gets canceled for groping a makeup artist.*

My little saint, she wrote back with a red heart emoji.

Time passed more slowly as a sober person. When my waiting room was empty, I took Russian lessons on my phone.

"Moy muzh finansist," I enunciated. *My husband is a financier.*

A green check mark chirped, and a new statement appeared.

"Moya sestra lyubit tantsevat," I said. *My sister loves to dance.*

"Only if your financier husband is paying," Debbie would have said.

I closed the app. It was six in the morning, and there was an hour left in my shift. I tried reading my novel but had to stop at the part where the best friend is found dead in an icy lake. I snapped the hair tie on my wrist and thought about texting Shirin to grab lunch, but we hadn't seen each other since I started working nights, and our last conversation hadn't gone well.

"No one's forcing you to take the pills," she said. "Can't you just sell them?"

"I can't be around them at all, Shirin."

"They don't teach you self-control in Narcotics Anonymous or whatever?"

"I don't really go to NA."

The few times I went to a meeting, I found everyone depressing: the woman whose three kids had been taken by the state, the one who'd been molested by her uncle since she was three, the man who spent his son's college fund on heroin and lived out of his car.

"Maybe you should," Shirin said. "The world's not going to sanitize itself to make your life easier."

"I know that. I'm sorry. I wish I could help."

"It's fine." She let out a long sigh. "You do you."

"We can still hang out. You can still use my apartment."

Shirin laughed. "When, at nine in the morning?" Her phone pinged and she texted someone for the next several minutes. I got up, sensing I'd been dismissed.

"I'm sorry," I said.

She waved me away. "Good luck on your journey."

I was too self-conscious to go to Sasha's after lying about her being my girlfriend. I was afraid she'd read it on my face, and of what would happen next.

At home, the air was lifeless and smelled of wet cardboard. I lit a candle Sasha gave me that smelled like redwood, lime, jasmine, and yarrow. It was called "Los Angeles" and was meant to evoke *overgrown bougainvillea, canyon hiking, epic sunsets, city lights.* Bougainvillea reminded me of Sasha, but canyons and city lights reminded me of Debbie. I blew it out.

I was lonely and my breasts hurt. The universe seemed determined to shoo me out of the house. In the evening, I put on clean clothes and made my way to the bus stop. It was both windy and rainy, a rarity even in December. The wind nearly blew me into oncoming traffic like a plastic bag. My hair slapped my face, braiding itself into my mouth and eyes. I got to the stop as the bus was pulling away. A little girl pressed her face against the glass, tongue flapping like an anemone until the bus turned a corner. The next one wasn't for eighteen minutes. By then, surely the bus stop, the old man waiting there eating a brown banana, the whole fucking city would be blown away. I began walking, waiting for the universe to take me in its jaws or to forget me as usual.

●

I knew what I was doing when I found myself on Mulholland Drive alone at midnight, clothes drenched, hugging the canyon side of the twisting road. I knew what I was doing when a man I didn't know pulled up beside me in a beat-up white sedan. And I knew what I was doing when I got into the passenger seat, smiling as the lock clicked shut.

The driver was in his thirties and had flappy ears that reminded me of Russian pastries. He had a stubbly beard and dirt under his fingernails and the kind of checkered shirt worn by two-thirds of the men in every bar. He was attractive in a sloppy, hometown-boyfriend way. In the backseat, a garbage bag with a long wooden hilt sticking out of it. A shovel.

How funny would it be if Debbie's alive, and I'm the one who gets murdered? I started texting Sasha. Instead, I shut off my phone.

"I'm getting your seat wet," I told the driver.

"Don't worry about it," he said. "There's a sweatshirt in back if you're cold."

The daisy-patterned yellow hoodie had clearly belonged to a woman.

"What's the shovel for?" I asked.

"What?" He looked in back. "Oh, right. My cat died."

The car jerked as he drove over some mangled branches that had blown into the street. The rain had subsided, leaving behind debris and a glossy black road that unspooled before us like the tongue of some beast.

"I'm sorry," I said. "Was it old?"

"Not really. She had this throat tumor that made it so she couldn't swallow. I fed her through a tube in her belly. But her electrolytes got out of whack, and she got an infection. Or maybe that was unrelated, I don't know. She died today. Her name was Golda."

"Great name" was all I could think to say.

"My ex left her with me when we broke up. I've been driving for an hour, looking for the right place to bury her. My apartment doesn't have a yard."

I was in a story about gentrification or the ways we fail as caretakers or recklessness as feminist rebellion. I was in a car with a dead cat and a strange man and a shovel, coiling around the canyons in the dark. My pulse beat my carotid like a strobe light. I wasn't afraid. It felt good to get to the bottom of something, to pull back a mask and see either a face or a hole.

"Do you want to see her?" he asked.

I assumed he would show me a picture on his phone, but he pulled into an overlook, in front of the same sign as the last time I saw Debbie, NO PARKING AFTER 9 P.M. I got out of the car and walked to the edge of the canyon. The view was one of my favorites. Without having to turn your head, you could see the houses of the rich—the Hollywood elite, the plastic surgeons, the oligarchs from Europe and the Middle East who bought mansions using shell companies—and the skyscrapers that denoted downtown, which meant gastropubs and music halls, but also skid row, the free clinic that sent undocumented immigrants who couldn't afford insulin to my emergency room.

The driver popped the trunk. It was full of garbage. Empty water bottles, credit card applications, mud-caked sneakers. I turned back to the view. It was hard to fathom that I was looking at both the hospital where I was born and the apartment complex where Nina and I were molested by the handyman. There was my grandmother's

Section 8 apartment, the television blaring news from a long-abandoned country, the counters sticky with fresh-squeezed juice.

The driver came up beside me holding a shoebox.

"You sure about this?" he asked.

"Show me."

He opened the lid. The thing inside looked like raw chicken. It was hairless and shriveled and reminded me of chewed gum. I stared into her open mouth. If I had never seen a dead body, I might have thought Golda died in terrible fear.

"My ex inherited her from her rich grandfather last year," the driver said. "He left her sister his Porsche and fifty thousand dollars. And he left my ex his cat and just enough money that she couldn't contest the will."

"Weird."

"He was losing it toward the end. He insisted the cat was worth hundreds of thousands of dollars. He kept saying that if we got her in front of a TV camera, we'd be made."

"Why?"

"He thought she was the last survivor of her breed. Supposedly, she's something called a Chelmno hairless."

"Do you think it's true?"

He shrugged. "We tried looking it up and didn't find anything. I asked a vet and emailed someone from the Natural History Museum. Nothing."

Below, tiny cars darted in opposite directions. Their pulsing red and yellow lights reminded me of toys, fireflies, batteries. All the people driving to work the night shift, or heading home from a concert, or leaving their cheating lover. Our puny indignities. Our timecards and UTIs and dead cats.

"He said Chelmno hairlesses were believed to be spiritual mediums," the driver said. "During seances, the person being summoned would inhabit the cat's body. You could pet your dead grandma. Tell her you loved her. His psychic told him that right after he got sick."

Sasha claimed ninety-nine percent of working "psychics" were charlatans. The real ones clued you into truths nearly no one else would care about, certainly nothing that could be monetized. But the good scammers steered clear of big promises too, opting for safer predictions about changes at work, a dark-haired lover, a minor family secret. "Most people don't care if their psychic is real," Sasha told me. "They just want someone to promise they'll be okay." That wasn't all I wanted from her, but I didn't know how to voice the rest.

Beneath the full moon, Golda was the color of a pencil eraser. She looked so small in her Nike box, too small to carry the legacy of her ancestors. I felt a useless urge to warm her against my chest.

"Ready to head out?" the driver asked.

"You don't want to bury her?"

The ground didn't have much give, but there was looser dirt beyond the railing. It would take great care not to lose my footing and tumble down the canyon.

"Not here," he said. "Seeing the city all splayed out like this would bum her out."

The stranger, the witchy cat, the punishing blue of the sky, the road spiraling like a mollusk—the evening was taking the shape of the painting Sasha had given me. I wanted to dig a big hole with a man I'd just met. I wanted a one-off spiritual communion with the last in a long line of survivors. I wanted Golda to channel my sister.

Instead, we got back in the car. I directed him to Sasha's apartment, and we drove mostly in silence. When he pulled over, Sasha's light was on.

"You should talk to a librarian," I told him. "They could help you research if there's anything to this Chelmno hairless thing."

"Maybe," he said.

"Don't bury her. What if it's true, and a museum wants to display her? What if she's some kind of missing link?"

He laughed. "Maybe you'll see me on TV showing off a new suit and a Rolex."

I got out and thanked him for the ride. He waved and drove off, his car illuminated like a tooth.

Sasha was waiting for me on the couch, drinking kefir from a tall glass in her underwear. A Russian ice skating reality competition played on mute. Without the music, each ill-timed gesture was exaggerated, each mistake a garish display.

"You know I hate when you hitchhike," she said.

She had a milk mustache. I pulled a tissue and wiped her face. On TV, a woman with blood-toned eyeshadow wept. Her partner threw his arms in the air, knifing the ice with his skate. Sasha closed her eyes and called me her durachka, little fool. I kissed her head. I half carried her to bed after she fell asleep.

I got in beside Sasha and switched off the overhead light. Headlights flashed across her ceiling, punctuated by brake pedals, the crunch of leaf beneath tire. It began to storm again. Enormous fronds hurled themselves from the palm trees, landing on balconies and cars, splintering glass.

Sasha jolted awake. She looked adorably disoriented, and I was so overcome with longing I felt my cells begin to smoke.

"Do you want tea?" I whispered, brushing hair from her face.

She nodded.

I made mint tea and returned to bed. We didn't speak, as though out of respect for the wind, the thunder, the projectiles slamming into her building like planks from a destroyed ship. My heart synchronized with Sasha's breathing. Lightning illuminated the blue of her eyes, the points of her nipples against her thin cotton tank. It was a deep V-neck. As Sasha leaned into the window to count the time between lightning flashes, her breast fell out. We'd never undressed in front of each other. But she was someone around whom I always felt naked.

Sasha's nipple was the pastel pink of bridesmaid gowns. It made me shy and also protective. I reached out to cover it with her shirt. Maybe my hand lingered there a moment too long. Maybe Sasha had known this was coming. She held my hand there. A bizarre thought, *Don't betray me*, ran through my head. She nodded as if she understood.

I kissed her first. Her eyes already closed in anticipation, mouth parted and tasting of mint. She breathed my name into my neck, hands scrambling up my shirt. My desire to be soft for her, to treat her gently, dispersed with the next thunderclap. I rolled on top of her, pinning her with my hips.

She bucked, nearly throwing me off the bed. I clung to her and let her pull me against her chest. I flung off her shirt. She tugged my underwear to the side. I groaned when she touched me, surprising myself. I'd never been vocal during sex; the performance embarrassed me. I felt ready to perform for any audience Sasha wanted, to open the windows so her neighbors could hear me over the storm.

I pulled down her underwear, but she stopped my hand.

"Not yet," she said.

She put her mouth on me, the lightest touch of her tongue. The mint from our tea had a cooling effect that made me shiver. *She's going to kill me*, I thought, as she began to suck.

Only after I came with such force I nearly blacked out did she let me touch her. We fucked through lightning flashes, our bodies disappearing and reappearing in a strobe-like haze. She was harder to please. She kept adjusting my fingers, telling me which way to move my tongue. I came again going down on her, her fingers mashing me into orgasm after orgasm until I lost count after the eighth. When she finally came with a little sigh, I almost burst into tears.

She fell asleep with a hand tangled in my hair. I barely slept at all. I needed to sit vigil over her until the storm quelled. If I closed my eyes, the universe might take her back.

I thought about Golda, how lonely it must feel to be the last survivor. I saw her in a candlelit room, surrounded by women speaking a language I didn't understand. The clutching of hands, the burning of herbs. A sharp inspiration. The pressure of a dead woman's soul entering her body, a feeling that should be cold but wasn't. The brown of her eyes going blue. Debbie's voice leaving Golda's mouth. So many hands on her small body. I fell asleep like that, petting her.

I awoke before Sasha with stiff hands, as though I'd been clutching something in my sleep. In the shower, the drain blinked up at me. Sasha's hair snaked out like a tiny rope. I felt too shy to face her, and so lingered in the shower, plugging the drain with my toe. As the water level rose to my ankles, I saw the driver from last night visiting the public library. He wore the same checkered shirt when he showed the librarian a photo of Golda. She typed into a computer, wrote a number on an index card, and told him to follow her. She led him to a distant stack. She pulled an old leather book from a shelf and laid it flat on a mahogany table. He held his breath. She flipped to a page near the end. She pointed to something. I withdrew my toe from the drain.

25.

When I stepped out of the shower wrapped in her towel, Sasha was waiting on her bed. She'd made black tea for us both and was wearing a face I'd never seen before. She looked uncertain. It made me wonder if I had power over her. I locked my thighs to keep from dripping onto her floor.

"Hey," she said, holding eye contact with her tea.

She'd put her top back on. The bed was made, any suggestion that something happened between us there erased. I was ready to pretend, like so many other times, that the escalations of the previous night hadn't happened or that they'd been some kind of bit.

"I should get going," I said.

"Why?" Sasha asked. "You better not pull away from me now."

And then we were kissing and tugging open my towel, our tea going cold on her nightstand.

Over the next six months, we spent nearly every day together. I'd sleepwalk through my night shifts, aiding people who'd forget me as soon as they left my waiting room, and I them. I had entire conversations I could barely recall hours later with people who couldn't stop shitting themselves, who'd taken a bar dart to the eye, who wanted an HIV test at four in the morning. Glamorously disheveled women passed through my waiting room looking like they'd licked the devil's asshole for some bargain that may or may not pan out. Sometimes I thought about Debbie. I thought about the private investigator, the number I'd memorized despite never calling him. But mostly I thought about Sasha.

I'd take the bus straight to her apartment and crawl into bed with her in the morning. I'd wake in the afternoon to her painting in her underwear. I'd read on her couch and watch her paint for hours. Sometimes, she handed me a brush and said, "Pretend you're me." I painted abstract blobs, lines that went from sharp to chaotically smudged. She never told me what she thought of my creations, but they usually ended with her hands up my shirt, my tongue in her ear. On weekends, we made smoothies, browsed the indie bookstore by her apartment, tanned by my building's shabby pool, walked the city arm in arm. She distracted me when I felt gripped by cravings. She held my hand when I called my mother. I'd never been so happy.

Sasha was my best friend, my spiritual everything. I was falling in love. But I was uncomfortable with how much I needed her compared to how little she needed me.

"I don't want to be a parasite," I told her one night in bed. "I want to be equals."

She promised it wasn't like that. When I pressed her, she said she wasn't perfect, that she'd done some shit in a past life she needed to atone for. She wouldn't tell me what, only that she would be psychic for the next four lives at least, using her gift to help others as penance.

"Penance?" I said.

"What's wrong with that?"

"I thought, after your mom caught you with that girl, becoming psychic was a kind of resilience. That it's an extension of your queerness."

"I want to believe that's the case. But that doesn't mean I'm innocent."

"I didn't realize you being my amulet was a punishment."

"Don't think of it that way," she said, massaging my shoulders.

I leaned into her touch. She was determined to release a knot I'd had in my upper back since I was fourteen. She dug her elbow behind my shoulder blade, kissing up my neck until I shivered.

"It's like being sentenced to community service instead of prison," she joked.

Sometimes that phrase went through my head when we fucked.

But mostly, it didn't. I felt lucky to be with her at all.

I didn't call the private investigator. I was afraid to let Debbie anywhere near us.

26.

We landed in Kishinev as the sun was rising and took a bus from the tarmac to our terminal. I hadn't slept on either of the flights and felt the edges of reality ungluing. The bus was stuffed to the windows with blue-eyed children waving American coloring books, women in sweatsuits carrying knockoff purses, and men wearing gold chain necklaces and is-this-my-life faces. Or maybe they liked their lives just fine. My grandmother said that in the former Soviet Union, adults who smiled at strangers were either imbeciles or were mocking you. Maybe she was onto something. Maybe some of the worst things that happened to me—the ones I'd courted and the ones I hadn't—could have been prevented by not smiling at the wrong person. I felt a surge of gratitude for my dour brothers and sisters of Air Moldova, for our brief, disposable interactions.

At baggage claim, posters advertised Moldova's varied offerings: three elderly women in babushka headwraps held out a platter of bread; two elderly women in babushka headwraps played folksy string instruments; a white peasant blouse with blue stitching swayed on a clothesline. By the carousel, a screaming toddler yanked the hem of her mother's dress. Her mother tried to reason with her, before giving up and slapping the girl's hands.

Our cab driver was a middle-aged man named Stanislav who chain-smoked the entirety of the ride. The city was old and green. Wildflowers in vibrant pinks and oranges dotted the cratered sidewalks. Cars zipped past each other in a game of whose-right-of-way-is-it, and when a Tesla cut us off, Stanislav called them a skatina under his breath. He told us the few luxury cars in the city were owned by oligarchs who'd paid four times their value in import costs, more wealth than many families would see in their lifetimes.

"We don't have technology here to update Tesla software," he said. "So they drive car with cool features off."

The cab lurched over a pothole.

Stanislav smiled. "It is funny to watch rich person ruin fancy car on our roads."

We drove along a boulevard flanked by symmetrical high-rise apartments. Chunks had peeled off the once-white buildings, exposing gray skin.

"The gates of the city," Sasha told me. "Built in the seventies, like most buildings here. World War II destroyed almost everything."

We asked Stanislav for a lunch recommendation, and he dropped us off at a café known for its sushi and hookah. We sat on the terrace, near a glittering statue of an armless woman like Venus de Milo if she were made of disco balls. A thin calico cat padded over from a neighboring table, playing with my shoes as I flipped through the twenty-page menu. I couldn't read much Russian, let alone Moldovan, but there were photos of each dish. All the sushi seemed to feature cream cheese. Embarrassing to have expected borsch and stuffed cabbage, to be shocked that landlocked Moldova had sushi at all. Sasha ordered two kinds of sushi, tomatoes with mozzarella, berry pavlova, bubblegum hookah, and a pot of bergamot black tea to share.

She still hadn't explained what we were doing in Moldova. Three weeks earlier, she told me she'd purchased plane tickets on a whim and wanted me to come with her.

"I have unfinished business," she'd said, silencing my questions with her mouth. We were entangled on her couch, and she smelled sweet and a little smoky, like a candle that had just been snuffed.

"At least give me a hint," I said.

"There's a Russian proverb that goes, 'So much is ruined by saying it aloud.'" She kissed me on the nose and left the couch.

"How do you say that in Russian?"

She didn't answer. I wondered if she'd made the expression up.

"And I'm paying, obviously," she shouted from the bathroom, addressing the anxiety I hadn't vocalized.

"No way."

"We both know you can't afford it. Don't be difficult."

Sasha had never spoken of my finances so bluntly. Her voice had an impatient edge, like she knew I'd end up agreeing and wanted to skip to that part of the conversation. I protested a bit longer, if only symbolically. By the time she rejoined me on the couch, I'd already sent a time-off request to my manager.

The thought of traveling with Sasha, of glimpsing the facets of herself she so closely guarded, was intoxicating.

Even more intoxicating was her demanding I join her, the mystery of what awaited me there. My unspoken role in her plans hung between us like an enchanted mist, promising everything. And now we were here, watching a waiter set up our hookah.

"So," she said, once he left. "What do you think?"

"It's so green. I wasn't expecting that."

She took a drag and exhaled bubblegum. "You were expecting Kishinev to be all potholes and crumbling buildings?"

"Honestly, I couldn't picture it at all."

She passed me the hookah, and I took a deep breath. The stray cat began licking my ankles. There were spots of blood around its back and neck. I removed my sneaker and stroked it with my toes.

"Try this," Sasha said, cracking the pavlova's gauzy shell. She swept up meringue, a fluff of cream, and a raspberry with her spoon.

I opened my mouth.

Instead of feeding me, she passed me the spoon.

We were alone on the terrace but within view of the diners inside. Prior to our trip, I researched LGBT life in Moldova and was met with a warning: *Moldova is not accepting of homosexuality, on a government or an interpersonal level. According to polls, two-thirds of citizens are in favor of removing all LGBT people from the country, and 95% state they would never be friends with an LGBT person. Though homosexuality was decriminalized in 1995, it is wise to keep a low profile given the country's traditional values.*

"Fuck," I said, spooning the pavlova into my mouth. "That's incredible."

Was anything more erotic than watching Sasha eat blistered tomatoes? How she bit into them, rather than taking them whole. How they burst against her lips, glossing them with juice and seeds. The juice dripped through the table slats, wetting my foot. A warm buzz came over me, a little hit of joy.

Later, in our hotel room, I noticed my left foot was coated in dried blood. The wetness I'd taken for tomato juice—it was cat blood. My foot hadn't been below Sasha's mouth. I adjusted my life's parameters like I was editing a photograph. I scrubbed the blood off in the bidet.

In bed, Sasha spooned me, and I inhaled the citrus oils of her hair. She worked the knot in my back. We drifted in and out of each other's dreams.

•

We awoke at three thirty in the morning, our circadian rhythms completely fucked.

"Let's get some tea," Sasha whispered into my neck.

I didn't move, savoring the sensation of her nuzzled against me. It was excessive, embarrassing, how ravenous I was for her. This wasn't normal hunger. I couldn't tell if it came from a place of deprivation in me, or something withholding I sensed in Sasha. My body responded to her touch like it was something to stockpile.

"Come," she said, tickling me with her toes.

Downstairs, the dining room was empty. A widescreen television played Russian music videos on mute. Quivering glossed lips, little green men emerging from a refrigerator, a babushka flooring a convertible into a lion's den—they had a hallucinatory quality that no degree of jet lag could account for. Sasha made us chamomile tea, and we drank it in front of the TV.

"I hate this shit," she said, as a platinum-blond woman with enormous breasts furiously kissed a man who looked like a contract killer on a frozen lake. This morphed into her gyrating for a stadium of screaming women, and then watching herself weep in a vanity shaped like a gold sturgeon.

"I kind of love them," I said.

The more over-the-top the video became, the more palpable the singer's pain. She was all these women at once. I felt close to some epiphany about poorly reflective surfaces as metaphor for the unknowability of the self, about sex as performance—but performance of what?

Sasha laughed. "You wouldn't love these as much if you grew up on them. Who would you be in the video?"

"The boyfriend." It wasn't a lie, exactly, but I couldn't get myself to name the singer, or how watching the video made me miss Debbie. I'd hated her theatrics, how she sucked the air from a room. How, after she disappeared, I stepped in as her understudy. She'd left behind all this potential energy; it had to be released somehow.

"Ew, really? He looks like a prison guard."

I made another cup of tea. I could feel Sasha's gaze breaching my skull. "You wear your emotions like a name tag," she once told me. She and Debbie were the only people

I knew who felt this way. Ronnie had once tearfully confessed that my resting face frightened him, that intuiting what I was thinking was like trying to interpret patterns in driftwood.

"Well, better the boyfriend than the singer," Sasha said.

"Why?"

"She isn't long for this world."

I smoothed the creases of the tea bag wrapper. "The singer herself, or the character she's playing?"

"Both. She feels too much."

Sasha's face had the open quality of a leaf stretching toward the sun. She was being a tease, reminding me she knew this level of detail about my future too.

"Don't tell me," I said. "I don't want to know."

She walked her fingers up my thigh. "My sensitive one."

I wanted to know Sasha more deeply than I'd known anyone, and for that knowing to fix me. I wanted her to teach me about myself and about how to live with that knowledge. But that's not what she was offering.

"We should try to sleep," I said, turning away.

I did a lap around the dining room, looking for a place to bus my mug. Apparently, Moldovan hospitality rendered it shameful for a guest to deal with their own dishes. I stood idiotically by the coffee machine, holding the cooling mug to my chest.

"Did I upset you?" Sasha said.

"No." I flipped through the tea bags displayed in a cherry wood box. Bergamot, rosehip, spearmint. "Okay, yes."

"I'm sorry. I shouldn't be so blasé about this stuff. I do care, a lot."

I turned to face her. "About me or the singer?"

"Both. About everyone."

She tied her hair in a messy bun, escaped strands falling on either side of her face. She wore her sexuality like an afterthought. The less she tried, the more she undid me. She knew it, too.

"It hurts, knowing this stuff," she said. "I can't control what comes to me. Sometimes I don't want to leave my apartment, so I don't have to pass someone on the street and know who broke into their car, who raped them, what complications will come from their sister's botched surgery."

"Stop. Please." Desire and revulsion were making a cursed stew in my stomach. She'd never expressed this anxiety to me before.

"Who's going to be transplanted the wrong organ," she continued, "whose brother will fall off a horse and onto a puppy, who will blow their life savings on a con artist who can't even properly eat pussy."

I laugh-cried. It was so Sasha to transform a chilling revelation into a farce. "Ti yesho tot frukt," I told her. My Russian app had just taught me that one. It means *you're a piece of work*, but translates literally to *you're a real fruit*.

"Look at you. Pretty soon your grandma will be able to berate you in two languages." She pulled my hair from its tangled ponytail, running her fingers through it. "I'm sorry. I don't like upsetting you." She kissed my ear, my neck, my bare shoulder scented lavender from the lotion she massaged into me after our shower. "How are you both the most innocent and the most experienced person I've ever met?"

I wanted to believe survival meant something, that

suffering wasn't an end in and of itself. That Sasha was more than my amulet, and I meant as much to her as she meant to me. I thought of the woman with Shoah grief, who both knew and didn't know what her family had endured. How I knew only a sliver of what Debbie had endured at home, at the club, with our pediatrician.

Sasha took my hand. We took the stairs back to our room, letting go when we heard footsteps, fumbling for each other when there was only our breath.

27.

The sensation of unreality didn't dissipate in the following days. It was Sasha's first time back since immigrating when she was seven, and our itinerary was as frenzied as an everything-must-go sale. We visited the hospital where Sasha was born, a white-and-brown building called Institutul Mamei și Copilului, which made my hospital look like a luxury hotel. Several windows appeared to use white construction paper in place of blinds. Air conditioning units dangled from the building's façade like unsocketed eyes.

A young couple exited the building cradling a bundled baby. They took selfies next to a chalice-shaped planter whose curly vines resembled bubbling champagne.

"My mom shared a room with seven other women when I was born," Sasha told me. "Their milk hadn't come in yet, but my mom's was gushing. She ended up breastfeeding half the babies in that room."

"Explains why you're such a boob guy now."

"A boob guy?" she laughed. "You really are a baby queer."

I had debated whether to tell Sasha she was my first, not wanting to seem like even more of a project. I confessed a couple of weeks in, after spending forty-five minutes failing to make her come.

"I'm sorry," I blurted, resting my face against her thigh. "I'm still figuring this out. I don't have, like, a system down."

"It's not you," Sasha said, caressing my cheek. She shifted, my fingers slipping from her ass. "It's always taken me forever to come. Sometimes I just don't. I'm used to it."

"I want to make you feel good," I whispered.

"Don't overthink it. If you were bad at sex, I would make sure you knew."

I believed her, but I also remembered all the times I faked it with Ronnie. How he mistook creativity for acumen, how I was able to look past this until I wasn't. I couldn't stop picturing Sasha coming wildly with other women, women who brought each other to orgasm with a kind of graveness, a shared understanding that every throb of pleasure was a needle in the eye of someone who didn't want you to have it.

The next day of our trip, Sasha and I took an hour-long bus ride to Orheiul Vechi, an ancient city on a river housing caves, fortresses, and an old monastery where we groped each other. Endless sunflower fields. I photographed Sasha there, six-foot-tall flowers hugging her beneath a piercing blue sky. The photos came out overexposed, her eyes glowing an ethereal blue, the same tone as the sky. It was like accidentally photographing a god.

"More like seeing Jesus in a grilled cheese sandwich," Sasha said, deleting the pictures from my phone. "I look deranged."

I recovered them while she was in the bathroom.

"When will we see your family's old apartment?" I asked inside a stone-walled café as we waited for our placinte to cool.

"At the end of the trip. I need to prepare myself," Sasha said, sipping her tea.

"For what?"

"You ask too many questions, my love. I need you to just be here with me."

I wanted nothing more. I could even see myself being talked into moving to Kishinev. Jeff would find a new renter; the hospital would find a new secretary. I could try and squeeze more hours out of my mother's health aide, guilt my grandmother into getting more involved in her daughter's care.

"Okay," I said, biting into the fried dough stuffed with sour cherries. "Whatever you need."

It rained the day we visited the Jewish cemetery. It was overrun with weeds, and we had to bushwhack with our hands. Nettles and dried branches scratched our arms and legs as we forced our way around the headstones. They were old and worn and many names were unreadable. Most looked like shards of sidewalk—gray blocks cut at jagged angles and plunked unevenly atop the ground. Others resembled cement tree trunks with severed branches. Some were emblazoned with portraits; the people pictured didn't smile. Even in death, they looked as though they were applying for a job in a factory or nagging their grandchildren to finish their soup. Wild berries and the blue labels of discarded water bottles were the only reprieve from the cemetery's gray, brown, and green palette.

A groundskeeper prowled around the periphery, half-heartedly pulling weeds and hacking up phlegm. Aside from the three of us and the bodies in the ground, the place was deserted. I had the sense that everyone buried there had been forgotten. That this was where Jews were sent when there was no one left to claim them. But when we spoke with the groundskeeper, he said some families who lived abroad sent him monthly checks to tend their loved ones' graves.

"He cleans the stones and sends the families pictures," Sasha translated. "Every month, they get photos of their loved ones' headstones."

"If he's doing his job, isn't it the same picture every month?" I asked.

"That's not the point. It's about showing that he was here, that everything's taken care of."

"It must not be many families. Most of these graves look like shit. What does he do all day?"

The groundskeeper muttered something malignant-sounding. It was unclear if he was speaking to us, to himself, or to his companions in the ground.

Sasha winced. "He says the weeds serve a purpose—that obscuring the headstones protects them from being vandalized or stolen for use as building material."

"God," I said. "That's so grim."

"Jewish cemeteries all over Europe look like this," Sasha said.

If I looked for my relatives in Saint Petersburg's Jewish cemetery, I might find that weather, graffiti swastikas, and half a century of neglect had eroded their names too. The ones fortunate enough to be buried in a cemetery, anyway. No one was paying to keep their graves tidy. Then I realized that if Debbie were dead, none of us would know where her body was.

"I should have warned you," Sasha said. "I forgot what it's like to come here for the first time. The guilt, that you live the way you do, that this is where they ended up." She pushed aside a branch from which dried leaves hung like the wings of terrible insects. "The first time my parents brought me here, right before we immigrated to the U.S., I wept. My mother shook me until I stopped. 'Remember this, Sashenka. Remember this is how our people lived. You are so very lucky you will grow up in America, the land of the free. No more crying in front of our dead. They deserve to see you happy. They deserve to know you will honor their sacrifices.'"

"She sounds like my grandmother," I said. "What's that Russian expression for laying stones on your soul?"

"Lazhit kamni na dushu," Sasha said. "Exactly. They dump all this horror on you, and then act affronted when it fucks you up."

She began plucking weeds from the nearest grave. Mangled underground roots pushed the headstone out of the ground like a crooked tooth. It belonged to someone named Lyudmilla Yevgenevna Korbatova, who'd died in her forties, leaving behind two children and no spouse. Instead of a photo, her headstone had an etching of a violin. I wondered if her husband had left her, if she'd never had a husband, if she was gay.

"Did you know her?" I asked.

"No."

I got on my knees to help clear the weeds. I saved the yellow wildflowers and laid them atop the soil. We might have been the first people in decades to touch Lyudmilla's grave, to say her name out loud.

"Okay," Sasha said, brushing the dirt off the knees of her jeans. "Let's go see my babushka." She took my hand.

From my periphery, I saw the groundskeeper watching us, frowning, until we were out of sight. I felt the dead watching too, revolted by our love, or perhaps on some level relieved that future generations of Jews had attained unimaginable freedoms.

Sasha consulted a folded paper on which she'd circled the locations of several graves. She rotated it a couple times, reorienting herself to the cemetery's layout.

"Okay," she said. "This way."

The graves grew increasingly decrepit the deeper we went. We stopped before a cracked cement headstone with Cyrillic etchings too faded to read. No portrait. It looked well tended compared to the ones around it: the weeds had recently been cleared, the headstone washed.

"Hi, Babushka," Sasha said, running her fingers across the top of the headstone. "Before we immigrated, my mom used to come here every week. My grandma's name was visible the last time I was here."

"What was her name?" I asked.

"Rita. Rita Davidovna Lebedinskaya."

Sasha extracted a pebble from her pocket and placed it on the headstone. I had done the same when visiting my great-grandmother on her yahrzeit—the anniversary of her death—with my grandmother. She'd hand me a white stone to place on her mother's grave while she recited the

Mourner's Kaddish. Our last visit together was four years ago. I was so rarely sober in her presence, it was possible she'd invited me to accompany her since. It was possible I'd promised to come but forgot.

"She was a baby during the war," Sasha said. "When my family fled Kishinev, they took their black cow with them. Her name was Nochka—little night. A few weeks in, Nochka stepped on a land mine."

"That's awful."

"And then Baba Rita got dysentery. Everyone thought she was going to die. No one had eaten in days."

She touched the spot where her grandmother's name had been and brought her fingers to her lips.

"Her aunt was clumsy and watched her feet when she walked to keep from tripping," Sasha said. "One day, she noticed a potato half buried in the ground."

"A potato."

"Yes. She chewed it up and fed it to my babushka. And she ate the potato and lived."

"She survived displacement and bombing and dysentery because of a potato."

"Yes."

"That's . . . kind of magical. A sort of deus ex machina."

A pinched look crept over her face, as though she'd smelled something foul. "This isn't a fucking movie. She had digestive problems for years. She was too young to remember the evacuation, obviously, but it was always with her. She was a jumpy woman, and she used to cry if I didn't finish my food. She called herself a human trash bag, because she wouldn't allow any food to go to waste and would eat everyone's leftovers, to the point of feeling sick."

"You're right. I'm sorry," I said. "I never know how to react to Jewish trauma. To its extremity."

"I'm aware that a potato shouldn't have saved my grandmother, but that's the story I was given."

"I get it. I'm sorry."

Sasha was still stroking the headstone, dirt darkening her fingertips. The rain started up again. Slow at first, and then torrential. We pretended not to notice. We stood there until the groundskeeper found us and demanded to know—I'm assuming—if we were crazy. He gestured for us to follow him, and we did. He led us out of the cemetery.

28.

Baba Rita's potato stalked us the rest of the trip. I awoke each morning with Nochka's ghost on my chest. My hands, no matter how many times I washed them, smelled of potato. Starchy, earthen, like they were of the cemetery. It was in my hair, my clothes, Sasha's hands, Sasha's hair, Sasha's clothes. I smelled it on the Barbie-doll woman manning the hotel reception desk. The long-abandoned banquet hall turned jungle where Sasha's parents married. Every taxi.

I asked less questions and just went along with Sasha's itinerary. My favorite food quickly became mamaliga, polenta dripping with feta and garlic butter. We turned down a lot of wine, which I learned was one of Moldova's main exports. We visited Sasha's preschool and elementary school ("There was this family of hedgehogs that lived in the bushes. I used to sneak them strawberries."); the clinic where her father was treated when he was bitten by a pregnant, rabid dog ("They gave him the wrong antidote and he ended up with serum sickness."); the medical school her mother would have attended if they didn't have a quota for Jews ("Love what they've done with the place though—the marble bust and giant fountains are very chic.").

I was thinking a lot about the woman with Shoah grief.

I could feel her gloating, beaming *I told you so* from across the world. But told me what? That my suffering was historic, that my sister's disappearance was the latest iteration of a trauma imprinted in my bones, that when Debbie walked the balcony railing at the nightclub, when we gave parts of ourselves to men who saw us as disposable, when we stuck things in our noses and throats and beneath our tongues, it was because, in 1950s Leningrad, our great-grandfather was shot in the street, and this was why our grandmother was so hard, why her love felt like cold hands shaking me awake, why our mother lived in this world but also in the other world, where neighbors were still spying, and hints of the horror to come flecked the media, and the firing squad was always around the corner?

Sasha and I didn't speak about any of this. I was afraid of breaking whatever spell had enveloped us like plastic wrap. Maybe the potato smell and cow on my chest were an inoculation. Against what, I didn't know. When she was young, Sasha was immunized against tuberculosis through a procedure that left a scar on her arm like a hole punched in paper. My grandmother had the same one. I liked the idea of being marked by Sasha.

Or maybe it wasn't an inoculation, but an activation—an awakening of dormant cells. Considering this made my lungs feel as if they belonged to someone else. Since childhood, I'd wished for the reprieve of blunted senses, for the ability to think and feel less. I was too sensitive to the energy of a situation, and I let that energy stand in for knowledge. Debbie walking the balcony railing was chaotic, memorable, deadly. It was sex and narcissism and pain and rage. The men who watched her saw a parlor trick. The women knew better; they saw a bleeding ulcer. I don't know what I saw, but it was more than I wanted. All this was energy, and none of it was knowledge. I wished I could ask Debbie what question tightroping across the railing answered. I used to think she was acting alone.

29.

Our last full day in Moldova began with an Elton John concert blasting from the hotel dining room. The couple at the next table were glued to the television. The husband wiped away tears; the wife held a hard-boiled egg before her mouth for several minutes, forgetting to bite.

"What were they saying?" I asked Sasha after they left.

"Oh, they're obsessed. Post-Soviets love a diva."

"I thought they only tolerated the closeted ones."

"As long as they don't have to see him making out with another dude, they can treat his gayness like a persona. He's so extraordinary, they're willing to look the other way." She gave a close-lipped smile and bit into a buttermilk pancake she'd drowned in apricot preserves.

After breakfast, we taxied to the apartment where Sasha had lived with her parents and grandparents. It was an old building with an exhausted gray exterior. The windows looked like they hadn't been washed since the building's construction. Laundry swayed from balcony clotheslines, women's underwear and baby socks and dishrags. There was something claustrophobic about seeing past white lace curtains into a room of aloe plants and sweating tangerines, about watching three old men drink beer in the courtyard at one in the afternoon. Benchers, Sasha called them. Behind them, a small playground, someone's paisley rug air-drying on the swing set. Turetskiye ogurtsy, Turkish cucumbers, was the Russian name for the design. I was nearing the end of the beginner's course in my Russian language app.

The building had five floors with eight apartments on each. A cat sunned itself on the windowsill in a third-floor unit. "That one was ours," Sasha said, pointing to a second-floor apartment with vertical blinds. There was an eight-point star mosaic with several tiles missing beneath the window. In an adjacent apartment, a shirtless man was curing salmon on his balcony.

I tried to commit the building to memory before remembering I could take photos. I photographed Salmon Man, the playground, the benchers, the entire courtyard from several angles, suppressing the thought that there was symmetry in the way I hoarded details about Sasha's life and the way my mother hoarded newspapers, first aid supplies, canned food.

"Is it like you remember?" I asked Sasha.

"Sort of. I mean, I was seven when we left. I barely remember any of it."

"Oh. I thought maybe, you know. Maybe memory worked differently for you."

Sasha scrunched her eyebrows. "I'm not omniscient. My memory is nothing special."

I wondered what other assumptions I'd clung to. I'd never asked Sasha if we were exclusive, if she was an amulet to others, if she would leave when her work with me was complete. We'd been saying *I love you* since early in our friendship, and that had carried over into whatever we were now. This was easier in some ways—less pressure to experience the admission as a milestone. But it was maddening to never be certain what she meant.

"Let's see if we can go in," Sasha said.

The entrance was locked. There was a call box, and for a moment, I thought she might ring her old apartment, ask her seven-year-old self to buzz us in. One of the drinking men called out to us in Russian. They eyed us with curiosity and suspicion. Two were heavyset and balding, and the third was very tall with white hair and reminded me of a cigarette. All three wore tracksuits—either black Adidas or gray velour—with a tank top underneath. One of the heavyset men spoke in a rapid, pressured way and kept gesturing at me. He clutched the crucifix around his neck.

Sasha took a seat on the bench across from them. She pointed to the apartment and to me and said some things I didn't understand. They said some things back I didn't understand. I heard *vedma*, witch. Their exchange went on for several minutes, becoming progressively less heated. The man let go of his crucifix. He laughed and offered us beer, which we declined. I sat across from the skinny one who, up close, smelled not like cigarettes but rosemary.

"Vlad lives on the fifth floor," Sasha told me, lifting her chin toward the man with the crucifix. "He owns four apartments in the complex. Sergei and Genady live on the fourth floor. They're brothers-in-law."

"Cool," I said, nodding at them. "Do they know who lives in your old apartment?"

"It's empty," Sasha said. "Whoever bought it after we left

never moved in. They don't even sublet or use it as storage. They've never seen anyone checking the mail, never heard a sound coming from inside."

"Weird. It's been, what, almost twenty years?"

"Yeah. But last year, Vlad was coming home tipsy from a party when he saw what looked like a lightning storm in that apartment. A naked woman stood in front of the window while electricity flashed all around her."

"What? Was it the TV?"

Sasha asked Vlad, who responded sheepishly and drained his beer.

"That apartment has no TV," Sasha said. "Vlad is friendly with the super, and he let him peek inside. Totally empty."

"He'd been drinking, right?"

"He knows what he saw," Sasha said with a cryptic smile.

"What did she look like?" I asked Vlad.

"Petite," Sasha translated. "Brown hair. Big eyes. Frighteningly alive."

I erupted in goose bumps.

"Did he ever see her again?" I asked.

"Only in his nightmares," Sasha said. "And a moment ago, when he thought you were her."

Sasha's expression was unreadable. She got this way when she was testing me, feeling out what I could handle. *Are you sure you can't cast lightning?* her eyes asked. I thought about the night we had sex for the first time. I'd wanted to touch her so badly, it was as if my desire summoned the storm.

"Why are you making that face?" she said.

Genady tried to hand me a beer. "Nu?" He pantomimed drinking it.

"Are you suggesting I'm the woman he saw in the window?" I said.

"What?" Sasha said, laughing. "Okay, that's not what I thought you were going to say."

"What were you expecting?"

"I was just translating what he said. I thought you'd get a kick out of it."

"But you were acting like you believed him."

"No, I wasn't. I'm just humoring him."

"I never know with you." I picked at my nails, looking for loose skin to rip off.

"Are you upset with me?" Sasha said.

"No."

She cleared her throat.

"I'm not," I repeated. A drop of blood the size of a matchhead surfaced from my thumb. I sucked it clean. "It's not a big deal. We can talk about it later."

"Okay." Sasha squeezed my shoulder in a friendly, sexless way.

A charcoal cat approached the bench, pawing at the empty bottles beneath our feet.

"Kish!" Sergei said, stomping the concrete.

The cat took refuge in a bush by the building's entrance, flooding me with déjà vu. Was this a past-life memory? A photograph I'd seen in my grandmother's albums, her and her parents wearing overcoats outside a similarly run-down building, a stray at their feet? I vaguely remembered going home with a Ukrainian man from Salvation who'd lived in an apartment like this—or had we hooked up in the bathroom? I cut my lip on his Star of David necklace. I couldn't tell which, if any, of these memories were real.

I pictured Debbie in the window of Sasha's apartment. It sounded like a sitcom: My sister, down on her luck, cutting ties and fleeing to one of the poorest countries in Europe. Working at a winery for the employee discount. Modeling for local businesses—podiatrist offices, bridal shops. Buying Cornelian cherries and persimmons from open-air bazaars. Smoking hookah in cafés with a gaggle of friends. Befriending the daughter of the couple who bought Sasha's old apartment. Sneaking in to do I didn't know what.

But there was no reason for her to know Kishinev existed, and she was more likely dead than living here.

Sasha was laughing with the old benchers as though they'd grown up together. "When you're done daydreaming, do you want to go inside?" she said.

"To your old apartment?" I said.

"Vlad says we can bribe the super with ten bucks."

If we weren't sitting in a Moldovan courtyard with three geriatric strangers, Sasha might have touched my hair. I might have asked her to explain the lightning lady. She may or may not have obliged, but at least her hand would find my leg, my head her shoulder.

"Okay. Let's go," I said.

While Vlad went in search of the super, the other two downed their beers. Sasha giggled at something Sergei said. Genady lit a cigarette. Then, Vlad appeared on a fifth-floor balcony, waving above the white undershirts and fading underwear with stretched-out waistbands hanging from clothespins the color of Easter eggs. He bit into an apricot and smiled, closing his eyes. Witnessing the little ways the elderly cared for themselves devastated me. My paternal grandfather rubbing gardenia-scented lotion into his gnarled feet. My grandmother slicing lemon into her tea, no matter what kind of tea it was.

Sasha and I followed the men inside, taking the stairs to the second floor, where Vlad and the super waited by a green door. The super wore a chunky gold pinky ring and could have been anywhere from fifty-five to seventy-five. He smelled, not unpleasantly, like the preppy clothing store at the mall for teens whose parents did insider trading. He and Sasha exchanged a few words, and she handed him a ten-dollar bill.

"Tridtsat minut," he said. Thirty minutes. He unlocked the door with a master key.

"Spasibo," she said, thanking the benchers. She smiled at them, hand lingering on the doorknob. "Spasibo bolshoye," she repeated.

They exchanged prolonged pleasantries, clearly hoping to be invited inside. Eventually, they wished us health, success, and many children and grandchildren, and we wished it back, and they began slowly descending the stairs.

"Ready?" Sasha said. She opened the door.

There wasn't a stitch of furniture inside. The living room and kitchen were a compact, multipurpose space. I could see where a pull-out couch and television might go, a miniature bookshelf that functioned as an end table. A glass dish for mints and hard candy. An ashtray on the windowsill in need of emptying. It was how my grandmother described the apartment where she'd lived with her parents.

I followed Sasha into the only bedroom. Another empty space, aside from a few naked hangers in the closet where her grandmother's wool coats would have pressed against each other, above boxes of leather shoes with mother-of-pearl buttons, suede lattice sandals, black kitten heels. A sensitive document—something related to Judaism?—stuffed into the toe of a loafer. Her grandparents arguing over whether to attend the neighbor's New Year's party or who had asked whom to close the window. Shouts dissolving into laughter. The bed where her grandparents would have slept beneath a woven coverlet, matching terry-cloth slippers on either side. Sasha and her parents on the pull-out in the living room. Tobacco and cotton and spiced perfume.

In the tiny bathroom, the sink was practically inside the toilet, which was practically inside the tub. "The bathroom was so small, you had to take your pants off in the kitchen," my grandmother had said. Our reflections in the rusted mirror reminded me of daguerreotypes. We looked beautiful and dangerous, as though we'd just robbed a bazaar or snuck into Putin's booth at the ballet. We were wily bitches of the nineteenth century, and we were us, months from now, if we ditched tomorrow's flight. The super might let us squat for an affordable bribe. I would work as a nanny or an English tutor, become fluent in Russian. We would visit Sasha's family at the cemetery every week, research where my family was buried and visit them too. We would feed each other tomatoes and crouch together in the tub, in an apartment filled with stone fruit and books and Sasha's paintings.

I touched our reflection, reaching for mirror-Sasha's hair. The surface was spotless, as though it had just been sprayed down. I peeked into the tub. It was wet.

"Maybe a plumber came by earlier," Sasha said.

"You think?"

She shrugged.

"Or it's our witchy friend," I said. "Maybe she was sore from inflicting neighborhood terror and needed a good soak."

"Hot. Too bad she didn't stick around. This would be an unforgettable place for our first threesome."

Seven months in, I couldn't believe Sasha was mine. No one had warned me how terrifying it was to get what you want.

"You're cute when you're freaked out," she said. "Get in the tub."

She stepped out of her sandals and pulled her dress over her head. Though she'd dressed in front of me this morning, it was intimidating to face her green bralette, her cotton-candy-pink thong. I almost fell into the tub. The hem of my top was in her fist. She pulled it off as if she were waving a ribbon. We were kissing, I was shimmying out of my still-buttoned shorts and underwear, she was on top of me in the bath, lukewarm water rising like an omen. Her fingers in my mouth, my breast in her mouth. Sasha lifting my ass, me pulling her hair. My eyes closing, the water warming, sensations shifting as more of us was underwater.

Violence was the wrong word for what we did, but how else to describe how my body spasmed, how I flipped her over, both of us banging knees and elbows against the tub? How we uncoiled each other like knots, making and unmaking each other. When Sasha laughed, it was violent. I heard the rattle of the rabbit I'd used to hoard pills, my mother recounting a story about a friend who'd long since abandoned her. I kissed Sasha's neck, down her back, and lower still.

"Sex is supposed to be unsettling," she'd told me early on.

With past lovers, it was the blankness that unsettled me. The way, with Ronnie, I could leave my body entirely, or how with Franklin, I could come over and over and feel so much and nothing at all. With Sasha, it was the embodiedness that scared me. We were tender, and we were brutal. When I withdrew my tongue, I was punishing her for withholding so much from me. When she groaned, "You bitch," and drove my face back to her ass, she was punishing me for reminding her I had power over her too. She murmured a drawn-out "Fuck," splashing water across the floor.

"I almost murdered you for a second there," she said, panting.

I ran my fingers through her hair, massaging her scalp.

She laid her head against my chest and held it there.

Eventually, I said, "The super will be back soon."

"No, he won't."

"Are you just saying that to keep me here?"

"Guilty," she said, twisting to kiss me. "Don't let it get to your head."

She extricated herself and walked barefoot from the bathroom.

I stayed in the tub until the water drained, remembering Sasha's mother screaming about the terrible life she'd have as a lesbianka, and I wondered if fucking here was a kind of exorcism. It felt cringey and dishonest to assign myself such a pivotal role. Maybe this was why Sasha was so private, why our relationship was a wrestling match between vulnerability and opacity. What did self-disclosure feel like to someone with access to the innermost lives of others? A surgeon had once passed through my emergency room with a headache and ended up diagnosed with a brain tumor. He wore the role of patient like a newborn giraffe learning to walk.

In the living room, Sasha air-dried naked in the sun. I lay next to her beneath the open window. The warm air felt amazing on my body. "It feels like a hug," I said, only a little embarrassed at how earnest it sounded.

"Mmm," Sasha said. She took my hand.

I was aware that people might see us but was too blissed-out to care. I fell into twilight sleep.

"Time to go," she said at some point, pulling me to my feet.

We picked our clothes off the bathroom floor. I wondered why the tub was wet when we got here. Why, without even a folding chair, the apartment didn't feel empty. "The past isn't a bag of kittens you can dump in a lake," my grandmother might have said.

30.

We were quiet at our last dinner of beef mititei and mamaliga. We ate from wooden bowls on a patio with enchanted forest vibes. Fairy lights, faux animal hides, a leafy canopy above our heads. Around us, families laughing and drinking, children chasing each other through the trees. Cats nipped at fallen meat. Sasha was soaking up garlic sauce with her bread, staring into space.

"What are you thinking about?"

She flinched at the sound of my voice. "My parents. It's weird being here without them."

I nodded, waiting for her to say more. But that was all I got.

We ordered a napoleon for dessert. A toddler waved seeded bread beneath his chair, and an albino cat swiped it in one smooth motion. "Max!" the boy's mother reprimanded. "Nyet!" When his eyes watered, she kissed his cheeks.

Our appetites abandoned us. The napoleon sat uneaten on its plate, Sasha poking holes in it with her fork. Its layers of puff pastry reminded me of her Soviet apartment building, everyone stacked on top of each other, silent witnesses.

"You okay?" I asked.

She shrugged and took a bite. "I feel weird is all."

"Weird about what?"

"I don't know how to explain." She picked at a chip in her manicure.

"Try," I said.

"The whole time we were here, like from the moment we got off the plane, I haven't felt it."

"Felt what?"

"I'm used to sensing something almost every day. Even the smallest revelation. This trip is the first time since I was a kid that I've had a break from all that."

"What about the woman from the music video?"

"I've seen it before. That was an old one."

I didn't know what to say. "Have you enjoyed the break?"

"I don't know. It's unnerving."

"I get that. Maybe your body needs to rest."

"It's like I'm constipated. And I don't know if it'll go away on its own or turn into a fatal obstruction."

"Most people don't die from constipation."

She didn't laugh. "Since when am I most people?"

"Maybe once we get home, it'll start up again," I said. "Maybe Kishinev is some kind of block. Or something here needs your attention more than your, uh, spiritual duties."

If we were alone, I would have held her hand. She was still picking at the napoleon. I interlaced the tines of our forks.

"What if it's gone for good?" she said.

"How would you feel?"

"Unfinished."

"Or maybe your work is complete, and you can live in service of what *you* want."

"I'm not done," she insisted. "I know I'm not. I told you, there are things I need to atone for."

All I wanted was to say the right thing. "Okay. Then you're not."

"I knew coming here would mess me up. You can't go back like it's nothing. You can't hold your grandmother's grave in the rain and conjure her traumas like she's not listening."

"Well, why did you want to come here?"

She watched a band of cats chase each other between chair legs.

"I don't know," she said. "It was just a feeling. I felt a pull."

This whole time, I thought Sasha was obscuring why we were here. I thought the reason for the trip—and the reason she'd wanted me here—would reveal itself. Maybe she did too.

"What kind of pull?"

"You know what I mean."

I supposed I did. "What can I do?"

"Nothing." Sasha dragged her fork across the dessert plate, creating tire mark swerves in the cream.

"It looks like one of your paintings."

She smiled a little. "It does."

I reached for her hand and pulled it under the table. No one looked at us. They were busy with their mountains of food, their escaped children, the cats licking their ankles.

We held hands beneath the table until the check arrived, letting go when Sasha reached for her wallet.

On the ride back to our hotel in the humid marshrutka, arms sweating as they pressed against other passengers, I wondered about her power. What utility she saw in organizing her life around resolving ancestral traumas that were, fundamentally, unresolvable. I would not live in service of my dead's vision for me, a descendent they never knew, who'd never asked them to sacrifice what they lost. I wanted to believe I could honor them by living the life I chose for myself, by making choices that, for them, were never even on the table. That there was a world where my dead saw me—a recovering addict with a psychic girlfriend and a missing sister, estranged from Judaism and unable to speak any of their languages—and felt proud.

31.

We woke to news that a queer activist had been murdered in Saint Petersburg. She'd been stabbed eight times and strangled, her body abandoned in the bushes near her home. Her name had circulated on a website encouraging vigilante hunts for LGBT people in Russia. Friends revealed that she'd been threatened with violence and death many times over, that her police reports had been brushed aside. Russian state media cast doubt that she'd been killed because of her sexuality, insisting that she was an antisocial addict who'd courted her own death. That her murder was a drunken brawl between degenerates, nothing more.

We read the news in bed, clicking around various websites as though combing the beach with metal detectors, uncovering nothing. We did this until we needed to pack for the airport, and even then, we were fused to our phones, freezing at each notification like deer.

"Saint Petersburg of all places," I said, looping my headphones around my fingers.

Sasha stopped folding a blue jumpsuit. "What do you mean *of all places*?" Her voice was thick, and it made something in me jump.

"It's where I'm from," I said.

She left the jumpsuit on the bed where, an hour earlier, she'd spidered her nails up and down my back with the hand she wasn't using to scan the news. "What are you saying? That if your family had stayed, this could have been you?"

"I don't have a thesis," I said, biting my thumbnail. "I'm just saying, it's a weird coincidence."

"Coincidence?" She gave me a mysterious smile; it was almost Debbie-like, except there was no humor in it. She looked out at the oak tree shadowing our room. "There's nothing coincidental about a bisexual woman being murdered in one of the queerest cities in Russia."

Our door was shut but not locked. I could hear the businessman next door blowing his nose.

"It's a backlash," Sasha said. "These fuckers hate everything the West espouses, and killing queer people is practically patriotic. She demonstrated against Russia's seizure of Crimea too—did you read that? Against war and domestic violence and Putin. It was probably a contract killing." She tossed the jumpsuit in her suitcase with her dirty laundry. "She was a real person. Her murder isn't a metaphor."

"I never said it was." I'd wrapped my headphones too tightly, leaving blue ridges in my fingers. I didn't understand why we were fighting.

Sasha's phone dinged, a WhatsApp message. She took it with her to the bathroom and shut the door.

The mood in the dining room was obscenely cheerful. Guests went to town on blueberry blintzes, sighed at the earthly pleasure of hot coffee. They refilled their porcelain teapots, braided their children's hair. On TV, a toddler played the piano in a talent competition while the audience wept with delight. I wondered what would happen if I threw a plate at the TV. If I shattered the screen and popped a shard into my mouth, blood lighting up the spaces between my teeth.

Sasha and I took the table farthest from the other guests. She hadn't stopped texting since the first message came in. "It's Jenny," she said gruffly when I asked. Who was Jenny? Then someone named Masha, whom I also hadn't met, and then the three of them in a group chat.

I ate nine blintzes. I found Jenny's Instagram, stared at a photo of her sporting a yellow beanie and a septum piercing, and became irritated at how self-assured in her queerness she appeared to be. I scrolled my contacts for someone to text, each possibility more unhinged than the last. *Did you hear about this?* I wrote to my high school friend Kim, linking the article. We hadn't spoken since that night at Salvation with the fake art buyer. Then I deleted the message and typed, *hi*, before deleting that too.

Sasha rested her teacup against her cheek. The heat left behind an angry pink splotch. "Can we stop by my old apartment again?"

It was the first thing she'd said in an hour that was longer than two words.

"Of course," I said.

She gutted her blintz with a flowered knife.

In the cab, I willed her to run her hand across mine on the middle seat, low enough that the driver wouldn't notice. She didn't. I held my own hand. We passed the abandoned circus, her mother's elementary school exploding with purple hydrangeas, near-identical arrays of brutalist apartments. I rolled down the window, my hands clammy, chest tight.

The taxi deposited us next to a bush that bore swollen green berries. Sasha plucked one and sniffed it. I reached out to touch it, but she'd already let go. We watched it roll across the courtyard like an eyeball. It was late Tuesday morning, a sweaty July day. The sky was the same radiant blue as the day I photographed Sasha in the sunflower fields, and this felt like a betrayal. The paisley rug no longer hung from the monkey bars, replaced by a child in a strawberry-print dress. An older child was giving a gray dog licks off her ice cream cone. The dog was missing an ear. The benches in front of the building were empty, and no one was out on their balconies, and there were no candlelight vigils, there were no protests.

An old woman in curlers shambled out of the building. Sasha caught the door, and we took the stairs to the second floor. Her apartment was unlocked. The air was thick like the liquid within snow globes. I felt slow, amniotic.

"What's going on?" I asked.

She lay beneath the window, where yesterday she'd held my hand, and shut her eyes.

"Sasha?"

I lay next to her and touched her hair, her ear, her shoulder.

It was hot in the apartment. I opened the window and felt the first crest of a panic attack. I breathed through my abdomen, one hand on my belly and one on my chest. I counted five things I could see—Sasha, the open window, a gold doorknob, an ancient oven, a radiator—four things I could touch—my eyelashes, the warm floor, my carotid artery, a chip of paint that had unpeeled from the wall—three things I could hear—a child crying outside, footsteps above us, my own deep breaths—two things I could smell—a vegetal, musty odor like grave dirt, my own sweat—and one thing I could taste—blueberry acid between my teeth.

"Sasha, why are we here?"

She looked as if she were astral projecting to some other place entirely, somewhere I wasn't welcome. Somewhere I'd never be welcome. The strange energy in the apartment was forcing me to acknowledge what I already knew—I could squeeze some interiority out of her on occasion, but it would always feel coerced. She would decide what I was and wasn't ready to hear. How quickly I accepted whatever she offered me, like a stray begging for table scraps. I couldn't name another person so willing to believe it wasn't her business if her lover was psychic. Sasha could have engineered this trip, this break in her power, as a means of dropping the ruse. How quickly I'd reverted to being a knife block.

It didn't matter if she was grifting, or if she believed every word she'd said. I'd played by Sasha's rules the same way I'd played by Debbie's. I understood then why my great-grandfather was willing to die for his religion. Why I was willing to risk it all for Sasha, and before her, for Debbie. Banish one god, and you'll end up worshipping another.

I sat next to Sasha, and she continued to ignore me, and I felt more alone than I'd felt since the night of my miscarriage. A door slammed, the one-eared dog howled. Then, something in my brain clicked off, and something else took over, like nurses swapping places at change of shift. "I can't keep doing this," I heard myself say.

Sasha placed a hand on my thigh, and already it felt foreign, as though it belonged to the TSA agent who'd patted me down. "Yes, you can," she said, eyes closed.

"No. Look at me." I gripped her hand. "I want to be with you, but I don't want to keep feeling like this. I don't want to feel lonely in my relationship."

"How can you feel lonely?" she said, finally meeting my gaze. "We're together all the time. I brought you to Kishinev. I've never been back, and I brought you with me. You think I'd do that with anyone?"

"I don't know. I don't think so. But I honestly don't know."

Her hand went limp in mine. "How can you say that?"

"There's so much you won't tell me. You know everything about me, but you won't let me know you."

"You know me," she said in a thin, tinny voice.

"I love what I know. But I want more."

"We always want more. We're never content with what we have." She raked her fingers through her hair, pulling out a clump.

"What happens when you're through with being my amulet?" I asked.

She rolled the hair into a ball.

"Sasha."

"I don't know, okay? What do you want me to say? I don't know every fucking piece of the future." Her eyes were wet. I realized I'd never seen her cry.

"It's okay." It came out flat, affectless. I tried again with more warmth. "It's okay."

"Stay here with me." Her voice wobbled like glass at a table's edge.

"What?"

"I'll teach you Russian. We'll visit a new city every weekend. I'll . . . try to be more forthcoming."

The smell of fried meat and onions drifted in from outside. The dog barked harder, nearly drowning Sasha out. Neither of us moved. "You're staying?" I asked.

"I can't go back like this. I need to figure out what's wrong with me."

"I don't think anything's wrong with you."

She exhaled roughly, and something set between us like cement.

"But I get it," I said. "Kishinev has power over you. You're not ready to leave. It's okay."

"Stay with me. We'll go to Saint Petersburg. We'll try to find where your great-grandfather was buried, where your grandmother lived, if anyone who lives there knew your family. I'll help you."

"Saint Petersburg is the last place I want to be right now," I said, thinking again of the murder.

Half my organs were screaming that I was making a terrible mistake, and the other half were urging me on. I couldn't tell which of us had betrayed the other. Or there was no betrayal, only recognition. For once, we were equals.

I cupped her cheek.

She let me.

A child laughed, a car blasted Russian rap, a sapphire balloon floated past our window.

“You’ll miss your flight,” Sasha said.

I nodded but didn’t move.

“Will you take care of Apples for me?” she asked.

“Of course.”

She squeezed my hand. “I love you.”

“I love you too.”

Hearing her say it first drained the remainder of my life force. I crossed the room. The glassy look on Sasha’s face reminded me of Debbie, how in her eyes I saw my future. It turned out nothing like I’d expected. Except for the part where I end up alone.

IV

32.

I don't remember the flight or how I returned to my apartment. I don't remember baggage claim, if I had aisle or window or middle seat, what I ate, if I ate at all. I don't remember changing planes in Frankfurt. I don't remember going through customs. I don't remember if I slept. If I cried. If I got up to pee.

I awoke late afternoon, after sleeping thirteen hours, to my neighbor with emphysema hacking. On the balcony across the street, a beer-bellied man smoked in his underwear. I rolled over onto my hand and stayed there until it went numb. Somehow, hours went by.

Then it was dark, and my stomach ached like a limb waking up. Next door, someone was either having a dance party or blasting terrible pop songs to cover up a crime. I made Cup O' Noodles soup, which tasted like middle school. I used to buy them from the vending machines when I was too tired to prepare my own lunch in the morning. Sometimes I'd treat myself to a cinnamon roll for dessert.

"Your ass cheeks are going to stick together if you keep eating those," Debbie would say.

It was a rough translation of a Russian idiom our grandmother picked up from her mother. Something about enjoying sweet things in moderation. I didn't know how to say it in Russian.

Around midnight, I was back in bed, debating taking a Benadryl or turning my apartment upside down to search for benzos I knew weren't there.

Eventually my neighbor stopped coughing. My other neighbor cut their music. The man across the street quit chain-smoking and deserted his balcony. Even the street-lights were quiet. There was only the muffled sound of a car slowing before a stop sign. I wanted police sirens, a teenage girl shrieking outside the group home, a slammed door, the screech of an ominous bird. Someone calling someone an asshole. Glass splitting against a wall. A television falling over. Shattering, or not. Someone screaming, "Look what you've done!" or not.

It was two in the morning. I defrosted a slice of bread and ate in the dark. Even with the windows open, the city was too quiet. I put on jeans, a fraternity tank top some guy left behind.

I took the stairs to the lobby, where a security guard I hadn't seen before monitored the entrance.

"Good evening," he said. He looked behind me, as though expecting a leashed dog.

"Hi," I said. "I don't think we've met."

"I started last week," he said.

I wondered if something had happened while I was gone. "We didn't use to have security."

"Usually that's the case before hiring a guard."

It took a few seconds to realize he was joking. If we'd passed each other in the daytime, we would have maybe nodded at each other. The rules were different at night. We were buddies. Chums. Comrades. His name tag said DARRYL.

"See you later," I said.

I couldn't decide if I wanted him to be cool with me taking off alone in the middle of the night, or if I craved a lecture on personal safety. *Tell me to carry a rape whistle*, I dared him. *Tell me to hold my keys between my fucking fingers.*

Darryl held the door for me. "Be safe."

It was warm and the night air dripped with the honeyed scent of magnolias. A light breeze made the palm trees shiver. I followed them downhill toward Hollywood Boulevard, walking beneath the palms. Their bark was crunchy and thick. I wouldn't have minded a coconut conking me on the head.

At Sunset Boulevard, I passed the European café that stayed open until three in the morning. They had an entire soufflé menu, and Debbie once convinced a real estate broker smoking hookah at the next table to buy us one of each. He clearly expected the night to organically progress into a threesome, and we let him believe this, slipping out while he was in the bathroom. I turned left on Sunset and passed my supermarket. Russian delis, a gold exchange, a Brazilian restaurant. The public library where I discovered porn. That day, Debbie and I were killing time while our mother was at a doctor's appointment. I'd already pawed through several puberty books, a children's guide to world religions, and a manual for casting spells. I did a lap to look for Debbie and found her at one of the computers.

"I'm so bored," she huffed. "I don't know how to get to the Teens page."

Both of us still in elementary school, we flitted around the AOL Teens page like undercover journalists. There were games and advice columns and saucy message boards.

"Maybe teens.com?" I said.

The page loaded a photo of two naked women licking each other's breasts. Each boob a perfect water balloon. Then, a popup of a naked woman with her face between another woman's legs. The volume was off, but I could tell they were making pained sounds. More popups of women with women, women with men, men with men, women with breasts and penises. Each partly obscured the ones that came before, and I'm not sure how many I saw before Debbie shut down the computer. I stared at the black screen. Behind my eyes, I could see the flickering lights that had moments earlier been nude bodies, sweaty and desirable in a way I found frightening.

"Um," Debbie said.

We looked at each other. No one around us had noticed. We burst out laughing.

I walked into a twenty-four-hour burger place and ordered a cheeseburger and fries. Two women in sparkly slips were laughing over a shared milkshake. I wondered which bar they'd come from. If they'd dressed this way for the burger place as a bit. If they were lovers. I laid waste to my cheeseburger in five bites and continued down Sunset. I passed a bar hidden inside a fake sex shop, a theatrical shoe warehouse, a movie theatre, trendy hotels. The Mediterranean restaurant whose owner killed his wife and sister in a murder-suicide. Eventually, the places I passed stopped registering. I turned a key in a lock, and then another lock.

Sasha's apartment smelled like someone had shut the windows and touched all her things. I kept the lights off. Opened the windows. Fell into her bed. The sheets didn't smell like us.

I dreamt I was late to work and was mistaken for a patient. I was wheeled into an operating room, where Debbie waited in scrubs and a mask, cradling my knife. I was in Kishinev, in Saint Petersburg ("Leningrad," my grandmother corrected). My great-grandfather extracted the bullets from his body and handed them to me. My grandmother waited for me to sew the keys back into her piano. Golda the Chelmno hairless began to speak. "Find Debbie," she purred.

◍

I awoke dehydrated and sore around two in the afternoon. I drank water from the tap. Made Sasha's bed. Took a shower. My phone had no messages and work wasn't for several hours. I opened and closed Sasha's freezer until I lost my appetite.

A loop of scenarios played in my head. Debbie in prison for impersonating a pharmacist. Debbie murdered while hitchhiking or inducted into a cult that lived off the grid. She'd been gone for over two years. She could have had a child with someone who loved her. She could be stripping in New York. She could be homeless. She could have won the lottery. She could be dead.

I replayed the last time we saw each other and wondered whether I'd been the hospitalized one. Maybe I had stabbed my own arm. Maybe I had tried to kill myself. It scared me that I could entertain these questions.

I regretted not calling Debbie after the hospital. I should have asked about her medical bills, if she needed pain meds or help showering. But I'd never been able to resist her, and I wouldn't have then. She wasn't someone I could keep at a distance. Debbie was like those possessed toys that lit up even after you took their batteries out. If I ever saw her again, she'd make sure I didn't see it coming. I'd show up at my therapist's one morning, and Debbie would be waiting beneath a jacaranda tree in the parking lot. Or I'd drop groceries off at my grandmother's, and Debbie would be inside having tea. Then I remembered Sasha saying these were the best-case scenarios. I had no evidence Debbie was alive at all.

33.

The woman with Shoah grief was back in my emergency room.

Of course. Since returning from Moldova, everything and everyone felt out to get me. The shower drain, the bus driver who asked how my day was going, Shirin, who texted me yesterday, *hey are you still sober? had an idea I wanted to run by you*. I responded, *I'm listening*, and then blocked and unblocked Shirin's number so many times I missed her follow-up text, if she'd sent one at all.

Shoah Grief Woman looked pale and wore a T-shirt emblazoned with a cow's face. The cow had a real bell around its neck. With each step, it made an awful ding. Was this bitch seriously referencing Sasha's grandma and her exploding cow? Why else would she wear such a hideous shirt, if not to fuck with me?

I couldn't sleep after my last shift and had spent hours researching Jewish hauntings. I read about dybbuks and golems and intergenerational curses. I read about Nazi treasure hunters and time travel and skimmed a book that claimed conspiracy theories made the staggering horror of the Holocaust more approachable, that secret tunnels and buried heirlooms were more palatable than bodies heaped in mass graves. I wanted to ask my mother if she believed in psychics, in Jewish curses. If she ever felt like the scooped-out insides of a fish.

"You still work here? I thought you'd quit," the woman said by way of greeting.

"Why's that?" I said.

"I was here last week, and some other girl was manning the desk."

"I was out of town."

"Vacation?"

"Sort of." I wanted to unburden myself to her, and I wanted to triage her as fast as possible and never see her again.

She shifted from one foot to the other. Her stupid cow bell dinged. "Well, you know the drill."

She hadn't found a therapist she connected with, and the latest supply of benzos the hospital gave her had run out. She wanted to know if any Jewish doctors were working tonight. I said I had no idea which doctors were Jewish beyond guessing based on their names.

"Really?" she said. "They're your coworkers. You've never talked about it?"

"Hasn't come up."

I typed her information into the computer so fast the form glitched. I wanted to tell her about Moldova, how uncomfortable I'd felt rubbing up against someone else's Jewish trauma when I felt so estranged from my own.

She was humming a melody I vaguely recognized. Some klezmer song I'd heard my grandmother hum while cooking. The sort of thing I hadn't realized lived in my body until I encountered it in the world.

I wanted her to tell me it was not only okay but imperative that I live for myself. That the dead had no stake in my desires. But if she'd believed this, she wouldn't be in my emergency room.

A nurse approached her then. "Esther?" she asked.

"That's me," the woman said. She nodded at me. "Until next time."

"Bye," I said. "I like your shirt."

"Thanks. Bought it to make my granddaughter laugh, but this is the most serious ten-month-old that's ever lived. She's carrying the collective weight of the Jewish people on her shoulders."

Aren't we all, I was tempted to reply. She might have laughed. "Have an easy night," I said instead.

34.

My shift ended at seven in the morning. I rode the bus home and stared at the private investigator's number until my vision blurred.

Not looking for Debbie wasn't going to release her hold on me. In the time she'd been gone, her grip had loosened, yes, but I was never going to not care if she was dead or alive. Resisting something isn't the same as not wanting it. Despite all we'd been through—and all she'd put me through—I wasn't done with Debbie. Not even sobriety, happiness, or love would make it so.

A firework of adrenaline coursed through me. I was going to find my sister. I was going to find my sister without surrendering to her, without abandoning my recovery. Cutting her out of my life hadn't fixed me. Our bond couldn't be severed with a knife. It was cellular, metaphysic. I needed to know if my sister existed in the world. What I did with that knowledge was up to me.

I dialed the PI's number. The call went to voicemail. I tried again. Voicemail.

"Hi, this message is for Mark? I'm calling to get your help locating someone. My sister. It's been a couple years since she left Los Angeles, and I wanted to see about finding her. Please give me a call if you can help. Thanks."

I felt very hot and then very cold. "You're okay," I told my reflection in the bathroom mirror. With black eyeliner, I traced the person I saw on the other side of the glass. I followed the curve of her eyelashes, the thickness of her bottom lip, the soft V of her cupid's bow. She smiled at me. "I've been looking for you," I said.

35.

A few days later, the PI hadn't called back. I wondered if he'd retired or gone missing himself. PIs had to have enemies. Disgruntled ex-husbands, exposed scammers. My adrenaline morphed into anxiety. I engrossed myself in kennel club dog shows, hoping a constant drip of television would keep me from calling Sasha or texting Shirin or asking my former psychiatrist for an Ativan refill. I watched the shows from the moment I got home until I fell asleep. When one ended, a related video auto-played. The video running when I awoke was never a dog show. The first time, it was an old sitcom about a middle-class family cosplaying happiness. The next, a sniveling rant about the leftist agenda to outlaw gender, and then a Ritz cracker commercial spliced with clips of women fainting. I watched to the end as a kind of meditation, playing them on the bus and on mute at work.

Therapy wasn't for three days. I kept reminiscing about the warm buzz of Oxy and Ativan, how they made me feel held. I drew myself a bath and cried when it reminded me of Sasha. I showered instead and pumiced a layer off my feet. I watched another dog show. I got to work early, pacing the stairwells until it was time.

The PI called back that night. It was ten, and the waiting

room was dead. There was only one woman, asleep on a rolled-up scarf.

"This is Mark. You left a message for me."

"That was me. Hi."

"About your sister."

"Yes. Debbie."

"Debbie."

I waited for him to speak, but he didn't. "She's been gone a couple years," I said. "I was staying overnight with her at the hospital, and when I woke up in the morning, she wasn't there. I . . . didn't check in for a few weeks."

He stayed silent.

"By the time I reached out, her phone was disconnected, and she'd left her stuff behind. I've done some digging, but I haven't turned anything up."

"And this was how long ago?"

"Two years, three months."

"Two years, three months," he said. "Doable."

"Yeah?"

"Yes. Well, depending on a few things. I'm going to need more information. Can we meet for coffee?"

The call lasted eighty seconds. My only patient was sleeping in the same position. Her scarf was patterned with gray rabbits.

◐

I awoke to a Halloween makeup tutorial. A college student transforming her head into a jack-o'-lantern, contouring grooves into her face from forehead to chin. It was the dumbest shit in the world, and she was having the time of her life.

I wished I had known girls like her when I was growing up, that I knew them now. I wondered what Sasha was up to. My ribs began to ache. I hummed the telephone hold music from the hospital. I ate what remained of my nails.

At four, I arrived at the café Mark had chosen, a mom-and-pop place in Boyle Heights. I ordered black tea, which made me think of Sasha, so I switched my order to coffee. The radio played Spanish pop music and ads for predatory class action lawyers.

I was halfway done with my coffee when a short man with salt-and-pepper hair walked in. He nodded at me and ordered a drink at the counter. I waited awkwardly at a two-person table until he joined.

"Mark?" I asked.

"Yes. Nice to meet you."

He opened a leather case and took out a legal pad and a pen. "So, here's how I roll. I'll start off by asking you some questions. Anything you say stays between us. I'll take some notes, which I'll store in a secure location. That sound all right?"

I nodded.

"Great," he said. "So. Your sister."

"My sister."

"Tell me about her."

I started with the last few years—the drugs, the wild nights, the dangerous edge to our encounters. I told him about high school, the strip club, our mother's psych stuff, our father's affairs.

"So, she's an addict. Unpredictable. Lives for the drama,

even or especially when it becomes a threat. Tell me about the last time you saw her."

I told him about detox, the party, the overlook, the knife.

"And you stabbed her, why?"

"She said something to me. Or she didn't say what I wanted her to."

"She said something?"

"It wasn't just that. We had a complicated relationship. It wasn't about what she said or didn't say. It was an accumulation."

I went on about the childhood indignities, ditching me in the ER after my miscarriage, the black holes eaten away by things we'd taken or my mind protecting me from knowing what I'd done or what had been done to me.

"Are you currently using drugs?"

"No."

He cleared his throat.

"I'm not. I got clean a year ago. I take Suboxone."

"Which is—?"

"It's a replacement for opioids. It binds the same receptor."

"Got it."

I swirled my finger around my coffee. I couldn't decide if I liked him.

"Don't take the questions personally," he said. "I need to know who I'm working with. Tell me where you've already looked."

It took only a few minutes. It was embarrassing, spelling out how little I'd done.

"Your sister sounds like an agent of chaos."

I liked the sound of that, like something out of a fantasy novel. "That's right."

"Here's what we'll do. I'm going to email you some documents. There will be a rate sheet of what I can offer you. I'll highlight the ones I think are relevant here. And there's a contract. Take a look, let me know if you have questions, and send it back indicating what you want me to pursue."

"Okay," I said.

"You're a secretary?"

I nodded.

"We'll start small. I'll pull some documents, see what I can find online."

"All right."

"I don't do payment plans or sliding scales. You'll need to pay half up front and half after I deliver. Is that going to be an issue?"

"No," I said, hoping it was true.

He had a forgettable face. He could have been an optometrist or a parking lot attendant or a middle school friend's dad.

"I'll email you the rate sheet and contract tonight. Whenever you're ready, we can start."

"Thank you." I got up and bussed our mugs.

"Where did you park?" he asked.

"I took the bus."

I thought he might offer me a ride and was relieved when he didn't. He shook my hand and said he would be in touch. He didn't ask why I hadn't gone to the police. I decided it didn't matter if I liked him. On the bus, no one spoke to me.

●

The air in Sasha's apartment was sour and smelled like being smothered with an old pillow. I removed her landlord's card from the fridge, wondered if she would extend her lease. A paintbrush lay on a wood tray hand-painted with a Russian folk pattern. Khokhloma, it was called. My grandmother had a bowl in a similar pattern, and every bazaar and souvenir shop in Moldova sold plates, spoons, keychains, and jewelry boxes like these. I put the paintbrush tip in my mouth.

I hadn't been inside her apartment since my night walk a few weeks earlier. The only other time I entered the building was to pick up Apples from Sasha's neighbor, and those ten minutes were enough to poison the day.

I'd watched all the dog shows I could find and had moved on to cats. Anytime I wasn't working or watching TV, panic enveloped me like a plague of locusts. I held Apples while I watched, but he didn't like the cat shows or being in my arms. We struck a deal: I maintained Sasha's regimen of spoiling him with live crickets and fruit, and he endured my clinginess. Disdain radiated off his skin like a heat lamp. One especially fraught afternoon, I spent an hour researching variations of *Is my iguana a misogynist?*

Mark's contract was all numbers and disclaimers. I wired him two hundred dollars for the first part of his search, which he would conduct online. It was low-commitment enough that I could back out with most of my savings intact. He was searching for name changes, property purchases, run-ins with the law, "digital footprints."

I teared up at a rum commercial on a pirate ship that played during one of my cat shows. Sasha had lent me a book right before our trip, about a secret love affair between teen boys in France. The narrator was cerebral and well-off, his lover closeted, practical, working-class. It was a book of longing, a book of the body. *Shipwreck* was the word the narrator used for the pain of seeing his secret lover at a party with someone else, the pain of knowing he had no claim over him. I began dreaming of the sea, of running toward enormous waves, which receded each time I lunged. I dreamt of falling asleep naked on a doomed ship, of opening treasure chests and finding decapitated heads—Sasha's, Debbie's, my own. Dreams where I threw myself overboard with such force I landed back on the ship.

I moved on from cats to exotic pets. Those competitions were an absurd free-for-all: toucans versus chinchillas versus capuchin monkeys versus sugar gliders that could fit in my palm. The pets were ranked by looks and talent. I thought the monkeys had an unfair advantage, but their trainability was used against them. Scylla and Charybdis, the two-headed snake, head-butted a miniature soccer ball into a goal. Dr. Manhattan the lemur made vegan meatballs. Jeremiah the toucan painted watercolors with his beak—messy, abstract shapes that bore an uncanny resemblance to genitals.

36.

A few days later, Apples and I were watching an exotic pet competition in which an iguana named Bananas operated a forklift.

"What do you think of that, buddy?" I said. "Jealous?"

Apples ignored me as usual.

The phone rang.

"This is Mark. I've finished the online portion of my search."

My stomach seized. "And?"

"I didn't turn up anything definite. No arrest records or death certificates. No signatures on legal documents."

"Okay. What does that mean?"

"If she's alive, she's kept a low profile."

"Do you think so? I mean, do you think she's alive?"

"Hard to say at this point. If she's not, her body hasn't been identified."

I pictured the villain from a detective show Debbie and I watched together. He had a scarred face and looked like the result of ten generations of inbreeding. "Very on the nose," Debbie had said. "It's so boring when their outsides match their insides."

Mark told me he'd flagged a few things in his search.

News clippings of anonymous acts of grandiosity that sounded like things my sister would do. A police report filed by our pediatrician. And there was a woman in Boston named Debbie Eva whose only appearance in a legal document was after Debbie disappeared. Eva was Debbie's middle name.

An icy spasm coursed through me. "Send those to me. Please. I'll look over everything and get back to you about next steps."

"Alrighty." He hung up.

It was an awfully casual way of ending a conversation about someone who might be dead. He was probably desensitized to his clients' suffering—what was another missing person, another family member with their own secrets trying to find them. It wasn't so different from my job. Every shift, someone within a hundred feet of me was having the worst day of their life. I tried to harden my heart against them, but there was always someone whose suffering I metabolized.

"It's a beautiful thing," Sasha told me early on. "Most people only possess a third of the empathy they think they have. Not you. You're very aware of who claims space in your heart."

She returned to chopping celery. We were making tortilla soup. I kissed her bare shoulder. The smell of citrus flooded the room—her hair was wet.

•

Apples and I watched the last of the exotic pet contests and ate cheddar popcorn (me) and Lexapro bread (him). A voluptuous flamingo named Marilyn won; we suspected her of doping with eyelash growth serum. “Remind me to look up if that’s allowed,” I told Apples.

I called Sasha’s landlord. I said I was Sasha’s sister, that she was traveling with little cell service and asked me to confirm when her lease was up. There were four months left.

I wondered what would happen if she didn’t renew. Would the friends I’d never gotten to meet move her stuff into storage? Would the landlord trash her things? She and Debbie felt like mutually exclusive presences in my life. I’d never envisioned that when I searched for Debbie, if I searched for Debbie, it would be Apples by my side.

“Will it get easier?” I asked him.

He blinked, eyes like bathwater circling a drain.

37.

I procrastinated opening Mark's file, heart pounding as though the cops might kick down my door. I marinated in dread, afraid I would recognize her, afraid I wouldn't.

"We'll go through it later," I told Apples. "After work."

After work, I took the bus to random stops, sloping through the Valley, the Hollywood Hills, neighborhoods Debbie and I ended up at in what felt like a past life. I passed the turn for the estate that hosted masked sex parties that women could attend for free while men had to pay thousands of dollars and pass a video interview. Debbie went once and said it was boring, though she made off with a pair of Cartier cuff links that she pawned for a hundred dollars. There were streets that tugged at vague memories I'd blacked out, driveways that made my hair stand on end.

I ended up back in Hollywood, outside the apartment complex where I was assaulted in fourth grade. There was the switchboard to buzz in, the fluffy trees that lined the property. The semicircular balconies that delighted me at nine and gave me a vertiginous feeling now. I wondered if the handyman still lived there. He victimized multiple girls who lived in the complex, their friends too. If there was a lawsuit, I'd never heard about it. I have no idea how the story ended. If it ended at all.

Back home, I spent hours on message boards for the families of missing persons. The threads for finding people who didn't want to be found hadn't been updated in years. One website aggregated information about cold cases. Debbie wasn't featured. I clicked through profiles at random: A thirty-five-year-old woman who vanished after a biopsy; by the time the results confirmed metastatic cervical cancer, no one had seen her in three days. An Auschwitz survivor with dementia, whose wallet was found at a Holocaust memorial thirty miles from his nursing home. Teen runaways who, it was later discovered, had been talking to older men online. A mother of three who drove to work at a soda factory and never returned. Sometimes, suspects were named—almost always abusive exes. There were striking details: a close friend who went missing the same week, whether the missing person was a *known hitchhiker*, a cold pizza left untouched on a kitchen table. The details of someone else's disappearance shed little light on what might have happened to Debbie. If anything, they confirmed our ridiculous, shared reality: a person could abandon or be pulled from her life like a loosed balloon.

◐

Stitches, pneumonias, broken arm, aspirin overdose. Around three, when the only person in the waiting room, a man whose mother was getting IV antibiotics for a UTI, left in search of coffee, I downloaded Mark's file.

The document was nearly two hundred pages of news clippings, police reports, convoluted documents ranging from housing applications to commercial real estate agreements to contact information for people of interest. I went through it line by line. When I reached the last page, there were fifteen minutes left in my shift. I stared at a crooked photo on the wall of a bee humping a tulip. It was hard to summarize what I'd read. The frenzied assortment of people, places, and events defied paraphrase.

But in that entropy, I felt Debbie.

Most of the file was boring legal bullshit with the faintest connection to Debbie—a name that could have been an alias, a contract for something she might have pursued. The best parts were the unsolved crimes. All over Florida, a beautiful woman with brown hair and wild eyes was spotted driving a stolen car; multiple men claimed she'd flirted with them, and that they'd paid for her gas. The car was recovered in a high school parking lot in Boca Raton, the woman believed to be at large. In San Francisco, a woman smuggled dozens of animals out of a pet store. In Los Angeles, a children's dance instructor stole jewelry, electronics, and an heirloom Fabergé egg from a pharma heiress's home. In Houston, a substitute teacher gave a comprehensive sex education lecture at an abstinence-only middle school. She was escorted from the premises, but the school's temp agency had no record of a teacher being dispatched that day.

I stopped breathing halfway through the police report filed by our pediatrician. Two weeks after the last time I saw Debbie, he came home to find nine of his watches missing. Someone had broken into his house, disabled the alarm, made off with a quarter million dollars' worth of watches ranging from Rolex to brands I'd never heard of, and set the alarm on their way out.

There was a copy of a rental agreement for a small storefront in Boston, signed by the woman with Debbie's first and middle names. I flagged that file, the police report, and some of the news clippings for a closer look.

The chaotic vigilantes of Mark's file, with their glamour and wit and manipulation and grandiosity, all sounded like Debbie. They were facets of the same crystal, minus one facet that was missing. All the people made to suffer arguably deserved it. Even those who hadn't actively committed evil were complicit in something—the opioid epidemic, confining animals in overcrowded cages, the patriarchy. There were no innocent victims here.

But what had I done to deserve what Debbie put me through? Not looking for her when she went missing was the obvious answer. It was as though Debbie had been punishing me my entire life as preemptive payback for this betrayal.

Back home, I searched for social media accounts belonging to Debbie Eva. That didn't turn up anything useful. Neither did entering her name in several search engines.

"Fine, one more thing," I told Apples, who was half asleep in my lap.

Searching the address from the commercial real estate application would be quick. The internet would either list a business or it wouldn't. If there was anything notable, Mark would have told me. Probably the place never opened, or it was something that made no sense for Debbie. A dowdy maternity shop, a Scientology bookstore, a travel agency. I imagined entering the address and being redirected to a picture of Debbie's coffin.

Apples clawed my arm. I hadn't realized I was shaking.

"Sorry," I mumbled.

I was too anxious to face an official website. I typed the address into an online map instead, selecting satellite view. A red pin indicated a location but didn't provide its name. On the same street: a Starbucks, a Chinese restaurant, a stationery store. On the other side: a nail salon, a dry cleaner, an ice cream shop, a jewelry boutique. I switched to street view. I saw a four-story brick building with several storefronts. Trees bursting with vibrant leaves, an explosion of red, orange, and yellow. A blurry American flag above the stationery store; it must have been waving. A windy fall day.

I zoomed in, looking for the suite number from the rental agreement. It had a glass façade like all the others. A UPS truck and a tree obstructed my view inside. I saw only a sliver of the storefront, white space, and an abstract lilac shape. The letters *N*, *I*, and *C*.

A white curtain had been drawn inside the shop. What was Debbie doing in there? Or not Debbie. Hope is a tricky thing with missing people, the message boards told me. Losing it is bad, but so is having too much. What was it that Emily Dickinson said? "Hope is the thing with feathers." At a reading Sasha took me to, one of the poets said, "Hope is the thing with teeth." That feels more honest to me.

What kinds of spaces were blocked off with a curtain? Maybe a medical office. The neon sign didn't feel medical, though it did resemble a foot, or a hand. It could have been a nail salon, but there was already one across the street. Maybe an art gallery. The work being exhibited could have been light-sensitive or viewable only by ticketholders. Knowing Debbie, she'd probably display nudes with the zoom up so high you thought you were looking at sand dunes instead of foreskin. Videos of women self-harming to dance music. A statue made of broken watch parts, melted down into the shape of human feces and titled *This Shit Is Worth $250,000.*

Maybe fantasizing about the possibilities was better than dredging up the past. I could decide this store, whatever it was, was Debbie's. That she lived in Boston, that whatever she was doing, she was running the show. I could put an alert on her new name, and until I heard otherwise, could assume she was alive. I could move on. When I missed her, I could pull up the street view of her shop. I could look at the autumn tree, the UPS truck delivering the day's wares, the neon sign, and imagine what Debbie was up to inside. I could place Sasha in the fantasy as one of Debbie's artists. Everyone I'd lost could work or shop at Debbie's store. I closed my eyes. Took a deep breath. Held it, held them, and let it all go.

38.

I made it a week before looking up the address directly. I went to work, fed Apples, and eyeballed photos of the store. I virtually toured the surrounding area. Here was the Chinese place where Debbie grabbed takeout. The boutique that sold bougie candles and mugs with tits that Debbie occasionally shoplifted. She lived in one of the apartments above her store, a brownstone with original hardwood floors and eclectic furniture she'd thrifted or claimed in breakups. Sasha's paintings lined her walls.

Toward the end of that week, I role-played a scenario in which I called the shop using a fake name and haggled with Debbie over the price of one of Sasha's pieces. How would Sasha react when she learned an anonymous buyer from LA had made a big purchase? I'd insist on flying out to pick up the piece and on meeting the artist in person. Around the time I was brainstorming what to wear to a reunion with Debbie and Sasha, I realized I'd chewed my nails down to bloody tatters and hadn't showered in days.

I put on a pair of mesh gloves Sasha gave me to keep from biting my nails and forced down a glass of water. I searched the store's address online, closing my eyes before the page loaded.

There was a hit.

I thought it was a mistake. Then, a horrible sensation as though a vacuum had been shoved down my throat and let loose in my stomach. There wasn't a website, just a name and phone number. There was also a listing on a review site: three-point-five stars, seven reviews. The shop offered ten dollars off the first visit, another ten dollars off for referrals. Every review mentioned Debbie. *She helped me find my true path in life*, one reviewer wrote. *After only six sessions, I'm a completely different person.* Another said, *Honestly, I have no idea if I believe in this stuff, but she's very intense in a good way and I enjoyed talking to her.* One person complained about the lack of street parking and draconian cancellation policy. Another said she left her fiancé after her first session.

It was called Salvation Psychic.

There weren't any pictures of her, but I knew it was Debbie. It had to be. Debbie was living in Boston and masquerading as a psychic, her shop name an homage to the bar where we weaponized the worst parts of ourselves. I tried to breathe through my diaphragm, but the vacuum feeling was still happening, and my face was wet, I must have been crying. I pulled the silver rabbit out from under my bed, knowing it was empty. "Durachka," I could hear Debbie saying. "What kind of idiot doesn't stash any emergency Ativan?" Except that was Sasha's word, not Debbie's, and Sasha wouldn't call me a fool for taking sobriety seriously.

All I had were as-needed prescriptions for propranolol and hydroxyzine, which alleviated my anxiety about as much as you'd expect for pills designed to treat high blood pressure and itch. I jammed both in my mouth and kneeled before the bathroom faucet. I did my grounding exercises, naming my surroundings, describing them in my head. White sink. White-and-black tiled floor. My hair on the floor. Shampoo. Conditioner. Strengthening hair mask. Pink razor. Drain.

The name, Salvation Psychic, was the most obvious clue, but there was so much more, slipping through my hands like tiny fish, yes, but it was there. The audacity felt distinctly Debbie. I tried to piece it together. Debbie leaving the hospital while I was asleep. Silence between us for weeks. Gone by the time I reached out. The pediatrician's police report. Debbie reselling the watches. Moving to Boston and opening a psychic shop. And me, meeting Sasha, loving Sasha, getting clean, losing Sasha.

Debbie loved a scam, and a psychic shop was as good as any. She had the personality for it. She could slice through a person's psyche and hand their own brain back to them. She perceived primordial fears and desires, ones you didn't know you had. She was difficult to refuse, a skilled manipulator. But what did it mean that the two most important people in my life were psychic or posing as psychic? Debbie's shop felt like a mockery of the happiness I'd experienced with Sasha, a suggestion that both were a scam. None of it made sense. I had no proof the person who owned this psychic shop was my sister, but the possibility I was wrong rang so hollow I nearly slapped myself.

I called Mark, but he didn't answer. I emailed him saying I believed Debbie was the owner of Salvation Psychic. That she might also be the one who stole the pediatrician's watches. Some of the other news items sounded like stunts she would pull, but I didn't know for sure. Sending the email brought back the feeling of something unspoken having been decided with Debbie. The last time I felt it was after I stabbed her.

Mark called the following morning. "So, you think this is her?"

I'd gotten in bed hours earlier but was too adrenaline-high to sleep. "I do."

"Because it's a reference to the bar you used to frequent together?"

"Yes. There's something about it that's so her. She could easily convince people she's psychic. Plus there's the name on the rental agreement."

"Interesting. So, you want me to follow up?"

"I think I should go out there. See for myself."

"Someone should check it out, I agree. I have an associate near Boston I could ask."

"No." I surprised myself with how firmly I said it. "It needs to be me."

39.

I entered the Russian deli, expecting to immediately get clocked as an outsider. When I called my grandmother that afternoon, offering to do a grocery run, I assumed I'd be going to the supermarket a few blocks from her place. Instead, she sent me here. I walked the aisles, looking for familiar items I'd seen in her kitchen: cream cheese in tall glasses, green onions, frozen pelmeni, Belochka chocolates with squirrels on their wrappers. I lingered before a glass display of baked goods, waiting for a woman in cat-eye glasses on a rhinestone chain to take my order. She began speaking in rapid-fire Russian. Too self-conscious to try and pronounce what my grandmother asked for, I pointed to the sour cream cake.

"Medovik?" she asked, indicating the honey cake next to it.

"No," I shook my head, trying again.

"Bulka s'makom?" she reached for a poppy seed loaf.

"No, sorry. It's the . . . smetannik," I said quietly.

"Ah, smetannik." She pantomimed cutting it into different sizes, waiting for me to tell her when.

"That's good."

She sliced the cake into a neat square and laid it inside a

paper box. She weighed the box and stickered it with a price. "You said it right," she said. "Do not be afraid."

When I arrived at my grandmother's, she was making sour cherry vareniki.

"Go wash your hands and eat while they're still warm," she commanded.

A lightbulb was out in her bathroom. Her soap was shaped like a rosebud, and there was something so hopeful about it that I almost teared up. I caught myself just in time to avoid drying my hands on the off-limits towel. It belonged to her mother, who died nearly twenty years earlier. The towel was pale blue with braided tassels. It hung over a dedicated towel bar as though, at any moment, my great-grandmother might walk through the door with wet hands. As a kid, not being allowed to touch the towel was crazy-making. Sometimes I pretended to use the bathroom as an excuse to hold it to my face.

The television blared Russian music videos. We ate the vareniki in silence. When I finished, she spooned five more onto my plate. They were perfectly tart but had the occasional pit.

"I'm seeing Debbie in a few weeks," I told her.

She frowned and got up to fill a teapot with water from the sink.

"If there's anything you want me to pass along to her, let me know."

My grandmother scoffed. "Anything I want to say, I'll tell her myself. In person. Not by carrier pigeon."

"Okay." I was too full to finish the vareniki, which I knew would turn into an argument. When she had her back turned, I nudged them into a plastic baggie I'd brought for this exact scenario and hid them in my tote.

"She's finally coming back?"

"Not exactly. She has a few days off, so we're meeting in Boston."

My grandmother laid a handful of tea bags and a chipped porcelain cup nearly as old as her before me. I chose the tea with a hand-drawn lemon on its tag. She filled my cup with a shaky hand. I was going to ask for ice but thought better of it; our relationship worked best when we asked as little of each other as possible. As if reading my mind, she went back for her ice tray.

"I remember," she said. "Endless patience for finding a good man, a good job. But waiting for her tea to cool? Not this one."

"That's me."

She laughed, not cruelly.

The music video I'd seen in Moldova began playing. The diva watched herself cry in her gold sturgeon mirror. She kissed her scary lover on a frozen lake.

"She feels too much," I found myself saying.

My grandmother shook her head. "People like that are never long for this world."

"So I hear. Maybe she'll prove us all wrong."

"Wouldn't that be nice?"

As I was leaving, she extracted a hundred-dollar bill from her freezer and tucked it in my pocket. "For your trip. Come over when you're back, and I'll make you stuffed peppers. Oh, and don't tell your mother where you're going. It'll only worry her."

"I won't."

She sighed, the creases in her face vibrating. "There's a Russian expression for what it's like to try to talk her out of her paranoias: byitsa kak riba ob lyod."

"A fish trying to beat its way out of a frozen lake?"

She knit her eyebrows together. "I taught you that one?"

"I've been learning Russian."

My grandmother laughed. "Good luck. It's the toughest language in the world. Maybe by the time they're lowering me into the ground, you'll be able to string a sentence together." She tucked my hair behind my ear. Her hand was warm as it cupped my cheek. "You liked the vareniki?"

"I loved them."

"My mother's recipe. She used to say that if I ate too many, I'd become a sour cherry. As if life hadn't made the women in our family sour cherries already."

I kissed her cheek. "I'll be back to change your lightbulb later this week," I said, but she wasn't listening.

"When you see Debbie, tell her to come back soon. Enough is enough."

40.

The bus dropped me off half a mile from the psychic shop, and I walked the rest of the way. The wind blew my hair into my mouth and bit at my ankles and wrists. I wrapped my scarf around my face and head, body vanishing from sight except for a floating pair of eyes. Debbie loved that kind of cartoon logic. One time, we were wandering our neighborhood and ended up on the roof of a squat one-story house. I don't remember how we made it up there. At eight and ten, one minute we were attacking a lemon tree and stuffing the lemons down our shirts, the pointed ends sticking out like hard nipples, and the next we were on the roof, trying to kick loose a rain gutter for the shit of it. We were up there the whole afternoon, lying on our backs, watching airplanes unzip clouds. After a while, Debbie went quiet.

"What's wrong?" I asked.

"I don't want the future to come."

"What do you mean?"

"I have a bad feeling about it."

"What kind of feeling?"

"A *bad* feeling." She was pulling leaves from the gutter and tearing them to confetti.

"What, like you can see the future?" I snorted.

"I look at you, and I look at me, and I feel like I already know what's going to happen." She edged closer to the roof's lip, dangling her legs as if preparing to go down a slide.

"What are you doing?" I asked.

Her butt was halfway off the edge. She fanned her legs in the open air like ribbons. It reminded me of watching the Olympics on TV with our parents, of seeing a rhythmic gymnast toss her ribbon a million feet in the air. The ground catching Debbie like a gymnast's hand.

"Don't you love how, if we were in a cartoon," Debbie said, "I would only fall off the roof if I knew I was doing it? If we were talking, and I went over the edge by accident, I wouldn't start falling until I looked down."

"Debbie, stop." I crawled toward her, afraid I'd pass out if I stood. I paused a couple of feet from the edge.

"Live a little," she said. "Come sit with me."

I didn't move.

"You see that woman with the little dog?" She pointed to a woman in exercise pants and a purple sweater with suggestive cut-outs walking a poodle in a matching sweater. "What do you see when you look at her?"

"She looks, I don't know, intense?" I said. "Like she's trying to lose weight or something."

"Is she happy?" Debbie asked.

"No?"

"You're right. She's obsessed with what people think of her. Which is why no one likes her—she's fake."

"You can tell just from looking at her?"

"You can too. You already did."

I mulled it over.

"She got that dog after a breakup," Debbie went on. "Her last boyfriend dumped her for being too insecure. So will her next boyfriend. She spends all her money on vodka and kibble. She'll die alone. Now you try."

On the other side of the street, an old man smoked on his porch.

"That grandpa is really sad," I said. "His life is boring, and he's tired of doing the same thing every day. He hates how his grandkids are always crying and eating boogers. His wife died years ago, and he kinda wishes he'd died with her. He will, soon. From cancer."

Debbie laughed and started clapping. "See, you can do it too."

"It can't be that easy. How do we know we're right?"

"We don't. Does that make it any less true?"

Years later, Debbie's words arrived unbidden when I hooked up with people I knew would be dead before the next decade, when I envisioned the outside lives of those I encountered at Salvation and in my waiting room—their mortgages and suppressed sexual urges and the choices they'd made with a clearly defined *before* and *after.* It was how I felt looking at satellite images of the psychic shop. That my suspicions were unconfirmed had no bearing on my conviction that they were correct.

•

In Boston, I walked past a post office, a home goods store, a medical clinic. Bright yellow leaves, pretty, but nothing

I hadn't seen before. I liked the flower beds in people's windows, the brick buildings, the wool coats. I passed a cemetery full of ancient graves with worn-off names. The headstones' aura of neglect was part of their power. It would have you believe the past was long forgotten, only to end up choking on its ghost.

I stopped when I saw it: the tree from the map. It was even more glorious in person. Its leaves varied from crimson to ochre, transitioning between colors like ombré hair. I didn't want to face Debbie's shop yet. I touched a leaf. It was tender and a little crispy, a delicate, doomed thing.

It was 11:50. My psychic reading was at noon. I pictured Debbie with long acrylic nails, a headwrap, a Transylvanian accent. A thinly veiled con, but jeans and a sweater would hardly be more convincing. I stared at the tree, running its leaves between my fingers until it was time. In the shop window, the purple SALVATION PSYCHIC sign was flanked by new additions—neon stars and crescent moons. A sheet listing off services like a takeout menu hung by the door: tarot reading, psychic reading, palm reading, couples reading, tutoring for psychic children, aura cleansing, spiritual coaching, spiritual detox. I couldn't see inside. An ivory curtain patterned with silver stars oscillated behind the glass, dancing to a hidden breeze. I wished that I had Ativan on me, that I could pop a benzo only when I needed it, no big deal. I took the propranolol and hydroxyzine an hour earlier, but my stomach was still halfway up my throat.

Wind chimes chirped as I entered. Two green velvet chairs faced each other, a gold table between them. I took the chair closest to the door, trying to shake the paranoia that it had locked behind me. Twinkle lights hung from the ceiling, daylight filtering in through the ivory curtain. Soft harp music played over the burble of a stone waterfall that stood on one of several white shelves. The water was pale pink, like someone had dipped a bloody finger into it. Next to it were two female figurines, an ugly dark crystal that reminded me of a porcupine, and a cluster of jewel-toned potion bottles. One had tipped over and was dripping translucent aqua juice.

Something rustled behind me. I forced myself to stare straight ahead, not to face her until she faced me.

"Good afternoon," she said.

My body tensed as though I were about to be drawn and quartered.

She sat in the other chair and lifted her face to mine.

41.

Spending time with my sister, Debbie, was like falling for a psychic you met in the emergency room. You never knew if it would end with you and a new lover entangled in a bathtub in a former Soviet republic, or coming to alone in your apartment, your heart feeling as though it had been run through a woodchipper. Often, it was both.

When our eyes met, she was already smiling.

"Sister," she said.

Her eyes were softer than I remembered, her face fuller in a healthy way. She didn't look like a weapon. She reached out her hands, and I placed mine in hers.

"What did you come here seeking?" she asked.

"You."

I couldn't believe I was looking at her, touching her. The heat of her hands, the coriander of her perfume, flooded me, threatened to pull me under.

"But in seeking me, what are you really seeking?"

I didn't understand why she wasn't surprised to see me.

"Did you know I was coming?" I asked.

"Yes."

"How?"

She smiled. "Mark told me."

At first, I didn't understand. And then, it was obvious.

"You gave his number to our bartender, knowing I'd want it someday," I said.

"Yes."

"And you knew I'd use him, because it was easier than finding a PI on my own."

She nodded, looking proud of herself.

"But why?"

"Why do you think?" She was wearing the same rose gold lipstick as during our fight the day after my miscarriage.

"How would I know? I'm not the psychic."

My mouth went dry. I'd been caught in a Debbie-shaped trap.

"What is this place?"

"Salvation Psychic." She was still smiling, pleased her plan had fallen into place.

"Yeah, I got that part. But why are you here? Where have you been? How did you know I'd come looking for you?"

Debbie laughed, the same high-pitched scraping I remembered, like medical equipment. She wore a linen tunic, leopard-print black tights, ankle boots. She had new nose and ear piercings; a hand like the neon sign in her window hung from the cartilage of her ear. I ran my fingers over her chunky rings.

"Did you take Dr. Matthews's watches and sell them off to buy this shop?" I asked.

"Yes."

There was a reason the file Mark sent me had such Debbie energy. She'd designed it herself. One in-person meeting with a private investigator, some phone calls and emails, a few hundred dollars—of course it wasn't that easy to find a missing person.

Even from afar, invisible, Debbie pulled my strings.

"Don't be upset," she said. "I only wanted what was best for us."

"I had no idea if you were dead or alive. How was disappearing for two years and then manipulating me into finding you what was best for us?"

"I didn't manipulate you into finding me."

"You set me up with a private investigator."

"No one forced you to call him. No one forced you to find me. I just wanted you to have the option."

The darks of her eyes were electrodes scanning my brain. A sick feeling gurgled in my stomach.

"Was Mark tailing *me* this whole time?" I said. "Do you know everything that's happened since you left?"

"Of course not. I already told you—I wanted you to have a way of finding me. But I wanted it to be your choice. I didn't want you to feel pressured."

"How did you think I'd feel when I found out you tricked me? That what I thought was a decision I'd made for myself was actually one of your schemes?"

She sighed. "It *was* a decision you made for yourself, but it felt unfair to make you do all the work. I was afraid that without Mark, you wouldn't find me. That you might not search for me at all if his card wasn't shoved in your face. I'm sorry."

I looked away, fixing my gaze on the waterfall. She'd posed the two female figurines at the top, balanced at its precipice. They were moments from drowning or fighting their way out.

"That waterfall is very on the nose," I told her.

"You know I love a metaphor."

She'd apologized. Had she ever apologized to me before?

"Are you ready for your reading?" she asked.

We were still holding hands.

Debbie closed her eyes. "You're angry. Full of more rage than I've ever known you to be, except for the last time we saw each other."

"Of course I'm angry. You abandoned me and moved across the country to open a bullshit psychic shop. You up and left. You left me."

I was sweating through my top and undershirt. I unraveled my scarf and let it fall to the floor. My breakfast climbed my throat.

"Where's your bathroom?" I said, standing up.

She pointed to a beaded curtain behind me, which led to a small bathroom where I promptly vomited. I dumped a bowl of potpourri over it and flushed several times. I hoped her toilet clogged, her pipes burst, that she had to clean up gallons of puke and shit and piss because she didn't have enough watch money left for both a cleaning person and a plumber.

I half expected Debbie to be gone when I returned, but there she was, offering me a mason jar of water. I downed it and didn't say thank you. She gave me one of her old looks, and we were back at Salvation, both of us in short dresses and smeared eyeliner, halfway through the third set of drinks we had no intention of paying for, me telling her

Ronnie and I were happy, her watching me like a drunk oracle, shaking her head.

"Listen," Debbie said, taking my hands back in hers. "I know I've been a crappy sister."

My hand twitched. She held me tighter.

"Not that you've been so great, if we're being honest," she continued. "You made me feel crazy, like I was alone in the world."

"How could you feel alone? I followed you everywhere."

"You never asked what I was going through at the strip club, or with our pediatrician. You didn't want to know. You were too busying judging me, too busy playing the victim."

"What are you talking about?" I said.

"You got to enjoy the fun parts of having a fucked-up sister and had me to blame when things went south."

My muscles clenched, bearing down as if to entomb me in the dirt beneath her store. "You're always telling me who I am and what's wrong with me. Look in a fucking mirror."

"When I quit detox, you assumed I'd gotten kicked out," she said.

"Well, why did you leave detox?"

"They were assholes. I overheard one of the specialists refer to us as junkies. When I called him out, he said to prove him wrong. He turned it into a fucking challenge, like he wanted me to earn back my dignity."

I looked down at our clasped hands.

"You were the only one who objected to how people treated me," she said. "But you held those same objections against me. We were kids, I get it. We didn't have the language for what was happening to us. My point is, we've both been through a lot. We've both failed each other."

It was too much to process. I couldn't reexamine my entire life and her place in it in the remaining twenty minutes of my reading.

"You're my big sister," I said quietly. "You were supposed to protect me."

"And you're the smart one. Do you stand by all your choices? Did you make good decisions while I was gone?"

I scraped my boot across her hardwood floor, marking it with the rubber sole.

"But you're right," she continued. "I really regret not being there for you when you miscarried. I shouldn't have pressured you into hooking up with that rando, or freaked out the next day when you wouldn't give me back my purse. All those times I left you to fend for yourself. My whole life was organized around getting my next fix. There's a lot I don't remember. A lot I don't want to remember. But I know I led you to some dark places. You're my little sister, and I don't know half of what you've been through. I'm sorry."

I willed myself not to cry.

"You don't have to say anything," she said. "I just wanted you to know I get it. I wouldn't have looked for me either."

I stared at our clasped hands.

"Debbie," I said. I didn't know how to continue.

"If this is about that picture you sent Dominic, it's fine." Her lips twitched into a half smile. "It was, um, not that hot."

I groaned. "I don't even remember doing it."

"Don't be embarrassed. We went through some fucked-up shit."

She twirled her hair between her fingers. I used to think she did that to mock me, but now, it just felt like a gesture. She placed her hands back in mine.

"I'm staying here, in case you're wondering," she said. "I'm not going back to LA with you."

I hadn't thought that far ahead, but I was relieved.

"We belong to ourselves now," she said.

Before she vanished, everything was refracted through Debbie. Even her absence was a presence I couldn't shake. I thought about the woman with Shoah grief, and my mother, and my grandmother. Was belonging to yourself even possible?

"You know where I am," she went on. "And I know where you are. Maybe that's enough."

I didn't know what I wanted, but she wasn't waiting for an answer. And I had so many more questions. "Why Boston?"

"It's not that exciting. You remember that girl Pilar I was friends with in middle school?"

"Vaguely. Didn't she move to Texas or something?"

"Yeah, in seventh grade. She posted on Facebook that she was moving to Boston for a job and was looking for a roommate. When all that shit went down between you and me, I reached out to see if she was still looking. We still live together, actually. It's been kind of great."

"Was that you in the news clippings Mark sent me? The car-jacking, the pet store liberation?"

"I wish," Debbie said. "This girl Kayla from my support group said that when she's feeling down, vigilante justice makes her feel better. I thought I'd give it a try. Collecting stories, that is. I'm taking a break from being the vigilante."

"Your support group?"

"For addicts who have experienced sexual trauma. This woman runs it out of her ballet studio. We light candles and watch ourselves cry and eat donuts in front of the giant mirrors. It's kind of woo-woo."

I laughed. "I like that for you."

We sat quietly, hands clasped, waterfall murmuring.

"I see a bright future for you," she said, closing her eyes. "Lots of sex, a sick apartment, pets that are super into you. Sobriety. Books. Self-actualization."

"Sounds nice."

"It will be."

We sat there, exposed like cut frogs on a table. I thought about our privilege and stupid luck, how we'd survived each other, survived horrors that so many others hadn't. How survival was provisional. How progress could be reversed like a plastic bag. Outside, trees swaying like flames. Music bumping from a speaker. Drinks being poured. Mouths colliding. Powder dissolving beneath a tongue. Our sisters, singing along in their flawed human voices. Our brothers, lighting a match.

42.

At work, a teenager with box braids slept with her head in her mother's lap. It was nearly midnight. Her older sister had sliced her hand in chemistry lab and was being triaged down the hall. Their parents spoke in hushed tones to keep from waking her, but I could tell from the way her eyes moved that she was only pretending to sleep. Her parents knew it too. There was comfort in reverting to our archetypes—sister, mother, father, addict, lover, friend. Psychic. I shook my head, visualized wiping Sasha's face from a dry erase board.

An hour passed, and the older sister was released. The younger one leapt from their mother's lap to inspect her stitches.

"Let her breathe," their mother said, pulling her eldest daughter into a hug.

"Can we go home?" the girl said, yawning. She was in good spirits for someone who'd spent the night bleeding through two hand towels until a stranger found the time to stitch her shut. Grown men howled and cursed, smiting the entire hospital, for much less. She was wearing a sweatshirt when she first got here, but she'd taken it off, revealing a UCLA tee beneath.

"How do you like it there?" I asked.

"At UCLA? It's okay. Being pre-med doesn't exactly lend itself to *the college experience*," she said using air quotes.

"It's not UCLA's fault you don't drink and haunt the library like a gargoyle," her younger sister said.

Their parents cracked up, and both sisters rolled their eyes.

I placed the discharge paperwork in her good hand. We wished each other a good night.

Traffic was light that morning. On Fairfax, I watched a hunched woman draw back the metal bars of a Jewish bakery. I pulled the stop request cord. Inside was an assortment of challahs and pastries, dishes both sweet and savory. The warm yeasty smell brought back a memory of baking pierogi with my grandmother. Debbie kneading the dough, me laying the mashed potato inside, our grandmother painting the tops with egg wash. I filled a bag with chocolate, cinnamon, and poppy seed rugelach. Back on the bus, I bit into a chocolate one and skimmed UCLA's website. I looked up some other schools in LA and bookmarked their financial aid pages. I texted Kim, *Hey I've been thinking about you. Want to grab coffee?*

When I checked my mailbox, wedged between Bed Bath & Beyond coupons and another acting class invitation from the Church of Scientology was a postcard. I pulled it out, expecting a reminder from my dentist. It was a photo of a topless, ethereal woman, her breasts just out of view of the frame. She hid her face behind a conch shell, its pink center open like a vagina. It was from Sasha. *I'm proud of you*, she'd written. That was it. The card was postmarked in Kishinev.

In the elevator, I held it to my chest. A gaggle of Russian-speaking grandmothers got on at the next floor. I smiled at them, holding out my postcard.

"Isn't it beautiful?" I said.

•

Salvation burned down a few months later. One of the regulars, a chatty former accountant named Troy, smashed a kerosene lamp over his own head. I must have heard a dozen versions of how he lost his CPA license. A drunken car crash into the dining room of the Magic Castle, a fraudulent tax return for an ocelot breeder named Basil, a "sexually explosive but alas very toxic" affair with a member of the California Board of Accountancy.

I read about the fire online. Troy had died, and two others were in critical condition.

I hadn't spoken to Debbie since that day at her psychic shop. I texted her the article.

"Can I FaceTime you?" she replied.

I said yes.

It was late afternoon in Los Angeles, evening in Boston. She wore winged eyeliner and an amethyst pendant. A candle burned on her coffee table, shadows flickering across her face as though we were seated around a fire.

"Is that an iguana?" Debbie said.

Apples was asleep in my lap. Spooked by my absence while I was in Boston, he'd finally started to warm up to me.

"Yup," I said. "A story for another time."

Debbie took a sip from a steaming mug. "Do you

remember the time Troy got punched for talking to that Marine's wife?"

"Yeah."

"She wasn't even his wife. The Marine just wanted an excuse to beat the shit out of him."

"Sounds about right."

I tried to make out the art behind her. There was a line drawing of a rabbit, a holographic print of the moon's phases, DIY-looking collages of images torn from magazines. The collage closest to her featured women with disco balls for eyes, dismembered doll parts, luxury watches, the Los Angeles skyline, an array of glossed lips spelling out *THE BODY REMEMBERS.*

I wanted to ask if she'd made them herself, but I liked not knowing.

"The article was so short," I said. "No interviews or anything. You'd think self-immolating in a bar would get you more than two hundred words."

"Poor Troy, never quite sticking the landing."

The article didn't mention that he had two kids named Lance and Daisy, that he once performed the Heimlich maneuver on a guy who moments earlier had told Troy that if he kept running his mouth, he'd kick his ass so hard that Troy would shit footprints. I was floating somewhere up by the ceiling. The choking man's squeaks yanked me back like a balloon being tugged by the string. Troy dug his fist into the man's abdomen and dislodged a sinister mass the size of an egg. Watching the dark pearl shoot out of him, I felt I too had been purified. That salvation had finally come for us all.

"He wanted to have the last word," I said.

I reread the article after hanging up. It was accompanied by a picture of a burnt-out room that could have been anything. There was no mention of a motive. There was no need. We all understood. We were more interested in why he had chosen a kerosene lamp.

Acknowledgments

Thank you to my beloved agent, Mina Hamedi, for signing me as a baby novelist, for editing this novel within an inch of both of our lives, and for championing my work in every genre. Ours is a better partnership than I could have ever dreamed. Thank you to my incredible editor, Alicia Kroell, for understanding this book at the deepest level, for making it so much stronger, and for the laughs and friendship along the way.

I'm grateful to everyone at Catapult and Janklow & Nesbit, whose visions and hard work helped usher my book into the world. Deep gratitude to Jonathan Lee, Alyson Forbes, and Kendall Storey for believing in me. So much love to Megan Fishmann, Sarah Jean Grimm, Rachel Fershleiser, Kira Weiner, Dustin Kurtz, Alyssa Lo, Katie Mantele, and Miriam Vance for getting my book into readers' hands. To Gregg Kulick, Nicole Caputo, and Lexi Earle for their tireless work designing the dreamiest cover, featuring Cat Thomson's incredible photograph. Major thanks to Mikayla Butchart, tracy danes, Laura Gonzalez, and Wah-Ming Chang for the copyedits. Essay genius Tajja Isen has made me a better writer with each of our thrilling collaborations. Much gratitude to my film and TV agent, Will Watkins, and to CAA for seeing a future for *All-Night Pharmacy* beyond the page. Thank you so much to every bookseller, librarian, and reviewer for your thoughtful engagement and for spreading the word.

Thank you to *The Iowa Review*, *The Rumpus*, *Joyland*, and *7x7la* for publishing the short stories that I adapted into this novel and for giving me the space to live deeply with these characters. I'll always be grateful for the Tin House Summer Workshop and the friendships I made there. Thank you to my friends and colleagues at the University of Southern California, Harvard Law School, Massachusetts General Hospital, and UCLA Health for enthusiastically supporting my writing. To my teachers at USC, especially T. C. Boyle: thank you for your wisdom and encouragement.

So much love to the writer friends who read drafts, helped me work through craft and personal issues big and small, quelled my anxieties, and made me laugh: Diana Arterian, Leah Bailly, eae benioff, Jackson Burgess, Jean Kyoung Frazier, Ilya Kaminsky and Katie Farris, Zack Knoll, Lisa Locascio Nighthawk, August Luhrs, Billy O'Neill (who came up with the title!), Ben Purkert, Sarah Elaine Smith, and Hua Xi.

Huge thanks to Kristen Arnett, Jean Kyoung Frazier, Jean Chen Ho, Kimberly King Parsons, and Kyle Lucia Wu for the early blurbs. It's a gift for our writing to be in the same conversation. I'm so thankful for the growing community of the Cheburashka Collective, and especially to Julia Kolchinsky Dasbach, Maria Kuznetsova, Gala Mukomolova, Luisa Muradyan, Alina Pleskova, and Karina Vahitova.

Endless gratitude, suffocating hugs, mutual obsession,

and jokes that take it too far to the friends I've been lucky to know and love for half my life (and in Marli and Shushana's case, closer to three-quarters): Aaron and Bubba; Eric and Neil; Juliet; Laura and Matt; Layne; Marli, Zack, and Elliot; Nicole and Jared; Shushana. If I had to give up writing, my life would still be deeply satisfying because I'd have you.

My family has loved and supported me whether I was writing novels with commercial appeal or hermetic poems in defunct journals. I cannot emphasize enough that they are not the family in this novel! Big love to my little brother and best friend, Adam. I can't imagine a world where I didn't have you to exchange memes, cursed gossip, and the innermost corners of my soul with on the daily. So much love and gratitude to my parents, Dana and Michael, for making me feel like the most important writer in the world and for being the first people to tell me that I don't have to choose between being a writer and a healthcare provider. My beloved grandparents Yefim and Roza may not be able to read my writing in English, but I know they're proud of every word. Many hugs and sloppy cheek kisses to my aunts, uncles, and cousins, especially the Bikvans, Galpers, and Rabinoviches. Lots of love to my Phillips and Bisno families, to Isabel and Susanna. To Lena and to the family friends who have always felt like family. I write in loving memory of my grandparents Anna, Lev, and Samson; my great-uncle Izrail; and my great-grandmothers Frida, Sonia, and Anna. I am so grateful to have spent time with the ancestors I never got to meet while working on this book.

I ask for forgiveness and give thanks to anyone I've

neglected to name here. I promise to perseverate on my shame forever, regardless of whether you'd want me to.

All my love to my partner in everything, Adam Phillips, whose fingerprints live on every page.

And thank you, dear reader, for spending time with my diasporic drama queens.

© Adam F. Phillips

RUTH MADIEVSKY's writing appears in *The Atlantic*, *The Los Angeles Times*, *Harper's Bazaar*, *Them*, *Ploughshares*, *Tin House*, and elsewhere. She is the author of a poetry collection, *Emergency Brake*, and is a Tin House Summer Writers Workshop scholar. She co-founded the Cheburashka Collective, a community of women and nonbinary writers whose identity has been shaped by immigration from the Soviet Union to the United States. Originally from Moldova, she lives in Los Angeles, where she works as an HIV and primary care pharmacist. You can find her at www.ruthmadievsky.com and on social media at @ruthmadievsky.